ACCIDENTAL LIVES

By

Linda Kendall McLendon

Accidental Lives
©2013 by Linda Kendall McLendon

The characters and events in this book are fictitious. Any similarities to real persons, living or dead, are coincidental and not intended by the author.

WRB Publishing
Palm City, FL 34990
wrb1174@comcast.net

ISBN-13: 978-0-9896247-1-8

Also by Linda Kendall McLendon

<u>Unintended Lies – first in the series</u>

"Author, Linda Kendall McLendon, does an excellent job of creating likeable, believable characters, showing us their fears and flaws." Tyler R. Tichelaar, Ph.D. and award-winning author of *The Best Place*

Loved this book and can't wait for the second one! "The book is so easy to read and to get hooked on immediately. I loved all of her characters and how she wove the tale around them and their unintended lies. Each page had me wondering what would happen next and how would the book end? Once it did end, I wanted the next book right way so I could continue to be a fly on the wall in the character's lives. A terrific tale of love, comedy and suspense. Can't wait for book two." **Leslie Corcoran**

This fresh new mystery delivers: "**<u>Unintended Lies</u>** delivers compelling, fully drawn characters while at the same time depicting a strong woman pitted against a dangerous future. You fall in love with the heroine, Catherine DeLong. She's just as appealing in the boardroom as she is on the ranch, especially her transition from city gal to country ranch owner. The story begins with a dark ominous prologue and a first chapter that grabs readers and makes them read on until the final curtain." **Leona DeRosa Bodie,**
Amazon Bestselling Author of *Shadow Cay*

Clearly Written, Full of Energy, <u>Unintended Lies</u> is a Page Turner from the Beginning: "Two Protagonists living separate lives meet through a chance circumstance. The character-driven story presents vivid lifelike characters, each with a clear personality and agenda. We watch as the characters evolve and grow throughout the storyline. This is a fun read and full of suspense, drama and physical danger. Five stars for Linda McLendon." **Glenn Gardiner, Co-Author of *Glimpse of Sunlight***

PROLOGUE

Catherine DeLong believed everything happened for a reason, but now she was having a difficult time hanging on to that belief in the face of the horrific accident that had taken her husband away from her forever. Life had a way of sending people in unexpected directions. She hadn't recovered from the death of her husband, James, and had just begun her new life on her farm, when she headed to South Florida to care for her terminally ill Uncle Walton. She was glad to do it, needed to be there for him, but it had come at a time when she already felt completely vulnerable and raw.

She hardly took a breath and her uncle was gone. As soon as she returned to her farm in Highberry, she was knocked flat on her back by total exhaustion and a terrible virus. When she began to come out of it, she was shocked to discover her hired hand, a man she barely knew, had been caring for her. She was grateful to Zane Wheeler for what he had done, taking care of the animals, the farm, and her, but could hardly face the fact that he'd been, well.... She didn't want to think about it, but while she was sick, he'd seen every part of her. It was ridiculous, but at the same time, what would have happened if he hadn't been there?

Still reeling from the recent events, Catherine asked Zane to stay on until she could regain her strength and get her mind back. Perhaps unintentionally easing her loneliness and filling empty spaces that were so hard to accept, Catherine headed into the making of a love song in spite of the heartache she was hiding. She and Zane put their past behind them and began to build the lives they once could only dream about.

CHAPTER 1

Catherine DeLong sat on the sunporch at the back of her house, watching the horses as they grazed in the pasture. Friskie, her smallest dog, slept on the chair next to her. She silently asked herself the questions: *How long have I been like this? Where have I been?*

It felt like she had suddenly come out of a sullen long-lasting dream from a faraway place and no one even knew or cared that she'd been gone. The feeling crept in slowly and silently like a cat stalking a bird. Then it struck quickly, as if something burst to the surface to take a breath after a long deep dive. She looked up from reading and became aware that her eyes could suddenly see more clearly than she ever remembered. Several of the horses were in a cluster, picking at the short spring grass content after the cold North Florida winter. They took advantage of each other's tails warding off the miserable flies. Their coats glimmered in the bright sunlight. Two of the dogs, Scuz and General, wrestled in the corner of the porch, growling and playing bitey-face, having awakened from an afternoon nap full of energy.

What had kept her away from a moment like this? She had no clear answers. She shook her head as she thought about how she had taken in six dogs in such a short period of time right after moving to the ranch. She was having difficulty putting a time frame on it. She knew she had been attempting to fill the void left by the death of her husband, James, but she had also wanted to rescue them. Now she was the one who needed rescuing. Her life continued to feel a bit out of control.

Try as she might, she couldn't minimize what she had learned about her husband's deceit. The secrets he'd kept haunted her, especially because of the lack of closure. No one had contacted her in months about any progress being made to arrest his murderer. Now, every time the phone rang, the pain in her stomach struck again.

She was grateful for Zane. She couldn't have imagined falling in love this soon, let alone with the man she had hurriedly hired to look after her farm while she was away caring for her ill uncle, but the painful memories of James remained.

She hadn't equated a single thing with the fact that James wasn't just working for Robideaux Pharmaceutical or that his traveling had anything to do with the current world situation—certainly not anything to do with terrorists and world leaders. Catherine felt like a fool. She had simply moved through her life, feeling totally secure in herself and him until the whole thing suddenly came crashing down around her with the so-called accident that claimed her husband's life. She was totally knocked to her knees, but she had somehow staggered through standing in front of his casket, staring at something she couldn't even identify as him. She remained strong through the funeral and many unimaginably difficult days until she finally knew what she had to do. She fled everything that felt or looked remotely familiar and started a new life in the small town of Highberry, Florida. She had become totally angry at herself. How could she have been so stupid? She was intelligent, thought she was very aware, but she had somehow allowed James to do this to her. She was consumed with thoughts about what else she didn't know about him. Her gut told her there was more to come.

~~~~~

Zane Wheeler relaxed at the opposite end of the porch, pretending to read *Western Horseman* magazine, but he was actually watching Catherine. She had that faraway look on her face as she peered over her book out the porch window. The deaths of her husband and uncle had taken a toll on her. Following her debilitating illness, she had looked sullen, with dark circles under her eyes. Her auburn hair had hung thin and dull. Now, her hair was pulled to one side and she looked radiant in a deep turquoise blouse.

"Penny for your thoughts," he said, sucking in a deep breath as she came back to him.

"That's a small price to pay," she said, her lips making that little smacking sound he loved to hear when she smiled.

He knew she was dancing around it. She sighed that sigh she often did. She had to be thinking about the past and worse yet, most likely James.

"I don't know if I feel bitter or if I've turned completely cold. I actually looked up bitter and cold in the dictionary."

"And, what did you discover?" Zane asked gently.

"Well, bitter was defined as painful, caustic, cruel. All the definitions fit very nicely into how I'm feeling
~~~~~

these days about him." She had told Zane earlier that she couldn't even bring herself to say his name out loud anymore.

"And cold?" he pushed her.

"Frigid, without passion, indifferent. I think it's good because it means I've moved into more of the angry stage."

"It was inevitable, don't you think?" he asked, rather than suggested, coaxing her out.

"I know. I don't think I will ever understand how I became so naïve that I didn't see any of it. I didn't have a single clue. He was so good at deceiving me. That's where the pain comes in. It actually hurts my heart when I think about all the lies he told and how long he had been doing it."

"I'm sorry you had to go through it, but I think you're at the right place now to get past it."

He never expected his life to turn out like this. He figured he might meet someone some day, but he hadn't given much thought to dating or pursuing a woman. He had been completely focused on his job as an operative for so many years that he didn't need much else. Then, he and his partner, Buck Matthews, decided to retire. He felt very lucky it had happened this way. It could have been a scene written for a movie—*"hired hand falls in love with the lady of the ranch,"* but in this scenario, she loved him back. It didn't get much better than that.

He continued watching her as she looked out across the field. He had never allowed himself to give a number to how many years it had been since he and his best friend, Buck, graduated from high school and took off for their careers with the United States Government. It was an entire lifetime ago. He couldn't begin to know how Catherine really felt, but lately when he thought about his mother and Montana, he did feel heaviness around his heart. He tried not to pay too much attention to it, but now that Catherine spoke of it, he understood what the phrase, *"It was tugging at my heart,"* meant. What he knew for certain was that he had fallen totally in love with this remarkable woman and he had to figure out a way to keep her life intact while he traveled to Montana to make amends with his mother. It didn't seem to be the right time for him to tell her that he needed to go home, but he really wanted to go and soon. If she found out the truth about James, there was no telling what it would do to her. They were standing at a precipice that would certainly change both of their lives forever.

~~~~~

As she and Zane waltzed their way into a new rhythm, Catherine couldn't help the memories that kept popping into her head. Little nagging moments crept in at the most inopportune times. Earlier that morning, she and Zane were in a beautiful part of her farm. He was riding Trouble and she was riding Sundy. Suddenly, she found herself thinking about a place she and James had visited. They were staying in a hotel when she overheard a strange telephone conversation that left James agitated. His usual calm demeanor had been shaken, and he abruptly told her he had to take a walk. She was looking out the window at the mountains when she spotted him in the parking lot in some sort of confrontation with a stranger. His arms were flailing and
~~~~~

she watched him hit the man and knock him to the ground. This was out of character for James. Later, when she asked him about his walk, he simply told her he had found a lovely garden and he would have to show it to her, something that never materialized because the next day through a maze of excuses, they checked out and immediately flew home. She never questioned him about it. Now, she wished she had.

She had this uncontrollable feeling that something was about to happen. Part of her didn't want to know the details about James' death. She didn't want to feel any of those emotions again now that she was gaining her strength and was finally finding happiness. Still, she felt a certain dread because of the "what ifs." What if someone contacted her and asked her a lot of questions about James? She wouldn't be able to tell the person anything that couldn't be read in the same report she had been given. They would come to the same conclusions that she did. She wondered why there wasn't any news on who was responsible for murdering James. Surely someone was still working on the case. It made her feel shaky inside whenever she allowed herself to think about it.

She glanced at Zane and forced herself to let it go. She wanted desperately to enjoy the moment with the horses and this amazing man.

CHAPTER 2

The morning sun filtered through the curtains on the back door creating beams of light across the breakfast table. Zane and Catherine sat next to each other in deep discussion. Catherine sounded like she was trying to convince herself of what she was saying, "I understand a lot better now why my mother made the decisions she made. She did what she had to do to survive. She found a good husband who could provide for her and her girls, and then she spent the rest of her life catering to his every need. They are still very much in love."

Zane gently began to rub the top of her hand and looked into her expressive eyes as he spoke. "My mother saw the poverty and heartache on the reservation and went after the life most Native American women could only dream about. I never realized how much she gave up until recently. I was so caught up in getting away from my father that I forgot about her. Now I realize how selfish I was. She never blamed me, and she never changed how she felt about me. She wanted a different life than that of alcohol, drugs, and instability."

He loved the way Catherine's face softened when she listened to him talk about his mother. He squeezed her hand and she took a deep breath and said, "Even though my mother was completely wrapped up in Hamilton's life, she took very good care of us, gave us everything we could possibly want. Children don't come with an instruction manual and the decisions parents make affect their kids forever. They provided my sister, Kiki, and me with excellent educations and taught us what we needed to know in order to go out into the world and be successful. Looking back, I think my mother was guarded. She didn't want to love us too much because when she was younger, everything she loved and believed in left her. It is easy to see it now, but I didn't understand that for a long time."

Zane took a sip of coffee and replied, "Same here. I never stopped long enough to consider why my mother did what she did for herself and for me. It had to take a lot of strength to walk away from her family and the closeness of her tribe. Three generations all lived in the same house—her grandmother, her mother, and her sisters. The house was always busy with cooking and sewing and children running around. There was either laughter or shouting. On the occasions when we visited, I felt overloaded with all the noise and activity. I was used to the quiet and steady pace of the ranch."

Zane watched her drift away as she stared at the floor. He waited while she sat there silently for several minutes.

"The best thing that ever happened to me was when my mother dropped me off at the savannahs for horseback riding. Mostly, we jumped on the horses and went trail riding. It was hot and miserable, and I loved every minute of it. I didn't even mind being all sweaty and black with sugar sand caked in the cracks of my neck and arms. My mother would shake her head at us and make us sit on towels in her car when she came to pick us up."

Zane chuckled.

"What are you laughing at?" she asked.

"Oh, just the thought of you as a young girl all sweaty and covered with dirt and looking like that."

"I didn't care. It was fun. I didn't even know I was a mess."

"I understand. When I was young, I would saddle up my pony, or later on, my horse, and take off across the plains. I knew someone was always watching me. My father would have a ranch hand, but mostly Parker Iron Crow, trail me, but I didn't care about that either. It was in case I got dumped or hurt or to keep one of the big cats or a bear from getting me. I loved the freedom of exploring every inch of the ranch. I even found a cave once, and just as I started to go inside, a hand reached out and grabbed me by the collar. Iron Crow stopped me. He said I had to grow a little in my wisdom before I was ready for the stories of the cave. He told me if I was patient, he would show me all the mysteries of its belly. It was hard to stay out of there. On my fourteenth birthday, he gave me a beautiful handmade pair of moccasins and told me to get my horse. We rode out toward the mountain. He taught me a ceremony and then we went down into the cave. And that story will have to wait until another day because I have chores I have to get to."

"No! No! You absolutely can't leave me wondering about what happened in there. That's not fair." Catherine tried blocking him from getting up. "You can't tease me like that. You can't."

Zane stood, smoothed the creases out of his jeans, and held her chin in his hand as he leaned down and kissed her.

"I love you when you look like that, and it will be worth it to make you wait."

He staggered back as she pushed him away.

"Hey!" He was chuckling.

"You really can't leave me wondering."

"I can, but I promise, it will be worth waiting for."

He headed out of the kitchen, grabbed his gray weathered hat from the hook and opened the back porch door wide for the dogs. They bounded out in all directions, except for Friskie, who remained behind with Catherine.

~~~~~

Catherine and Zane walked arm in arm, slowly down to the barn in the late evening darkness. The air smelled sweet from the heavy night dew on the freshly mowed pasture. The longer hours of sunlight made it seem like the days melted into each other. She watched as he tossed flakes of hay to the five horses. The dogs were off checking out the scents of the night creatures and doing what dogs do. Catherine snuck into the tack room to play with the cat. Sweetie was always happy to see them and would rub against their legs until one of them picked her up. She would immediately turn on the purring. She was no longer the little ball of fluff, but she was still very precious. They were hoping to let her become the barn cat once they figured out how the dogs would interact with her.

"The dogs know there's a cat in here. They are used to the idea of her. They just need to get used to her." Zane told her.
~~~~~

She knew Zane was ready to let the cat out of the tack room because it wasn't natural to keep a cat confined like that, but she was still afraid. "Do you think she'll be okay?" Catherine asked.

"Yes, I think she'll stand her ground and it will be all over in a minute. All she has to do is swat one of them and they will get the message."

"I wish I'd asked the rescue people if these dogs liked cats."

"You worry too much. They'll be fine. All she has to do is pop one of them on the nose and they'll figure it out."

"Oh, how I hope you are right. I don't want anything to happen to her."

"We can let her out a little bit at a time, when we are right here to watch them. I promise you, it will be fine."

Catherine wasn't sure about it, but she knew it wasn't fair to keep the cat locked in the tack room forever. That morning, she had seen a tiny mouse in the corner of the barn and even though it was very cute, she knew it had to go. Zane had reminded her that if she saw one, then there had to be a whole family. She absolutely was not going to put out poison.

All the dogs had come into her life from the shelter, except Friskie. She had wanted a dog to help her feel safe living in the house alone. That's why she had adopted Champ. He was big and looked like he would protect her, but he had quickly proven that Golden Retrievers are nothing but big Teddy bears. She had been vulnerable and heartbroken and he had filled a huge void. He also kept her busy, not allowing her to think too much. Her second dog, General, was a rangy-looking mutt with hair going every which way. He was quiet, well-mannered, and had short dirty brown hair with darker flecks. He and Champ were instant pals.

She hadn't intended to add any more, but she caved when the dog people called her. "She's totally timid, part greyhound with really long legs," the woman on the other end of the phone told her. She didn't like dogs with pointed noses, but how could she say "No." The sweet, gray dog with nearly yellow eyes never stopped looking at her. The dog had her eyebrows up, with a worried wrinkled look, and she was shaking uncontrollably. Her name was Scuz.

A week later, the woman at the shelter used the excuse that she was checking to see how the three dogs were adjusting. Catherine felt sick to her stomach and her heart was beating fast. *"I'll just say 'NO',"* she silently told herself, but she didn't.

The neighbors hadn't seen the man for two days. They had found the two little dogs under the covers in his bed, protecting his body. She was doomed. Peanut and Gem were caged together and sullen and wary. Peanut was the cutest, a little wire-haired gray terrier thing. He was feisty and curled up his lip and growled at her. Peanut was a spaniel-type with a beagle face and ears, black and white, but small boned.

That brought the total to five. She could barely believe it, but they seemed like they knew she saved them and miraculously behaved very well together. In fact, she couldn't believe how well. She imagined they had warned each other not to blow it. She could almost hear them saying, "We've got to stick together."

Then Buck, the guy at the feed store, had found the

sixth dog in the store's doorway in a cage. No one knew where the little dog had come from. His face was so fuzzy you couldn't find his tiny black eyes. He looked like a Chow, but was most likely a black Pomeranian. He was very small. She told herself and Buck that she would only keep him until the real owner showed up. The tiny dog had jumped up and down and pawed the side of the cage all the way home. She decided to call him Friskie until someone showed up to tell her his real name. When she was living in her New York City apartment, she had never imagined that some day she would be living with six dogs inside her house.

When she and Zane came out of the barn, the moon played its lovely light through the pecan and oak trees. Catherine loved walking from the barn to the house in the patchwork, especially when the trees were swaying in the soft night breeze. She would come out of their canopy and stare up at the big round moon and the stars in wonderment. Zane would catch her hand and they would walk silently together. There was no need for words to explain what they felt. They were totally together in the moment. More often than not, when they were at the back steps, he would turn her around to him and kiss her as the dogs impatiently waited for the door to be opened. She loved those moments, the feel of him against her and the smell of him in the night mist.

~~~~~

Early in the morning in the dew and fog, they rode off on Trouble and Sundy. The horses were frisky in the cool morning air. It took them almost an hour to ride up the lane between the fenced pastures and then back to
~~~~~

the barn. They were hungry for breakfast by the time Zane had the horses turned out and Catherine placed two plates on the table and sat down. She said, "That was the most invigorating feeling. I have never been so in rhythm with my horse. I never really focused on being one with them before. I was always too busy trying to stay on. Thank you for teaching me how to do that."

"You are very welcome. I waited a long time to do this my way. My father's methods of breaking horses were old style and pretty cruel. It was what he knew and he was unwilling to change. He was the typical cowboy— gonna break them and ride them or else. He had people right there on the ranch that knew better ways, but the damn fool had to have it his way."

"Well, how did you become so different? Didn't you want to follow along in your father's footsteps?"

"No. I had Parker Iron Crow as my mentor. Now that I look back on it, I see how wrapped up my father was in the cattle, the horses, and the ranch. He left me to my mother and Parker until I was old enough for him to use for chores. My father was okay with Parker looking out for me and keeping me out of harm's way. I'm grateful I had those early years with Iron Crow. We would go off on horseback up into the mountains and that's where he taught me a different way of doing things. One time, there was this horse they just couldn't break. They tied him up, laid him down, and the horse fought and wouldn't give in. My father told Parker to take him up in the hills and feed him to the coyotes. We did take him up there, but instead of shooting him, we built a pen and every day we would go up there and Iron Crow would work with him. Sometimes he would just sit with a bucket of grass and hand-feed him. Eventually, he put him in the river out pretty deep and slid up on him. The horse struggled against the water and the current and Iron Crow kept riding him deeper and deeper into the water. When the horse began to swim, Iron Crow kept with him. Eventually, they came back out. After that, the horse was done with his fighting. When we took the horse back to the house, my father never realized it was that same horse and no one ever told him."

"It must give you some peace knowing you and what's his name, Parker, were able to change the outcome for some of the animals."

"It wasn't enough."

CHAPTER 3

James DeLong swallowed two aspirin and lay in bed, staring at the ceiling. He was trapped in a nightmare. Being under constant surveillance in an unknown location and held against his will was taking its toll. He couldn't imagine not being married to Catherine or living anywhere other than their apartment in New York City. Now, he was being held captive in what he considered to be a dump compared to their luxury suite overlooking Central Park. He and Catherine had loved it because it was right in the heart of everything they truly cared about.

He never intended for things to turn out like this. It should have been a simple task. All he had to do was deliver the drug formula to the appropriate government contacts and then cover up any evidence that it ever existed. There could be no paper trail, no computer screw-up, nothing to tie anyone or anything to Robideaux Pharmaceutical or him. His buddy, Roger Halvesord, knew about all of it because he was the one who set it up. He had trusted Roger. They had been college roommates, and after graduation, Roger became his attorney and his confidante.

In the beginning, James believed it was his duty. He had to do it for his country, for everything he held sacred, but mostly for himself. The fact that he'd never served in any branch of the military had made him feel inferior. His discovery of the drug formula afforded him an opportunity to do something important. It didn't matter that no one would ever know. It was about his self-worth and feelings about himself.

In the end, it became his death sentence. Now the person he loved the most was far away and he feared he would never see her again. He hated what he had done to Catherine. If he could relive that one moment, would he have made the same decision? Could he have protected both of them? It was too late now. He was being forced to recreate himself, his life. The part that bothered him the most was that he had to deceive her. Everything about him had become a lie.

He clung to the sole idea that it had been the right thing to do. The terrorists were gaining strongholds all over the world, and if his concoction stopped some of their support and leadership, it would set them back and give the United States time to do something significant. He had done what anyone should do. The drug was simple and almost undetectable. It acted on the brain in such a way that the person appeared to have a stroke. It disrupted the pathways, rerouting them like a circuit board. Certain cell clusters would be affected, causing the brain to route the wrong signals and shut down others. No one would ever suspect anything. The diagnosis would always be the same—a stroke. It was uncomplicated and effective. When he agreed to give the United States Government the drug formula, it gave the CIA an easy method to bump off major players in the crazy post 9/11 world.

He had worked hard to make his way up through the ranks at Robideaux, quietly labored over his private research projects for years, and finally had this breakthrough. He had innocently mentioned to Roger the powers of his new drug, and Roger had taken it and run. Roger jokingly likened it to the creation of the atom bomb. It was clear to James that it would cause catastrophic changes, but only in taking out people who honestly deserved to be eliminated. That's why he decided to do it. He simply hadn't realized the impact it would have on his personal life, especially the loss of Catherine. It was eating at him because she still had no idea that he was alive. Right now, he was clinging to the hope that one day he could explain it all to her, face-to-face, and that she would forgive him. Meanwhile, life as he'd known it was over, and he was stuck in some God-forsaken place in the middle of nowhere until the government decided it was done with him.

Roger was the one who connected the dots with Robideaux. Then, the CIA orchestrated the infiltration of the important sites and chose the leaders to be targeted. James was assured he would never be linked in any way. That's what they told him. What infuriated him the most was how they had completely destroyed his life. He had no idea why they were still holding him. They simply told him he was being taken into protective custody. As they whisked him away, their plot to "murder" him was disclosed along with the plan to change his appearance and give him a new identity. They insisted it was the only way to keep him and Catherine safe. Roger had cautioned him about resisting, fearing that the agency might take a more permanent course of action. After all, they really didn't need James to be alive anymore.

~~~~~

James made one request of them, and when they brought beautiful Arianne to the small cabin in the woods, she made the long days easier to bear, although he still dreamed about and missed Catherine. He never asked Arianne if she had made the decision to come there or if they had grabbed her. He didn't care. He just wanted her to be there.

She looked different with brunette hair. He didn't like it or her excuse that she was trying to be "incognito." It didn't go with her green eyes and he missed her bouncing bright red hair. Red belonged on a woman who behaved like Arianne. Not brunette, which reminded him too much of Catherine. Yes, Arianne was beautiful, but spending so much time with her in such small quarters quickly began to wear on him.

He never should have allowed it to happen like this. He had some understanding of how the man who invented the atom bomb must have felt after it was dropped. There were no similarities, really, but it made him feel better to think that someone else had done something that seemed so much worse than what he had done. Still, the cost of what he did was very unfair and out of balance.

He didn't want this new life at all, but there wasn't a damn thing he could do about it. He was completely at their mercy. He was feeling intense remorse over the lies—even the simple lies of omission—that had sliced through his life with Catherine. He had cherished their relationship. He wondered how Catherine would react when she found out he was still alive. He wouldn't
~~~~~

blame her no matter what her reaction, even if she simply walked away. He'd much rather have her hit him, scream at him, but that wasn't Catherine. She would keep herself completely under control.

James and Arianne weren't allowed to have cell phones. Other than the local television shows, they had no contact with the outside world, until recently when the guards had allowed Arianne to leave the cabin and go into town. He was surprised when she came back with a jeep. He knew she had sacrificed a lot to be with him, and he wasn't sure what she thought about their relationship. They had been together briefly before he met Catherine, but at that time, it had been recreational for him. Now, she was convenient.

The cabin had been built as a bunk-house for railroad repairmen and was very old. The only remodeling that had been done was electricity and plumbing. The barely running water was luke warm. There was only one small window, a double bed, a night stand with a lamp, and a small closet and overhead luggage rack with a few places to hang clothes underneath. They had a small plug-in heater, which adequately warmed the small rooms, but that was little consolation. If you were using the commode, you could wash your hands in the sink at the same time. You hit your elbows on the sides of the shower when you tried to wash your hair.

They had created a makeshift kitchen by bringing in a microwave and small refrigerator, but Arianne had to wash their few dishes in the bathroom. They kept everything in totes piled up against the wall. Frankly, it sucked. Most of the time, the guards felt sorry for them and would bring them food from town.

At first, Arianne seemed okay with their situation, but now he knew she was restless. They were both anxious to get out of the woods and back to a normal life. The men guarding them told them it wouldn't be too much longer. Making things worse, James barely recognized himself when he looked in the mirror. His features had been altered, contacts changed the color of his eyes to hazel, and his hairline had been moved farther back on his forehead. He doubted whether anyone from his former life would recognize him.

When Arianne first arrived, his face had been swollen, distorting his appearance quite a bit, but as it resolved, she had told him, "It's not so bad. I still know it's you. It could have been worse, you know. You could have actually been in that crash. They could have easily decided to kill you. We have to be grateful you are alive. Don't you agree?"

He shuddered at the thought of what they were capable of, but he hadn't said a word to her. He simply climbed into bed with her. Afterwards, he lay staring at the ceiling. He wanted his old life back, but for Catherine's sake he was trying to move on.

~~~~~

Arianne shifted down into third, removed her hair clip, and shook her hair out as the wind whipped through the jeep's open windows. It was finally warm enough to enjoy driving on the ridiculously curving road near Glacier National Park. The small cabin up on Bison Creek was nestled far back in the woods. She hated it, but she was relieved to know exactly where in the world
~~~~~

they were. It has been a tough winter and they had been trapped indoors more days than she cared to think about. She never dreamed that her glamorous and exciting life would be reduced to taking care of James. She had even dyed her hair brunette in order to alter her appearance, not that anyone here in this remote part of Montana would have recognized her. It was the least she could do for her closest friend, what with his having died in the horrific accident and being burned and all. She had been furious with him when he'd sent for her, and she had discovered that he was actually alive.

"It wasn't me in that car," he said. "That was staged to protect all of us and keep Catherine safe."

He had explained everything to her. She couldn't help but feel sorry for him because she knew how much he had loved Catherine. As the story unfolded, she was sucked into feeling that she needed to be there for him. After all, every aspect of his life had suddenly changed. In fact, he had no life. The United States Government completely owned him once he'd given them his formula for that stupid drug combination. She tried to understand why he did it, but none of it really mattered now. All that had mattered to her in the beginning was that he needed her and she had immediately allowed them to take her to him. Now, well, she was pretty fed up with the small cabin in the woods and 24/7 with him. She simply didn't know how to quit him anymore than he had known how to say "No" to the government. They had both become victims by wanting to do the right thing.

She pulled the jeep to the side of the small cabin,

stepped up the two small steps onto the porch, and opened the door. The guard was sitting on the small front porch and simply nodded. James was propped up in the bed reading a book. That was all he ever did. He ate, slept, read, slept, had sex with her, and slept some more. He was in the thralls of the worst depression she had ever seen. She had gone to town to get him some new clothes and some real food. She only hoped that the things would fit him and give him a sense that this was going to end soon. He'd taken to being not so nice lately. She'd also bought herself red hair dye, not only because he told her he hated her as a brunette, but because it would make her feel better about herself when she looked in the mirror.

It still surprised her every time she looked at him. It was him, but it wasn't him. The work they'd done on his face did make him unrecognizable to someone like, well, Catherine. He was still sort of handsome, but in a different way than she was used to. His nose was smaller and slightly pointed at the end. His hairline was back and made his forehead seem bigger and shiny. His eyes appeared farther apart. She didn't know whether she would ever get used to him looking this way. He complained about sticking the contact lenses in his eyes and she hated listening to his protests.

"Why the hell do I have to wear these damn things when I'm not going anywhere?"

She told him the truth. "You have to get used to wearing them so you look natural with them in your eyes. We don't know exactly when they will turn us loose."

She understood how he felt. She had been stuck

there for months through the worst winter she'd ever seen. She had no idea it would be this long when she'd come to him. Her only consolation was that sometimes he was sweet with her when they made love, but that bothered her. She wondered if he was imagining Catherine when he was making love to her like that. Other times, he was rough with her. She didn't quite know what to think. Still, she didn't know how to let him go. She worried about what would happen to him if he were left alone. He seemed fragile. She hadn't realized how balanced Catherine must have kept him. She wondered how long this "job" was going to last. She had once liked him a lot, but now she didn't like feeling like she had to baby sit him. She missed the old James—the sexy, masculine, in control man he used to be.

~~~~
~~~~

CHAPTER 4

Buck Matthews flipped over the "Closed" sign and locked the feed store door. He stood looking down the street at the little country town he'd somehow landed in. Highberry was just west of Gainesville, Florida, and had been plumb full of surprises. He never imagined that old Mrs. Peters would be so prophetic when she claimed Deb Albom wanted him to be the father of her child. Now he was slap dab in the middle of that predicament; not that having a baby was an insurmountable dilemma—but the way it had happened was. One night stands, well...

He and Zane had been so young when they ran away from Montana and began their adventure as operatives with the United States Government. They had experienced more than most men. Now it seemed like they were getting a second chance at a real life.

He let out a low long whistle. He expected his mother to be shocked when he finally found the courage to tell her at this late date she was about to become a grandmother. He would wait for her question as to whether he had set a date for the wedding. No grandchild of hers was going to be illegitimate. He was certain of that. He flipped a bead of perspiration off his forehead and walked toward his truck. Sitting silently for a moment, he mustered up his courage and opened his cell phone. She answered on the second ring.

"Deb, this is Buck. I'm leaving the store. I'll pick us

up some grub and then I'll be at the farm. Would you care to join me?"

~~~~

Deb's heart started beating faster the moment she heard his voice. She had been hoping; waiting for his call. She finished buttoning her blouse, slid lip gloss slowly across her already red lips, and stared into the mirror, fluffing her long reddish brown hair. This would be one of those moments that would redefine her life. She couldn't imagine what he would say. All she could do was pray as she drove toward her future.

Deb Albom's life had taken a strange turn of events. She had come to this small remote town hoping to escape her past. It seemed easy to become a realtor. All she had to do was drive people around and help them find a new place to live. She hadn't banked on the turn in the road that would lead her to being very pregnant and single.

His house was a medium brown color, wooden with a veranda that ran all the way around. Four rocking chairs were placed on either side of the front door. There was an empty three-legged fern pot most likely left by the former owner. A small black bucket sat by the door, half-full of sand and cigarette butts. Deb was happy to see that he didn't smoke in the house. She banged the horseshoe door knocker.

As soon as he opened his door, the scent of his aftershave floated out and surrounded her. She could almost taste it. Buck was dressed in clean jeans with a crisp light blue shirt. His sandy colored hair, light brown eyes, and even his build took her breath away every time
~~~~

she saw him. He opened the door wide and let her step in. The entry opened right into the great room. They stood in the dim light looking at each other, and in an instant were in each other's arms. She was being kissed as she'd never been kissed before. He was tender and his lips were soft and delicious. It was a long time before they stopped.

Deb had never felt that hot in her entire life. It was almost embarrassing because her neck and face felt like they were on fire. He folded his fingers between hers and pulled her into his chest, wrapping their arms behind her back.

"I have a proposal of sorts for you," he said softly into her ear. "You don't have to marry me if you don't want to. It's not like that. It's more like this." Buck took a deep breath and said, "Miss Deb, would you do me the honor of moving in with me?"

He was searching her face, and before she could say a word, he added sweetly, "I think my mother would be proud to have you as a daughter-in-law. I think you are just what's been missing from my life. It didn't happen the way I thought it would, but we don't need to be in a hurry."

She didn't say a word. She had prayed and hoped, but deep inside, she had expected him to dump her. After all, this wasn't the way she had planned her life either, but he was trying to make it right for her.

"I know this ain't nothing fancy, but it's safe and we can make it work. I think we can do it. I really do."

She couldn't let him struggle for another minute. She stood up on her toes and kissed him square on the mouth as hard as she could.

"Buck Matthews, I would love to mmmmm—move in with you." She had let the "m" slowly roll off her lips trying not to say "marry."

She gasped as he picked her up and spun her around.

"I promise I will make this okay. I really will. And I am happy about the babies and when we are ready....."

She put her index finger on his lips. She had barely wrapped her own mind around carrying his children–his twins.

"Don't say it. Not yet."

She followed him as he took her hand and walked into the kitchen.

"Best way to a man's heart is through his kitchen," he smiled, as he quickly pulled plates and silverware from the cupboards.

She watched as he poured them each a glass of milk and dished out the fried chicken and potato salad. Before Deb knew it, they were eating their first meal as a couple. She couldn't help but think this was the best day of her life, so far. For the first time in a long time, she saw a man through eyes that weren't hiding all her fears.

~~~~~

Buck tried not to question the scenes in his mind as he watched Deb's belly grow, but his life had become somewhat of a wonderment. He was thrilled the first time he felt the twins move beneath his hands, and he was excited about the fact that he would soon be a father. It was something he thought would always elude him. The fact he was getting two kids at once was a bonus; plus he and Deb thought two would probably be
~~~~~

quite enough.

There was something bothering him, though. Deb hadn't seemed all that great when she first came into his feed store. She'd been a bit flirty, batting her fake eyelashes at him. There had been no sex appeal or magnetism whatsoever. To him, she had looked dumpy and wore too many clothes, layered like a gypsy. Then, that day she'd appeared at his door, she'd looked different. She was in tight jeans and her blouse was unbuttoned just enough and he'd lost his mind not once but twice with her. Damn, it had been sweet, but he never expected this. He just wished he could figure out exactly what it was about her that was nagging at him.

CHAPTER 5

The morning news revealed that an oil leak was looming in the Gulf of Mexico and it was eating at him. They kept calling it the "Black Tide." That bothered him too because the news photos clearly showed huge red patches of oil floating on the surface. It went as far as the eye could see with one slick the size of Texas. Catherine brought it up.

"I can't stand looking at the birds and other animals being destroyed by the oil."

"I know. It is the worst possible scenario for an area that has already suffered so much. Their best bet is a big storm."

"Are you serious? My God, Zane. That would be even more devastating."

"Sure. They have already lost so much from Hurricane Katrina, but the best thing for them is to get that damn thing capped off and then have a big storm blow in. It would break it up and be less destructive in the long run."

He could see by her face that she couldn't grasp the horror of another big storm hitting them. "History has a way of repeating itself. I was talking to Buck about it. I don't know why they call it 'Black Tide' when it is clearly red, except that then it could be confused with that nasty Red Tide micro-organism that creates the fish kills. It brings to my mind the red river of blood from the massive destruction of the buffalo herds. You do know the government decided that if they took away the one thing that sustained the Native Americans, the buffalo, it would destroy them. Without their source of food, clothing, housing, weapons, they would not survive. So, they very systematically desecrated the herds until there were only a few hundred buffalo left."

He watched Catherine as the tears began to well up in her eyes. She swallowed as if she had a lump in her throat and then she shivered. "That's horrible. I never knew that. It is heartbreaking."

"The Native Americans that fled either died trying to get away or gave in by surrendering when they were about to freeze or starve to death. Many of them were slaughtered along with their horses."

"Their horses? You mean to tell me they killed their horses too?"

He could see the shock on her face. "Oh, they had a reason. They knew it would break them down even more and give them no way to get away. I guess you don't know about the smallpox either?"

"Smallpox? I remember hearing that many of them died from the white man's disease."

"Well, they got this idea of contaminating the blankets they gave them."

"That makes no sense. No sense at all. It makes me sick."

"Well, now, here we are with these foreigners pumping our oil out of our ocean floor, and they cut corners, screw around, and accidentally blow up their rigging. Who pays the consequences? They think they can solve it with money. The blood of the fisherman, the restaurant workers, the hotel keepers, and on and on;

well, it is just like the blood of the Indians. That's what I mean by history repeats itself."

"James wasn't any better than those people who contaminated the blankets. They thought they were doing something for the good, just like he did. He created a very destructive drug and didn't care who it destroyed. Isn't it just the same? Zane, isn't that the truth?"

Zane sat looking at the floor for a moment. *Where was he in this picture?* He carefully chose his response. "No. Not really. James was trying to stop the worst of our enemies. He wasn't creating something to take out masses of people. His goal was specific individuals whose loss would mean a domino effect to that government. He thought he was protecting his country by his actions. He helped get rid of the problems one at a time."

"Well, didn't they think if they got rid of the Native Americans, they were getting rid of the enemy? I simply can't imagine him thinking like that. I had no clue."

"I'm not convinced James knew the sacrifices he would have to make. He really was a genius for putting those chemicals together. But, they used him. You will never know what was really going through his mind."

"That's why I can't dwell on it too much. I go round and round and always come back to the same conclusion. I decided I want to remember the sweetness of our relationship and forget about all the parts I didn't know. Then it doesn't matter what he did. It only matters how he was with me and I can move on from there."

"That makes it easier for us, but I don't want you

ever to feel like you can't talk about it to me or to anyone else. I understand that you had a life before me and I'm okay with that."

Zane loved her for her openness and her sincerity. He loved her for the way she lived her life. She was beautiful, had a gorgeous body, a great mind, but most of all, he loved her for her heart. "Catherine, it pains me that you had to live through that."

He watched her chest heave as she let out that low sigh and then took in a deep breath. She told him, "It is getting easier. It will never make sense, but it got me to today and for that and you, I am grateful."

She had finally started talking to him about all of it. That was enough for him for now.

~~~~~

Zane watched as she rode next to him staring at her horse's neck lost in her thoughts. He waited. He could sneak a look sideways at her without really turning his head. She hadn't caught on to it yet. He waited some more. He knew she was in that faraway place she sometimes traveled to. It was easier to leave her alone. He saw her shake her shoulders and pull herself back into the present. She simply looked up, smiled at him, and didn't say a word.

"Absolutely fabulous day," he said.

"Yes. Yes it is." She sighed. "I love this place so much. I never dreamed life could be this sweet."

They rode on silently. It bothered him that her phone didn't ring. She never seemed to get any mail, other than the usual bills, junk, and occasional packages from her accountant or attorney. It was hard
~~~~~

to understand how such a remarkable woman could vanish from everyone who had been in her past. But then, no one was looking to find him either. Except for Buck and his occasional phone call to his mother, he was marching solo too. He and Catherine were in some ways very much alike.

Their relationship was unlike anything he had ever known. If he summarized it in one word, it would be *EASY*. There were no conflicts, even if they had a difference of opinion. He took the time to listen to her and heard what she had to say. It was a pure exchange of thoughts, adult to adult, without judgment. The problem was it made him question how he'd handled himself in the past. What also bothered him was how he was going to find the right moment to tell her that he was going to Montana. It had already been too long. He and his mother weren't getting any younger. He wanted to pick a time when Catherine wouldn't feel too much pressure. The horses were spending more time out grazing and the days were getting longer so it seemed to be the perfect timing.

~~~~~~

Catherine loved the way she and Zane interacted with each other, but it made her analyze her relationship with her deceased husband even more. Try as she might, she couldn't keep James out of her head. The two men were at completely opposite ends of the spectrum. Zane had lived a rough life on the ranch and then been constantly on the move, working secretly, all those years. James had been gifted. He had been able to create an almost perfect life. Because he was uniquely
~~~~~~

intelligent, he found a way to obtain the support he needed to go to college and graduate with honors. Robideaux Pharmaceutical had been a perfect match for him. She was, however, beginning to understand how selfish and self-centered James had been as she fell deeper in love with this caring, loving man who accidentally came into her life.

She had been crazy about James. He was charismatic, took control of a room the minute he entered, and he had loved her deeply. She felt as if she were betraying that part of him, but the absentee, deceitful man was tearing her apart. How could she have missed all the signs and who had he really become? He had turned out to be such a liar. He had been working on something so significant to the country's welfare, but he hadn't trusted her with even a snippet of information. None of it made any sense. She shook her head.

"I'm okay. Really, I am," she said softly.

"I know you are," Zane assured her.

She hadn't meant to say it out loud. She had so many questions, but she was also afraid Zane would have the answers. She knew for now that these things were best left in the grave.

She had made a pact with herself to get up earlier this week to allow them to retreat to the porch in the afternoon. It also gave them an early start working the horses, which were in terrific shape from being ridden every day. Their coats were slick and glossy. She loved the easy pace of the farm and enjoyed watching the horses and dogs. She also liked watching Zane, especially when he worked Trouble. The way he rode was mesmerizing. She could see by Trouble's eyes that he wanted to please Zane, but more, he enjoyed the man and the job he gave him. They did some turnarounds and sudden stops that sent her head spinning. The black was absolutely shimmering in the sunlight.

Catherine took a deep breath. She felt like she needed to pinch herself. The spring flowers were absolutely brilliant and abundant following the early spring rains. When she bought the house near Gainesville, Florida, she had no idea the sparse and scraggly looking bushes were actually azaleas. Now they were in full bloom. It made her feel happy to look at the house with all the pinks, purples, and whites up against the almost white siding as they rode back from their ride.

This house had been in her dreams her entire life. She loved the French paned windows and the porch that ran the entire length of the back of the house. She recently purchased a nice love seat and a couple of comfortable cozy rocking chairs. An old trunk became the coffee table or footrest. The scattered rugs were favorite spots for the dogs. It was the perfect sun-room, and with a few African violets placed in the window sills, she felt almost ordinary as she went around with her little watering can. Her life had certainly taken a different path than she expected.

They dismounted in front of the barn and led the horses inside, cross tying them in the aisle. She couldn't help but smile, listening to Zane hum as he un-tacked his horse and carried his saddle, pad, and bridle into the tack room. She was much slower at it than he was, but it didn't matter. Life had taken on its own rhythm for each of them.

~~~~~

Zane had begun to feel less invasive when he entered her bedroom. He might have been fine in the guest bedroom, except that he'd grown very comfortable sleeping next to this beautiful woman.

"I love waking up while you are still asleep and listening to you breathing," he told her.

"I'm not so sure I love that."

"Why not?"

"Well, I probably snore or sleep with my mouth open." She was grinning at him.

"You don't."

"Well, that's comforting. But I do appreciate that you don't wake me up when you slide out early."

He would slip quietly out of bed, dress down the hall in the guest bedroom, and head to the kitchen. Sometimes, Catherine couldn't resist the smell of coffee and she would join him downstairs. Some days, he would bring her a tray and crawl back into bed with her. He knew exactly how lucky he was to have those moments.

"You don't mind that Champ still sneaks upstairs late at night do you?" he asked her.

"Of course, not. He acts as if no one knows. I am sort of jealous that he has accepted his place on the rug on your side of the bed, though, when he's supposed to be my dog. But, I'm glad I don't fall over him in the middle of the night when I paddle to the bathroom."

"Poor Friskie wasn't so easy to convince that the little doggie bed was meant for him. He really wants to
~~~~~

be in the bed with us."

"I know and I do miss cuddling with him."

"More than cuddling with me?"

She was smiling her silly grin, but didn't answer him. They had compromised by letting the little dog in bed with them on the lazy coffee mornings. She knew that Zane didn't really care, plus he told her, "Whatever makes it possible to keep that beautiful smile on your face is worth it."

The other dogs never attempted to come upstairs. They had their favorite spots and weren't as needy when it came to interacting with humans. He was certain they appreciated being saved from their various calamities and they showed it by being very well-behaved. When he walked around the pasture surrounded by the dogs, it made him smile because he had waited a long time for a dog and now he had her six.

Sometimes, he wished he could erase the memory of how mean his father had been about his wanting a dog. It brought back a flood of unpleasant feelings when he allowed himself to remember. It had been painful watching his father interact with the dog that he finally brought home. At first, he had been excited thinking the dog was for him, but it soon became perfectly clear that he was to have nothing to do with his father's dog. That was one of the most hurtful times, magnified by watching his father beat the dog when the dog only wanted to be with his father, much the same way that he did. The poor dog had been following his father into the training pen when it was trampled by a frightened horse. His father had no one to blame for that except himself because he had been in one of his moods and forgotten to tie the dog outside the pen. That was one of the deciding factors in Zane's leaving the ranch as soon as he could. Now, he was trying to put those memories in their place and create new ones with this remarkable woman.

CHAPTER 6

"Hello," Catherine said as she caught her breath after bolting down the stairs to answer the phone.

"Well, good morning, young lady; it's Buck. Is your boy around?"

Catherine wondered what "her boy" would think about Buck calling him that, just as Zane came through the back door with all the dogs.

She mouthed, "It's Buck," as she handed him the phone.

"Hey, buddy, what's up?"

"Hey, Zane, got a minute? I wanted to talk to you in person, but I'm stuck here at the store."

"Well, you got me now, so shoot."

Buck cleared his throat nervously.

"I guess I'll just say it."

"Okay."

"I swear, I only boinked her once and she's gotten herself knocked up."

Zane took a deep breath. There was never any telling what was going to come out of Buck's mouth. Plus, how could she get herself...

Buck continued, "Well, I'm not sure what she's gonna do. I think her mother wants her to come home."

"Well, Buck, what do you want her to do?"

"I swear, Zane. I never expected it, but I'm kinda excited. She's not such a bad looker either, you know. What the hell do you think?"

"I really don't know what to tell you. It's up to you two to work it out. You do have that big old house."

"But, hell, Zane, this is a life sentence."

"Nice way to put it. What else were you planning to do? Spend the rest of your life alone on that farm? You'll do the right thing."

"I know. I actually asked her to move in with me."

"So you have made a decision."

"Yes, I guess I have."

"Well, good luck with that, man."

"Thanks a lot. I'll let you know. It's twins. She's carrying twins."

"Wow, Buck. That's great!"

Zane was chuckling when Catherine came in from the back porch with her watering can. "Everything okay with Buck?" she asked.

"Not exactly."

~~~~~

It had been Zane's idea to invite them over for dinner. The table was set. The potatoes were in the oven. The salad was chilling on ice. All Catherine had left to do was put the final touches on the cake and change her clothes. He was finishing shaving when she slid her arms around his waist. He felt good against her body.

"You can use my bathroom, you know." She still had her arms around him.

"This is fine. It's cozy in the guest bathroom and I can belly up to the mirror."

"I'm excited and hoping it will be the first time I'll be able to talk to Buck without his roaming eyes."
~~~~~

"Yes, this will be interesting. Do you know this woman very well? Deb what's her name?"

"Yes, as my realtor, she was fine, I mean finding me this place and all. Oh, and the encounter at that café that time. She did seem a little wild then."

"I sure hope Buck knows what he's getting himself into."

It was a celebration of sorts—for all of their newfound lives and loves. It was Sunday and Buck's feed store was closed. It was a perfectly clear day, so Catherine had Zane set up a table on the sun-porch. She was busy setting the places and fixing the wildflowers that he had found up in the meadow. He overruled her on pot roast and opted for steaks, potatoes, and "greens," his name for a salad. They had prepared a corn medley and it was simmering on the stove. She popped dinner rolls into the oven.

It was almost hard to believe, but they were each living very different lives. Now they were about to see just how pregnant Deb really was. Catherine watched from the window as Zane shook Buck's hand and they patted each other on the back. Zane then nodded at Deb, holding out his arm, pointing toward the house as he guided them to the back porch door. They arrived with a lovely bouquet and a bottle of non-alcoholic wine.

Buck said, "I think you both know my..." He stumbled over the word for a second and then continued, "Deb." It was obvious he didn't quite know what to call her and his faced flushed a bright pink.

Organizing the dogs had been interesting. They put a gate over the porch entrance into the kitchen and left Friskie in the upstairs bedroom. He seemed content in his little bed. The brood quieted down once they realized they couldn't get to the guests. Only Champ voiced his protests with a bit of whining.

"He is gorgeous," Deb said.

"He's a rescue. They all are."

Deb patted his head over the gate, which seemed to pacify him. She looked amazing and different. She had been a rather nondescript red-head in her flowing skirts and baggy blouses, with sandals on her feet most of the time. Now Catherine saw a more defined and refined version. When she turned sideways, there was a very protruding baby bump, but overall, she was a lot slimmer. In fact, the Deb she remembered had been plump and wore loose unattractive clothes. For a pregnant woman, Deb looked great in her jeans and sweet flowered top that revealed quite a bit of cleavage. It was an apparent transformation in such a short period of time. Deb's fiery red hair had often been pulled away from her face in either a knot or ponytail that flipped around when she was involved in her overly animated behavior. The woman here now was not that rather chaotic person she'd spent hours touring the real estate market with. Deb's hair was now reddish brown and curly, framing her face softly and flowing over her shoulders and down her back. She looked very cute, and her green eyes popped. Catherine couldn't figure out how Deb had transformed herself, especially during her pregnancy. If someone looked at her from the back, they would never guess she was expecting.

Buck and Deb were beaming as they settled on the porch. It was clear something fairly serious was going on with those two. There had been an obvious shift in Deb's behavior and Buck looked very smitten by her.

"Welcome to our home," Catherine said. "Deb, you look fantastic by the way. Do you know if you are having a boy or a girl?"

Deb smiled and giggled as Buck answered for them. "It doesn't really matter to us; just so they are healthy."

Catherine looked at Zane, but he was looking at Buck.

"Zane, you didn't tell me they were having twins! Well, my goodness, congratulations." She nudged him with her foot.

The four of them fell into easy conversation at the dinner table about their farms, plans for Buck's house, and at last, the conversation turned to when the babies would arrive.

Deb said, "I never imagined this could happen, but I swear, I am going to do my damnedest. We discovered both of us have twins in our families, and so it was bound to happen. I can't believe it myself."

Zane spoke up, "I know you will do whatever it takes, Buck. I'm really happy for you both. Seeing you like this makes it all worth it."

Zane slapped Buck on the back and then quickly flicked a tear that was about to slide down his cheek before anyone could notice.

~~~~~

After Buck and Deb had gone home and the chores were all done, Catherine picked a quiet moment to ask Zane, "Was I seeing things or does Deb seem a whole lot slimmer than I remembered?"

Zane chuckled, "I was wondering about that. I don't
~~~~~

recall her looking so fit, and here she is toting around twins. Go figure. I saw you watching her."

"I know. I couldn't help myself. I was thinking the whole time that she must have felt it too. I just couldn't help it. Honestly, I don't think Buck has a clue what he's in for." Try as she might, she couldn't stop what she was feeling. It hurt. It was too late for her even to consider being a mother, and she couldn't stop the tears from welling up in her eyes.

"Well, Buck seems okay with all of it. I mean I've never seen him really happy before. Not like this."

"Yes, they do seem happy. That's the truth."

"Of course, I'm glad for them. I'm glad for all of us that things turned out the way they did."

She knew they all had a lot to be grateful for, but she simply couldn't wrap her mind around how Deb appeared to have lost so much weight while being pregnant and also the changes in her demeanor. Could Deb have been putting on some kind of "act" before?

She was also trying hard not to feel the pressure in her chest or the pang around her heart. She didn't want to feel a single ounce of jealousy toward Deb, but she did. She knew she would never be able to be what Deb was about to be—a Mom!

CHAPTER 7

Catherine and Zane sat on the loveseat on the porch, watching lightning from a huge thunderstorm. The rain was pelting the windows. She jumped when a lightning strike lit up the yard. "Whew, that was close," she said.

Zane felt her shiver next to him and pulled her closer. "Yes, it was. Do you want to go inside?"

"No. It's okay. Maybe it is all about me. I know I'm the one who keeps everyone at arm's length, but look what happens every time I trust someone. I really want to blame someone."

Zane didn't know where this was coming from, but he didn't care. She was talking. "I'm not saying I don't understand, Catherine, but I have wondered why your phone doesn't ring and your mailbox is fairly empty, but I don't think you should blame yourself."

"I feel like it is mostly my fault. I haven't exactly reached out to anyone. I don't write; I don't call. I'm the one who moved and I removed myself from their lives."

"Still, you would think someone would wonder how you are doing."

"I had everything well organized for them at the non-profit when I left. The Missing Link Foundation is very busy and they all do their jobs well. I'm not surprised, although they do occasionally enter my mind. I thought they'd at least let me know how they are doing. They are responsible for so many families, besides their own.

Plus, they network with all the other service providers. You know, it doesn't really matter. That's not my life anymore."

"You say that it doesn't matter, but I know you have a sensitive heart and I'm sure you do think about them."

"Of course I do. But I have a new life now."

Zane wasn't about to bring up James or her family. The Foundation was the safest topic of conversation for now. He pulled her even closer to him.

~~~~~

Some days, at first light, Zane would slip quietly out of their bed, quickly dress in the guest bedroom, and spend a few minutes in the bathroom across the hall. He would head out in the semi-darkness to greet the day. The dogs loved being turned out to search for fresh morning trails. Zane didn't mind tracking whatever had been nearby during the night—a fox, an opossum, or tiny field mice. He hadn't lost his knack for keeping an eye on certain nests or finding evidence of where an owl had eaten its prey.

He would return to the barn and groom the horses and have them ready for their early ride or head to the house and prepare a robust breakfast. Those breakfasts were one of the reasons Catherine began to fill out and lose that gaunt look in her face from when she'd been so ill. Her auburn hair was now thick and full of life. He wanted to ensure that she enjoyed every meal he prepared. He also insisted on fresh flowers on the table, wild or bought on their trips to the grocery store. He knew she loved the attention, and he enjoyed doing it for her. His goal was to have her radiant and healthy again.
~~~~~

~~~~~

In her other life, Catherine had been a totally different person. It was as if she had unzipped from her old body and was now walking around in someone else's—simply stepping out and entering into another world. Sometimes, she hardly recognized herself in the mirror, and it felt even deeper on an emotional level. She didn't fully understand how she had mustered the strength to move from New York City and into her current situation in a small town called Highberry in North Florida. Some days it felt surreal.

Catherine was sitting at her desk in the back room behind the kitchen, watching Zane through the window as he split oak logs and stacked them for firewood. She began to doodle on a notepad.

Zane Wheeler - Mother ? Father ? Siblings?

Best friend and co-worker — Buck Matthews

Mother/Father ? Deb Albom - Siblings ? Children ?

Catherine DeLong - Mother - Elizabeth -

Hamilton -Step-Father

Father - John (deceased) — Sister - Constance (KiKi)

Uncle Walton/Aunt Josey — Cousins — Waylon & Justin

Half-Sister - Celia — Celia's Husband ? Niece - Olivia

Celia's Grandmother
~~~~~

~~~~~

She was incredibly grateful and yet uncomfortably confused at times. If she truly loved her James, how was it that she was now living and sleeping with this other man—someone she actually barely knew? It had been so easy and the answer seemed quite simple. James was dead and she had fallen in love with Zane. She honestly couldn't help herself. It just happened, and she didn't care if it seemed to be too soon. She liked how she felt about him, how he seemed to be crazy about her, and the way they had blended their lives in such a natural and easy way. Life was no longer as complicated, and they were both incredibly happy together.

Her thoughts wandered. Maybe James had crumbled under the pressure. He let his guard down and that's how they were able to get to him. Most of the time, she could control her mind, her heart, and how she let herself feel. She knew how her love for Zane felt, and yet she was unable to let go of her dead husband. She hated it, but she couldn't solve it. Not yet. She knew Zane was aware of more details about James' death, but she couldn't ask the questions. It was the old, "Don't ask, don't tell" adage. What she didn't know wouldn't hurt her. She knew it wasn't an accident. James had been murdered. The word sent chills up her spine and her mind spinning. She pictured his face. Had he realized he was going to die as it was happening? What were his last thoughts? What were his last words? Was he really dead when the fire...? She shuddered. She had always been naturally intuitive and had recently begun to feel an uncertain dread when it came to James. It was
~~~~~

as if the fear of the unknown had kept her from tuning in to her deeper feelings.

~~~~~

When Zane came into the house, he caught her staring off into space. She should have been enjoying looking out at the pastures, watching the horses and her dogs. Instead, she was in that faraway place where her mind took her. He could see how painful it was, because of her face. It changed when she went away there. Her brow would get a deep furrow, her mouth would tighten, and she would clench her jaw. He could see her pain. He never knew whether it was about her uncle or about her husband or both of them at the same time. She hardly talked to him about it. In fact, she didn't speak to anyone really except for him unless they went to town or that one night that Buck and Deb had come over. She was cordial, but guarded. It bothered him that no one else seemed to care about her. He shook his head. When he touched her arm, she jumped. He knew the scenario.

Catherine said, "I was just about to drift off. It's so relaxing out here."

She was lying. Zane pulled a chair right up in front of her, took her hands in his, and sat, gently looking into her eyes.

"Catherine, tell me what is bothering you. Let me help."

"I can't bring myself back to all of it right now. I know what they said, but I don't want to hear anything else. If I hear it, then it will make it true."

He knew how fragile she could be. He had helped
~~~~~

her struggle back after her Uncle Walton passed away. He certainly didn't want to send her back there again, but it wasn't healthy for her to keep brooding on this, keeping it locked deep inside either.

"Tell me one thing today. Just one thing and we will do it that way. We'll take it one little step at a time. How does that sound?"

~~~~

She quietly searched his face. She wanted to trust him. She thought she had known James, but look at the lies he had created. Then what about Roger? He was no friend to James if he could behave the way he did toward her after James died. Roger was supposed to be his best friend. He had been no friend to her either. Her own father had abandoned her and her sister, Kiki, because of all the dead children he carried in his mind after the war. Now she was supposed to trust this man— another man. So far, Zane had done nothing to make her mistrust him, but still.

It reminded her of something Arianne had said, "Men are for recreational purposes only. They are kind of like an erector set. You know. Fun to play with, but then you take it apart and put that toy away." Arianne would giggle and smile after she said it. She hadn't actually realized what Arianne meant until now. Had Arianne been playing with James? With her? She thought they were just friends, Arianne and James. In fact, it was at Arianne's party at her apartment that Catherine had first met James. Now it was puzzling and she was struggling with making sense of any of it. Had there been clues that she had missed in that
~~~~

relationship as well?

Zane was patiently sitting in front of her as she took a deep breath.

"So much has happened in such a short period of time. First James died, then I moved, and then Uncle Walton. Plus, my life has changed a lot with you. Not that I'm not grateful for what we have..." Her voice trailed off.

He sat waiting, not saying a word.

"I love our life. I really do. I don't want to do a thing to change it right now, but I'd also like all the pieces from the past to fit. Then I wouldn't feel so disjointed or at least I think it would help me to move on."

"I completely understand and I am here for you."

CHAPTER 8

The monotony of picking the stalls gave him plenty of time to think. Zane was afraid if she knew all the details, she would become wary of him, worse yet, angry at him. She would know that he had known more than he told her. It was complicated. The government had a way of doing that to people's lives. They tangled everything all up and left you dangling. They had pushed James into a corner and he hadn't been able to get out. They screwed up his life and then they stood him on a cliff and told him to jump.

Zane could only compare her pain to his greatest loss way back when he was just a kid in Montana. Parker Iron Crow took him up to Sweet Grass one spring, where they watched a herd of wild horses for an entire day. At least Zane had thought that they were wild.

"Pick out a pony and we will catch it and take it home for you to train."

It had taken several days to set up a corral at one end of the ravine just past where the horses entered. They came to a spring fed watering hole. Once the horses were trapped, they let them settle overnight. Zane picked out a nice paint pony and Parker threw a rope on him. Then Parker roped himself a nice chestnut mare. They loaded them into the trailer, released the rest of the herd, and headed back to the ranch. What Zane didn't know was that the horses belonged to the neighbor, Allen Echo Talker, and were green broke and released to winter in that area.

Zane worked hard training White Cloud alongside Parker and his mare, Lady. Before too long, they were out working cattle and riding the ranch. Zane knew his father was watching him from a distance and tried not to feel too proud. It wasn't long before his father decided to sell his pony to a nearby family for their children. It broke Zane's heart and he never got over it; nor did he forgive his father. Zane just flat out hated him. He avoided him as much as possible. It was even worse the way the son of a bitch treated his mother. He kept that pain in his heart until the day the bastard stopped breathing.

All the anxiousness and anxiety Catherine was feeling dredged up that old stuff for him. He had never allowed himself to dwell on it, but it was suddenly coming up with such clarity that he was having detailed dreams about it. It made him think a lot about his mother, and it also made him realize how he had walled off so many feelings. He was able to do that for all these years until Catherine had unexpectedly come into his life.

At an early age, decisions were made by him that set up how he navigated through his life and how he treated people. He hated to admit it, but sometimes when he had to get rid of someone; it was easy to let that rage come out. He figured he was doing it first for his country, but secondly, to rid the planet of one more son of a bitch. It made it okay. It was what he signed up to do.

His mother had been furious at his father for selling

his pony. He heard them arguing, and he heard him slap her and heard what he said. "The boy has to learn, and I'm trying to teach him something. Better he learn it from me now than later on from someone else." He heard his father stomp off and his mother's footsteps as she came down the hall. He met her in the dim light, tears sitting ready to spill down his little face. She pulled him into her skirt and wrapped her arms around him.

"I'm so sorry, Zane. I know how much this hurts. You have to look at the good side of this. White Cloud will never want for anything with that nice family, and with the way you trained him, he will never do anything to hurt those kids either. I'm very proud of you."

He looked up at his mother's face as she pushed his dark hair out of his eyes.

"You did a great job. White Cloud will never forget you and you will never forget him either. That's all that matters."

Parker came out of the shadows, touched her on the shoulder and scooped Zane up. Then Parker had quietly hooked up the horse trailer and they'd gone straight up to that canyon in Sweet Grass. This time, Zane chose a horse. It had been that way every spring until he and Buck made their fateful decision. That year, Zane told Parker he was taking a break from training a horse, but the truth was he knew as soon as he graduated from high school, he would be gone.

~~~~~

Zane had seen first-hand the meanness that lives in the gut of some people. He witnessed the cold heartless murder of innocent people too many times. It made it
~~~~~

less difficult to do his job, especially if they got the bastards before they actually carried out their plans. He watched the powers chatting over dinner as if it didn't matter that someone's life had ended. They knew full well they were involved in a chess game where the winner wouldn't just declare checkmate. It made him sick to think how many scenarios were in motion at any moment across the planet while people as innocent as Catherine went about their normal days. It made him feel worse for her because her husband had been the major player in this pharmaceutical debacle. James had "lost his life" at the hands of some of the most devious people in the world. The fact that they were Americans made it even worse. There was no reason for her to know the details. It would be devastating to her and most likely their relationship. Things were too good right now.

James hadn't known all of the government's plan until he was too far into it to stop. If Catherine ever found out it wasn't James in the car that night, well, he didn't want to risk the outcome. James was gone and all that mattered was that he was never coming back to her.

Zane felt like he was the luckiest man alive, living on her beautiful farm and sleeping with this amazing woman. He wasn't about to let anything hurt her. The way he saw it, there were a couple of ways it could go. If she learned the truth, once the shock wore off, he suspected she would be furious. She already felt betrayed and lied to by James. Then again, she might completely flip out. After all, it would mean that she was still married to James, but sleeping with him. It might throw her into some kind of guilt over betraying her husband. Or not! What if she were so furious at James for yet another lie—the one about his not being dead, living another life somewhere else, with whom? He would take his chances. It was best to say nothing for now.

Then there was all that money. She received the insurance pay-out and then the other checks from the government. She'd be just the type to feel guilty and think she'd stolen the money from the insurance company. They would have to tell her that it was all part of the plot as well; the cover to make everyone believe that James was really dead. Otherwise, James would still be in danger because someone would be looking for him. It was the only way to protect him and, of course, her. The government had covered the insurance pay-out in order to keep it all quiet. At least, in the end, James had negotiated all of that very well, making sure that she was taken care of. Maybe if she knew that, she could forgive them both. James had a least done that for her.

But he still felt it was best if Catherine were protected from the truth. It would do no good for her to have all these details. She was handling the fact that James had concocted this secret drug to kill people. She was handling that he was gone, forever. He wanted to keep things the way they were as long as he could. The more time that elapsed, the better it was for all of them.

Buck and Deb were about to become parents, and Buck hadn't said a word to him about Catherine lately. Deb had done that for them. She and the feed store were keeping Buck occupied. It was all almost too good to be true.

He called the dogs and headed back to the house. She should be awake by now. It was one of his favorite parts of the day. The early morning walks and chores gave him the clarity that he needed. Plus, he enjoyed daybreak, and waiting for the sun to peek through the trees. He never knew what he would find in the early morning mist. He entered the back door in a burst with all the dogs around him. Catherine was standing at the kitchen window with a cup of coffee in her hand.

"I was lucky this morning. The dogs scattered off in different directions and I discovered a fawn curled in a fern bed up at the tree line. There was an azalea bud perched right between its ears on the top of its head. I had to smile, because I knew the deer had been right up against the house during the night."

"That's incredible."

"I wish I could have taken a picture for you, Catherine. I almost missed seeing it, except for the flick of an ear that caught my eye. The dogs might have passed right by it anyway because nature protects newborn fawns by giving them no scent at all in their first few days. I'm sure the mother wasn't far, so I turned around and headed back in another direction. There was no need to stress her out. Plus the dogs usually stay down in the meadow, if I do. Life doesn't get any better than this."

"I'm sorry I missed it, but I'm glad it makes you so happy."

~~~~~

Lately, Zane knew he was spending entirely too
~~~~~

much time lost in the insidious thoughts and the scenes that would creep in. He didn't know how to stop it. The hardest part was keeping everything from Catherine, especially when it came at night in dreams. He couldn't control what happened in his sleep. A couple of times, he jumped out of bed, but luckily it had been in the early morning hours and she had been in a deep sleep.

He had bought a book at a small used bookstore in Highberry and began to read it almost as soon as they got back home. He found it intriguing. *The Lucifer Effect* by Phillip Zimbardo put things in perspective. He'd been a mover, shaker, a doer his whole life. Now, in this quiet peaceful place, he could stop and reflect on where he'd been all these years.

He read, "When faced with some unusual behavior, some unexpected event, some anomaly that doesn't make sense, how do we go about trying to understand it?" That was precisely where Catherine was. All the evil-doers didn't care what they did with people's lives. It just didn't matter at all to them.

The death of two of the closest men in her life was devastating, but the betrayal by James clearly cut her to the core. James destroyed everything she believed in and caused her to flee. It was the fright/flight pattern seen in deer and in horses. She simply packed up and ran.

Her sudden illness following her uncle's death allowed her to crawl into a cocoon and heal. She came out of it weak, but with a new determination. She was functioning very well, in his opinion, but he could feel a terrible undercurrent that he worried would some day burst through. He was beginning to understand the walling off that people do and recognized it as what he did when he fled his own childhood.

The text was about how good people turn evil. He hoped it would help him help her. The bonus was in his understanding of his own behavior.

"You are not the same person working alone as you are in a group," he read. That was exactly what happened to him and Buck with the CIA and their training. They both changed dramatically.

"The powerful use the underlings to do their dirty work." He knew that was exactly the same story for her James. They were each simply doing their jobs, and they did them very well. He read Alison Des Ford's opinion: "The behavior lies under the surface of any of us. The simplified account of genocide allows distance between us and the perpetrators of genocide. They were so evil we couldn't ever see ourselves doing the same things."

It was the command structure of the United States that created the dysfunctional system that developed the strategies that played out with so much evil. The U.S. military, the CIA, the NSA, the government officials—they all knew the dirty little secrets. In any other situation, he and Buck would have never done what they had been able to do. He didn't feel like a hero, and yet, in the end, they had been lauded as such. Maybe now, in this particular arena, he could turn his life around and become a hero for her. He was willing to take that risk if it made this beautiful woman happy.

~~~~~

Over lunch, Zane related a story to Catherine from the book. "You should be really happy you left New
~~~~~

York. I was reading this morning and this guy did a social and community experiment. He parked two somewhat derelict cars—one in the Bronx in New York and one in Palo Alto, California. In broad daylight, twenty-seven different people stripped the Bronx car. In Palo Alto, no one touched the car. In fact, it rained one day and a man shut the hood so the engine wouldn't get wet. Then, when they drove the California car away, three people called to report the possible theft of an abandoned car. Imagine? Can you believe that? We humans are something else."

"I know," she said. "It is amazing how people act in certain situations. You really seem to be enjoying that book."

"I am. It is very interesting. It is so thought-provoking that I've only made it to page twenty-four so far."

"Well, I'm glad you found it in that old store and it's worth reading. I'm hard-pressed these days to find a book that doesn't include something disturbing. Maybe it's just me and my current state of mind, but I don't get these writers right now."

"Maybe you should work on your own book. Write what you want to read."

"I know. It's just finding the time."

Zane chuckled. "You have to take it. Set a certain time aside every day. I'll work around whatever you want to do. Silly, isn't it? Right now, all we have is time, Catherine."

There were so many things in *The Lucifer Effect* that stirred Zane's thoughts. He spent a lot of time comparing Catherine's situation to what the research revealed. When people feel anonymous, think that no one wants to know them or care about them, they tend to become anti-social and self-interested. They were both doing it. They were isolating themselves, and they were consumed with themselves. It wasn't very healthy, but at the same time, it didn't seem wrong.

The sky was an azure blue and the air was crisp, lacking the heaviness of the previous days' humidity. He stepped out toward the barn with a new stride of optimism and ideas for how to turn things around for both of them.

CHAPTER 9

Celia Fenmore sat in her car at the Jensen Beach Causeway, eating her lunch. Once her mother's secrets were revealed, they answered a lot of questions, but at the same time resulted in more complicated ones. Who was her father, really? Why hadn't anyone diagnosed her mother's brain injury?

She hadn't said a word to anyone about the fact that she had discovered she had a half-sister, not even to her husband, Cary. She didn't quite know how to explain her connection to Catherine DeLong. She and her grandmother, Mimi, had decided to keep it to themselves for now. It would be difficult if someone in town heard about their story. She didn't quite know what to do from here. Should she try to find out more about her elusive relatives or just leave it alone? She didn't know whether Catherine's family knew about her and her family. She felt as if she should call Catherine, but she was busy with the end of school year activities and she had no time to do anything, especially delve into a past that most likely would be full of unpleasantries.

She liked her uncomplicated life. Still, there was this nagging part of her that wanted to know more. Maybe finding out the truth about her father would prove disheartening, but at the same time, it could lead her on a clearer path to understanding her own history and the mystery of her half-sister. She decided the best route would be to wait until school was out when things settled down a bit before pursuing questioning her grandmother. Celia wasn't surprised that Mimi hadn't said another word about it. After all, she had kept the secrets for years. It pained her that her own uncle had been right in front of her and she hadn't even known him. She also wondered how much he had known about her.

When Celia first discovered the true identity of Catherine, an important part of the puzzle fell into place. She was amazed at the draw their energy had played with each other beginning from the first chance encounter they had at the Florida turnpike rest stop. It had been completely random—simply passing each other through a door. Her daughter, Olivia, immediately felt a connection. She had even told her mother that the lady looked like her. It was uncanny and a magical part of her precious little daughter.

Olivia had sensed it again at the grocery store when they bumped into the woman again. Celia didn't quite know how to describe it, but her daughter honed right in. She hadn't told Olivia yet. She had to work out the details in her own head first. Mimi agreed. They would wait to tell Olivia that Catherine was her aunt until the puzzle was more complete. Plus, she wasn't sure how Catherine felt about her new half-sister and niece. If only Catherine lived closer, it would be easier. There was also the question of how Catherine's sister and mother would deal with the news. They lived right in the same town. Maybe enough years had passed. Did anything really matter except that they were related and had somehow miraculously found each other? The Universe obviously wanted them to meet, but Celia couldn't make up her mind what she wanted to do about any of it.

Although she finally understood her mother's behavior, it made her feel sad. She couldn't help but wonder if Nyla's life would have been different if someone had known earlier that her mother had sustained a brain injury. What if there had been a medication that could have helped control her erratic behavior? It didn't matter now, and she certainly didn't blame her grandmother. Mimi had done the best she knew how to do for her daughter, and she had most certainly taken care of her and Olivia. She had to be grateful for the way things turned out. It could have been much worse if Mimi hadn't been there for them.

She struggled with how to tell Olivia about Catherine? That child was intuitive. She had already connected with Catherine, even before there was any inclination that there might be a correlation between all of them. Celia thought that Olivia would most likely take the news in stride and be excited to have a real aunt.

Celia and Cary Fenmore kept no secrets, except now that she hadn't had the conversation with him where she said, "Oh, by the way, honey, I have a half-sister." Some of the family members were living right there in town, and it might adversely affect Catherine's mother and sister. Celia had also heard that their biological father was involved with other women besides Catherine's mother and her mother, Nyla. It had been a long time ago, but small towns still enjoyed their share of gossip. She knew if she told Cary, it would make it real. There were too many decisions to make.

The fact that she hadn't heard a word from

Catherine made her question what might be going on with her newly discovered half-sister. She certainly didn't want to cause her any problems. The woman had been through so much, losing both her husband and uncle in such a short period of time. No, it wasn't a matter that needed to be addressed in any kind of hurry. It would happen in its own time. Meanwhile, she felt blessed.

CHAPTER 10

Buck Matthews stepped out onto his porch, dialed the phone one Sunday afternoon, and took a deep breath waiting for an answer. He heard the soft familiar voice of his mother and felt the familiar pain in his heart. He always missed her.

"Are you my mama?" he asked.

"Why yes I am. My land, Buck, it is so good to hear your voice."

"It's good to hear your voice too, Mama. I miss you."

His mother had never judged him. She hadn't questioned why he packed up and ran away from them with his best friend, Zane Wheeler, as soon as he graduated high school. She didn't beg him to come home, even though he knew her heart was breaking still. She had been joyful the few times he had gone home. They all knew ranching was hard, often lonely and isolating. She had accepted his decision, but he knew she didn't like any of it. Now he knew that with his purchase of the feed store and farm, he would most likely never be going home permanently. He had been putting off telling her all of his news.

"Well, tell me now, how is everything?" Her voice sounded older, melodious, and tired.

"Are you okay, Mama? You sound tired."

"Yes, honey, I'm fine. The calving has been pretty tough this year. We pulled a lot of calves for some reason. The barn was full of them. We had a late storm.

One poor calf froze to death. We just couldn't get to him in time. Now we've had the shearing team here. The sheep are doing well. I've been cooking for everyone. You know."

Yes, he did know. There were endless chores. Maybe that's why, as he stood on his porch looking across his land talking to his mother on this Sunday morning, he saw nothing moving. No cows. No horses. Not even a dog—just the green open spaces and the quiet that it brought.

"I do know, Mama. Maybe what I've got to tell you will put a little sparkle on your pancakes this morning."

"What's that?" she asked with a giggle. "I'm ready for some news."

"Well," he said as pulled in a breath through his cigarette, "how would you feel about being a grandmother?"

She was quiet for a few seconds, and then she said, "You don't mean it. Really? Well, I'll be. Honest to land sakes."

"I can hardly believe it myself, Mama. It was just one of those things that happened, you know. Yes, it has really surprised me. I guess I got pretty damn lucky, because it is turning out all right. In fact, she's moving in with me."

"Well, I declare."

Buck knew that Effie Matthews wasn't the kind of woman who would have behaved like Deb did, but he was hoping that she understood how much the world had changed.

"When is the baby due, honey?" She waited.

Buck inhaled the smoke from his cigarette deep

into his lungs.

"Babies," he said. "We are having twins—a boy and a girl."

"Both? Oh, my goodness. That's just something, now isn't it?"

"I know, Mama. It sure was a complete surprise. All of it."

"Well, twins do run in the family."

"Yes, I remember that, and in her family too. It was inevitable."

"So when are they coming?"

"Early August—the hottest damn time of the year. She will be miserable."

"Are we planning a wedding, Buck?"

"Yeah, I really think I am. It's the right thing to do, but more than that, I actually like her. It's quite the package."

She sounded delighted. "I think that's wonderful, honey. I'm so happy for you. Really, I'm happy for all of you. It is just what you deserve."

"Thank you, Mama. I wish I was a little younger, but I think it is going to be just fine. Her name is Deb."

Buck felt a lot different than he had ever felt before. He was happy. For once in his life, he wasn't going to mess up. The last thing he had expected when he moved to Highberry, Florida was a wife and two kids, but right at the moment, he was damn excited.

"I'll let you know what's going on, Mama. Okay? Tell Dad hello for me."

"That will be great, honey. And yes, I can't wait for your father to come in so I can tell him the news. I love you."

"I love you too. Yes, tell Dad. Okay, Mama? Talk to you soon."

~~~~~

Deb had a lot to be thankful for. She was pregnant, healthy, and she'd fallen in love. Her life was very different than she could have ever imagined. Things were looking very good for her and Buck. When she first arrived in this small country town, she had been on a mission, sent by Bill Brannan to keep an eye on Buck. She took a crash course in order to pass the real estate test and then set up shop, so to speak. It wasn't easy to break into the rhythm of the town, but she created a new persona. She put herself into places where the local people became familiar with her. It hadn't taken as long as she had anticipated before she was getting referrals. She had been in the right place at the right time quite by accident when Catherine DeLong came along. She purposely included Buck's feed store into as many of her clients' tours as she could. She needed him to feel comfortable with her. She knew his history, including that with the ladies, and so had dressed differently from her norm, making herself as unattractive as she could. She had played the role perfectly. What she hadn't expected was being attracted to him.

Once Zane had shown up, Bill Brannan warned her not to get personally involved with either one of them.

"They are very superficial when it comes to women," he said. "You know how long they were in the Agency. I'm sure they had women in every port. Be careful."

She had heard him, but a lot of good that had done her. She rubbed her belly and felt one of the babies kick.
~~~~~

This was a far cry from the hectic life she had been living before she quit all that government nonsense. Buck had no idea she was the red-headed woman who had worked with Bill and that she was well aware of his and Zane's past. She didn't dare expose herself. Not now, possibly never. Buck would be more than pissed since men like him didn't like being "had," especially by a woman. She knew she was walking on very thin ice, but the pay-off was a normal life with a man whom she really wanted to be with. Plus, she knew almost everything about him. She had done her homework on both of them. Maybe this was the payback for everything the three of them had done for their country. Maybe it was simply fate. What she knew was that she was very comfortable living this life and what she had done in the past now seemed worth it.

<p style="text-align:center">~~~~~</p>

Buck Matthews whistled a happy tune as he opened the door to his feed store and tromped across the wooden floor. He was about to throw his keys under the counter on the shelf when he noticed a pair of shoes backed up against the wall. His eyes moved quickly from the floor up across the man's body and onto his face. If he had been in his other life, he'd have grabbed his service weapon and pinned the intruder up against the wall with it at his throat or temple. But he didn't have his gun on him. He felt vulnerable until he recognized the chiseled features, the gray hair and the dark brown eyes of Bill Brannan, one of the CIA officials he'd worked with. "What the hell? What are you doing in here?"

"Waiting for you, Buck. Nice store."

"How'd you get in here—inside my store, Bill?" Buck was so angry he could feel the heat in his face.

"You know how easy this is." Bill smiled at him.

"Okay, so then why?"

"Why not? I happened to be in the area."

"Just tell me, you son of a ...." Buck took a step closer and bowed up at him as he tightened his fists.

Bill couldn't back away because he was up against the wall. "Steady. What's gotten into you? I thought you'd be glad to see me."

"I don't understand why you can't leave us alone or at the very least just come in the door like everyone else."

"There's something I need to talk to you about, and I didn't want to do it over the phone."

"Really? This had better be good." Buck pulled a stool from behind the counter and sat down, folding his arms defiantly.

"Look, Buck; I've known you a long time, and I respect you and I really don't want to see you get yourself into something you can't get out of."

"Just give it to me."

"It's about this woman, Deb, you are shacking up with."

"Now wait just a minute."

Bill's hand came up into Buck's face defensively. "Hear me out and try not to be too reactive. Give me a minute, will you?"

Buck drew in a deep breath and motioned for Bill to sit on the other stool at the counter.

"She's not who you think she is. The mind boggling thing about all this is how the heck all of you ended up in this damn little town. I don't quite get how it all happened."

"So what are you trying to tell me?"

"Deb Albom is the red-headed woman who was working with me. She's an operative. I sent her here to keep an eye on you."

"Keep an eye on me? Bill, is this some kind of a joke? I mean it. Really?"

"No, Buck, it's not a joke. She worked for us, with me."

"You thought I needed a babysitter? Are you serious? What the f--"

"Look, I was concerned about you, especially since Zane had taken off to who knew where. I was hoping he would eventually show up. I knew Deb wanted out before it was too late. She and I had a very personal conversation about how much she wanted a normal life. I don't think there was any malice in all this. She's actually a nice person once you get to know her. She thought this little detour would provide a great place for her to transition out of service. I never expected the two of you to hook up."

"And you are telling me all of this now because?"

"I'm telling you now because I don't want you to end up marrying her and then find out about all this later on. Since I'm the one who kind of sent her here to keep an eye on you, I don't think it would be fair for me not to tell you."

"Fair? Are you aware we are going to have two kids together?"

"Well, I'm not responsible for that, but I did want to be the one to tell you this before you went blindly into a situation.”

“Situation, Bill? I can't make my kids go away.”

“I know that, but I....”

“But I what? The deed was done months ago and this is how it turned out. I'm not sure where you are going with this.”

“I'm not sure either, anymore, but I didn't want you to find out down the line and be all pissed off at me and much worse, at Deb.”

Buck walked to the front door and flipped the “Open” sign over and checked to be sure he’d left the door unlocked. He turned and glared at Bill. “How well do you know her?” he asked.

“Not like that, Buck. I'm serious. Not like that. There was nothing going on between us, if that's what you are asking. She worked with me. That’s all.”

“Well, I have to be honest; she wasn't much to look at when she first came to town. She was pretty dumpy. I wasn’t much interested in her either.”

“I warned her not to make herself too appealing, but I hadn't seen her in a while.”

“Well, she was, I guess you'd call her flamboyant. She wore these clothes you'd see on like a gypsy. She was nothing at all to look at. I don’t even know why I did it, and I thought I'd really screwed myself until the day she came to talk to me about being pregnant. Something changed. She looked and acted totally different. Are you still working with her now? Is she still involved?”

“No. Not now. Whenever I worked with her she was always dressed in jeans and polo shirts ready for work. She kept up with the boys, if you know what I mean.”

“Who was she with?”

"With? You mean was she sleeping with anyone?"

Buck nodded.

"She wasn't. She wasn't with anyone that I ever knew of."

"Well, we haven't talked about the past. We're just moving forward. This has been a big change for me and rather unexpected."

"I bet, especially since you aren't exactly a spring turkey."

"I think it is chicken, Bill, spring chicken."

"Well, you get my drift."

"I have no idea what to do with this, Bill."

"Maybe you don't have to do anything with it—nothing at all. I just felt I owed you."

"I don't know what confronting her with this information would do. I guess she was afraid to tell me." Buck sat back down on the stool next to Bill.

"That's something you have to decide. I'm not in your boots."

"It has sure turned into a twisted web. None of us were expecting everything to get this tangled up. So, was she watching Catherine too?"

"Yes, I had her looking out for her and then when Zane showed up. But, say, look at the bright side. You are about to have two kids."

"I just told my parents. I'm not sure I want to mess this up for them. My mother is pretty excited."

"I understand."

"I guess I'll have to wait and see. Bill, you son-of-a-bitch, you always keep things stirred up."

"Yeah, Buck, but I'm hoping we can all finally settle down. I'm getting ready to sack it in too. I'll be retiring."

"You're not moving to Highberry are you?" Buck chuckled.

"Oh, hell no! I have a wife. We've been married thirty-five years. She wouldn't move here. Did you know I have five kids, all daughters? The last one is about to finish college."

"Congratulations. I hope retirement works out for you. Keep in touch. I'll let you know how this goes with Deb."

"So, no hard feelings?"

Buck nodded.

"Well, then, best of luck on everything, Buck; I mean it."

They shook hands and Bill Brannan walked out of the feed store through the front door and got into his car.

"Son of a fucking bitch," Buck said and kicked the metal trash can clean across the wooden floor. It banged loudly into the wall. "I fucking hate all this shit. Couldn't some fucking thing just be normal? What the fuck?" He spit a plug of tobacco into the cup he kept under the counter. He honestly didn't know what to make of this.

CHAPTER 11

Roger Halvesord created the perfect life with his private legal practice, beautiful women falling all over him, and a lifestyle that was envied. Now, he was enraged. After five and a half years of skillfully preening her to be his office manager, Eve Brodie had decided to walk. Part of his fury came from the way she connived her departure. He knew she had the names of all of his opposing counsel because he had ordered her to make the list. He was certain she had used that information to land her new job. He slammed his fists on her desk. He had been such an idiot to trust her. Every aspect of his life was falling apart.

When he first employed Eve, she had been a recent naïve high school graduate excited to be living in New York City. He was proud of her because she became an intelligent meticulous young woman. But when she gave her notice, he had a hard time controlling his behavior. Eventually, he figured out that she had been planning her exit for months, not only because it seemed rehearsed, but because she appeared to have everything in order.

She had very calmly, but strongly told him, "This isn't about you, Mr. Halvesord. This is for me. I need an opportunity bigger than this. Please don't take it personally."

Internally, he had been a raging maniac, but for once in his life, he held it together. Eve had been more than his secretary and office manager. She was like family. He couldn't speak to her because he didn't want her to see him as vulnerable. He actually felt something. In fact, he felt like he was having a fucking heart attack. He hadn't seen it coming and it was crushing. Things were caving in from all directions. First, it was the situation with James, next Catherine had moved to Florida, and now Eve. Son-of-a-bitch! He had just stood there looking at her. He felt his jaw twitch, his hands roll into tight fists, watched as she braced for it, but he held it all in.

Everything had begun to unravel when he'd encouraged James to stick his neck in that damn noose. If he was given a "do over," even though he hated to admit it, he'd probably do the same ignorant thing. He and James were sucked into the whirlpool and then James was taken away, leaving him to clean up the mess. It wasn't just about the money. This time, with James out of the picture, he thought he'd have a real shot at Catherine. He expected to be her knight in shining armor, rushing in just in the nick of time to save her. He let his desires for Catherine override all his common sense.

He had planned to shield her from the truth until he was ready to catch her when she fell. It was ironic that she chose the one place on the planet where those other assholes landed. How in the world Buck Matthews and Zane Wheeler ended up in the same town as Catherine was beyond his wildest imagination. He didn't know how to solve it, yet. The worst part was that she'd turned on him. Catherine had fired him. It was killing him. He refused to accept it, but for now, what the hell was he supposed to do?

~~~~~

Roger hadn't had any contact with James because the authorities forbade it. It made him furious that the United States Government could work so closely with them to complete their mission and then keep them isolated from each other. He had been told it wouldn't be much longer before he could contact James, but several months had gone by. Enough was enough. He'd get answers from the one man who would tell him the truth. Bill Brannan was their contact at the CIA and knew exactly what had happened to James. He was also connected to Buck and Zane. He picked up the phone and dialed Bill's number. He was surprised when he immediately answered.

"Hello, Roger. How's it going?" Bill asked.

"It's not going anywhere and you know it."

"Well, I have some good news for you and your buddy. Things are about to wind down."

"What does that mean?" Roger was irritated.

"We are very close to releasing James and Arianne. They will be free to move about as they please very soon."

"And then what?"

"And then they will become normal citizens again and be able to do whatever they want. We are in the process of clearing James. Arianne doesn't need to worry because no one will recognize him. They can do whatever they want."

"So who is he now?" Roger asked.

"He can catch you up on all that when we release
~~~~~

them. It's up to him to contact you and tell you what he wants. I'm not getting in the middle of it from now on."

"Well, you sure as hell were in the middle of this when it was going down."

"You can't be bitter about how we handled this. It was in the best interest of all the parties involved. You know that our intention was always to keep everyone safe."

"Of course I know that, but look at how many lives you screwed up."

"Roger, you have to consider the big picture. Look at how many other lives didn't get screwed up. This was a huge win for the CIA at a time when we were really being questioned. Not to mention what it did to stabilize several hot spots in the world. You have to think outside the box and look at it differently; otherwise, it will eat you alive."

"All I know is that things are never going to be the same for any of us. Certainly not for James and Arianne, and things are very rocky for me. My life is unraveling. Catherine, well, she's an entirely different story."

"You are all safe. There are never any guarantees in anyone's life, Roger. You know that. Move on."

"That's easy for you to say. Nothing changed for you."

"Things change every day all over the world. Listen; I have to go. Good luck and James will be contacting you, I'm sure."

"And if he doesn't?"

"Roger, just wait. I'm sure he will."

Roger wasn't sure about anything anymore. His

office was in shambles since Eve Brodie quit. Business had almost come to a screeching halt, forcing him to make some drastic decisions. He was in the process of closing his solo law practice and joining a firm that promised him new clients. Meanwhile, his lifestyle had taken a big hit. He'd downsized his apartment, dumped his expensive car, and was squeaking by on the last of the funds he'd received from the government. He really needed to talk to James.

~~~~~

James and Arianne both jumped when someone knocked on the cabin door. It was one of the agents who had been guarding them.

"I thought they took you off the case," James said when he recognized the guy at the door.

"They had me scope out the area before they release you. They wanted me to check around with the locals. The cabin is going to be advertised as available for rent since you'll be leaving. Everyone I've spoken to in this little town thinks you are a 9/11 survivor who came here to heal. Some are hoping you will stay in the community; others don't have an opinion. It's up to you two where you go from here."

"When do we get to do that?" James asked.

"You can leave as early as tomorrow, but you must be out by the end of the week."

He handed them a laptop and new identification papers for James.

"Let me know what else you need. I'm assigned to you until the end of the week and then you will never see me again. You can do searches on the laptop, but
~~~~~

you won't be able to send out or receive any e-mails. Not until you are officially released. Let me know if you need me to contact any place or person for you. Okay?"

James looked at his new driver's license. They had allowed him to keep the same first name. The license identified him as James Robert Campbell. There had to be enough men named James Campbell in the world to keep him obscure. Still, it was a hard pill to swallow. He'd never see anyone from his past again; rather, no one from his past would actually see him again. Not the "real" him. He suddenly realized that other than Arianne, he had no one.

~~~~~

Arianne stood silently next to James, listening to the conversation. She was trying to imagine starting a life with James. She wanted her apartment back, she wanted her friends back, and she wanted her life back. She'd have to tread lightly and see what happened. She finally spoke.

"Do you know what happened to my apartment and my real life?" she asked the guard.

"Oh, everything is right where you left it," the man said.

"So what are you telling me? I can return to my life and then what do I tell everyone when I suddenly reappear?"

"Tell them whatever you like. You aren't attached to James DeLong anymore. Tell them that the death of your dear friend sent you into a tailspin and you simply left the country. Tell them that your sole surviving relative called in the middle of the night and you had to
~~~~~

go to Europe to take care of him and he just died. Tell them you lost your memory and just got it back yesterday. We don't care what you tell them as long as there is no link to what really happened. You can handle it. Your biggest question seems to be whether you are going to stick around here or go back to New York? It's up to you."

"Can I go back to New York?" James asked in a soft contemplative voice.

"You can go anywhere you like, because it is very apparent that no one is going to recognize you."

"But what about Catherine?"

Arianne spoke up rather quickly.

"James, honey, Catherine is in Florida, remember? She's not in New York. I doubt very seriously that we are going to go to Florida. Are we?"

He didn't answer her.

"Look, you two; sit in it overnight. I'll talk to you tomorrow and if we have to, the next day, and the day after that. We'll figure it all out by the end of the week."

Arianne knew someone would be sitting in a car in front of the cabin all night and would still be there in the morning. She closed the door. The day they had been waiting for had finally arrived, but with it came the difficulty of making decisions. She hadn't addressed her issues because she was afraid she'd set him off. After all, his life was forever changed. She had hoped that things would be easier for her and it looked like they would. She had to stick it out with him for a little while longer, but she wanted to tell him the truth. She wanted to go home and be Arianne again.

James spoke, interrupting her thoughts. "It's not

like I haven't given this a lot of thought, Arianne. I know that you did this for me. I understand and I do appreciate it. I don't blame you at all if you want to go back to New York, especially now that you know your life is pretty much intact. I hate that they played that card as well, letting you hang in limbo. They should have told you."

"Think about it, James; they were afraid I would bail on you. Maybe I'd demand that I be let go sooner rather than later."

"I understand their motives, but they weren't very fair with any of us."

Arianne bit her lip and said, "I've had time to think about this too, you know. There isn't anything fair. And, there probably isn't anything right. We can't think of this in those terms. I know you don't think I'm very intelligent, but we need to be grateful that we all came out of this alive. I always thought this kind of men 'accidentally on purpose' bump people off. I feel very fortunate to be given the opportunity to either stay with you or go back to my former life. Do you want to come back to New York with me?"

"Maybe, but I just don't know if I wouldn't always be looking for...."

"Go ahead and say her name. It's not like I don't know about her. Remember, I introduced you two." It was the first time she'd actually seen him smile a real smile in a long time.

"Yes, you certainly did."

"Look, James; wouldn't you have rather loved her for the time that you did, instead of never experiencing her at all."

"I just never thought....." his voice trailed off.

"No one ever expects things to go wrong with their lives. Parents don't expect to bury their children. Kids seem shocked when their parents pass away even at a ripe old age. Life is just like that. Poof! In a heartbeat, everything is different."

"I didn't know you were so philosophical, Arianne."

"I'm not. I've just been stuck in this cabin watching you read books and sleep, wrestling with what happened. It gave me a new prospective on what's important."

"I think the word is perspective, but I understand what you mean."

"Well, James, I know we have to create a new normal for ourselves."

"Would you mind if we just went to your apartment for a while until we figure things out? It would at least feel familiar."

"Sure, James. No one is going to realize who you are. To them, you'll be just another man that Arianne dragged home with her."

"Are you sure you want to do that?"

"I don't care what people think about me. You should know that."

"I do know that, but I also want you to have a better life than you've ever had because of what you've done for me."

"James, I'm okay. You really are worth it, you know. You did what you thought you had to do for the country. Don't you feel like you fulfilled a dream for yourself by becoming a real life American hero, even if no one else knows you did? I know. You made a huge sacrifice.

That's all I need. Tell me, if I were the only person on the planet, would you have done it for me?"

She put her hands on either side of his mouth, stood up on her toes and kissed him.

"You decide what you want, James."

She didn't know why she told him that, because, regardless of what he decided, she was going home to New York.

CHAPTER 12

Catherine handed Zane a glass of ice tea, then sat next to him on the loveseat on the back porch and asked him, "Are you ever going to tell me the story about the cave? You gave me that little tidbit about when you were a young boy and you started to go into it and this hand came out and grabbed you. I know it was that Indian guy at the ranch that saved you, but won't you please tell me the rest of the story?"

"He didn't actually save me. I always tried to get back up there, but he stayed one step ahead of me. It was several years later when I was around fifteen or sixteen when we finally went up there together. He taught me a ceremony and then led me in."

"So will you tell me the rest of the story?"

Zane smiled at her for what seemed like a long time, took a deep breath, sat his glass on a coaster on the trunk in front of them and began. "That Indian guy is Parker Iron Crow and he was much more of a father figure to me than my own father. He was firm, but fair—an amazing mentor. I realize now that he's a medicine man, a healer. First, we had gathered sage and sweet grass a while before this happened. When it was dried, Parker simply told me that it was time. At first, I didn't realize time for what, but I dutifully got the horses ready and we rode off. My mother was standing on the front veranda as we rode away in the early morning mist. She didn't say a word—she just stood and watched us go.

"It didn't take me long to figure out where we were headed. When we got to the entrance of the cave, Parker smudged the area and us in a cleansing to prepare us for what was about to occur. Before we entered the cave, he asked me if I noticed anything. There was an old wooden box half-open to the right of the dark entrance. It was full to the brim with emerald green aspen leaves. He asked me if I knew how they had gotten into the box. When I didn't have an answer, he told me it was the pack rats. He said it was going to be a hard winter, and it did turn out to be just that. Then down into the cave we went, climbing down a short ladder made of aspen limbs. There were four rungs. I remember it vividly.

"We had to get down on all fours and crawl through holes in the rocks in some areas of the cave. I have to admit, it still makes me feel a bit uneasy. When we got to the belly of the cave, the small light he carried illuminated several large rocks piled in a sort of altar. Parker motioned for me to sit, and then he removed a small weathered drum from a deerskin pouch. He began to play a rhythmic beat. The light suddenly went out and we were pitched into total blackness—the darkest black I had ever experienced. Parker continued his drumming and began a soft undulating hum. I'm not sure if I had my eyes closed or if the dark was just so dark I truly couldn't see a thing, but out of the black came this mountain lion running directly at me up into my face. As it came straight at me it roared. I could see its teeth, its tongue, and down into its throat. It happened three times, and the third time, the big cat turned into a warrior. He had the top half of his face painted red, the bottom half painted black, and white circled his mouth. He had black bear fur all around his face and buffalo horns that were turned down at the side of his head. I was terrified, and yet I couldn't stop looking at him.

"The warrior suddenly thrust out his hand right in front of me. He said, 'The people are like the beads. They flow off your fingers in a beautiful pattern. So it is with the people. Now go and tell the people,' and just like that he was gone. The light suddenly came back on and Parker stopped his drumming and chanting. A cold wind came out of nowhere way down in the depth of that cave, and I got chilled all the way up my spine. Parker brought out some tobacco and we both made an offering there at the makeshift altar. I don't know if my eyes had become used to the darkness or what, but it seemed like the entire room was now illuminated. We stayed there for a few minutes and then Parker led me back out of the cave. I didn't say a word to him then about the cat or the warrior. At one point, when I was crawling through a hole, my hand grasped something that fit right into my fingers and the palm of my hand. I stuffed it in my pocket. When we were out of the cave, I discovered that it was a fragment of a bone from a deer leg. It made me wonder if a mountain lion had lived in that cave."

"Well, what did he say when you told him about it?" she asked.

"When I eventually told him a little bit about it, he said that he was pretty sure I had experienced a vision because he said when the light came on, I was as white as a sheet. I wasn't really scared by it. I was trying to process what the hell had happened."

"Did he give you any insight into what it meant?"

"He said that I had been chosen for a purpose and to be sure that I understood the responsibility of it. I don't think he minded at all that I chose to serve my country in an extraordinary way compared to joining one of the regular armed services. Many Native Americans join up and give the ultimate sacrifice with their lives. It's their way of still honoring Mother Earth."

"Thank you for telling me about the cave and also for clarifying something for me. I always wondered why a people who had been so persecuted and demeaned could then turn around and fight to protect the very people who had stolen everything that had once been theirs. It never made sense to me."

"I have done a bit of research on this. Historically, Native Americans have the highest record of service per capita when compared with other ethnic groups. They feel it is their duty. They have distinctive cultural values that drive them to serve their country. One of these values is their proud warrior tradition, including a strong willingness to engage the enemy in battle. Most, if not all, Native American societies have these inherent qualities: strength, honor, pride, devotion, and wisdom. These qualities make a perfect fit with the military. When they have powwows, the first thing they do is honor the flag and honor the men who serve it. Then they honor the elders."

"I want to know more about all of it," Catherine said, "especially now that I've discovered that I'm descended from the Blackfeet Tribe. How I feel about the planet seems to make a lot more sense to me now. I feel more connected in some way. Do you know what I mean?"

"Of course I do. You'd have to meet my mother to understand the real connection that she has. She knows things, and the only way she knows is because that knowledge is pulsing through her blood—that and the oral history of our people. She just is."

"Oral history? You mean the stories that they tell? Well, we will have to figure out a way to make that happen."

"What? Make what happen?" Zane asked.

"My meeting your mother."

"I don't think she's going to come to Florida, so we will have to go to her."

Catherine hesitated for a moment. "Well then, I guess we will have to figure out a way for us to do that."

"I'm not sure that can happen any time soon, what with all this to take care of."

"Zane, what are you talking about? You took care of it while I was, well, you know...while I was sick."

"Yes, but admit it. I'm one of a kind and what are the chances of finding someone to take care of all of them now?"

"Stop teasing me. I bet we can find someone. How about those guys that you lined up when you thought you were leaving? Buck knows them. What about those guys?"

"Let's just wait and see. I don't quite know how to say this, but I think maybe the first time I go home I should fly solo, what with being gone so long and all."

Catherine was quiet for a few seconds. "I didn't really think about that, Zane. I'm sorry. You're right. Of course, you are. I'm being selfish. You should have that time alone with your mother, to talk to her about all the things that you have done, things that have been bothering you, and, of course, to get reacquainted with Parker. What's his name again?"

"Iron Crow, Parker Iron Crow."

~~~~~

Zane moved from the loveseat to his favorite chair on the porch and soon drifted off to sleep. She thought he looked handsome with his summer tan against his light blue long-sleeved shirt. Catherine wanted to take the story he told and twist it around. She went into the kitchen, lit a small candle, and breathed the scent of lavender into her lungs. *"Help me write this story in a new and important way,"* she whispered. Back on the porch, she closed her eyes for a moment and then began to tap away on her laptop.

I am going to tell you the story of Charging Bear, who lived on this land many years ago. His mother called him ChaChuNee. He was a warrior, unique among his people, because he had lived with a mountain lion high up on a ridge in a cave. He first encountered the cub in the spring with his mother and siblings—there were three. It had been a good year.

One day ChaChuNee found the young mountain lion with his back leg dangling and gangrene. He never discovered what had happened to him, but it was the smell of the rotting flesh that brought ChaChuNee to the cat. History told him that he should swiftly put the cat out of its misery, but there was something in its eyes. The big cat tried to move, but he was too weak and the pain overtook his wildness. He lay motionless, attempted to
~~~~~

growl, and then fell unconscious. ChaChuNee called him Roaring. He fashioned a drag from some young aspen limbs. He used his rawhide laces to tie them together, spread a deerskin across, lifted the cat gently up onto the skiff and dragged him to the cave. It was there by the fire that he nursed the cat for several days. It was late in the season, but he located herbs, made a broth with venison, and dribbled the warmth into the cat's mouth. When the cat fell into a deep, deep sleep, ChaChuNee began to work on his leg. He cleaned away the dead and rotting tissue, used a poultice he made from clay and herbs he steamed, and wrapped it in a mix of leaves and aspen bark. He then encased the entire leg in a piece of deerskin. He was willing to take the risk. After all, he had isolated himself from the tribe for a while now. He had been on his vision quest, and perhaps the cat would reveal the mysteries that he sought.

This would not be easy, but ChaChuNee continued the task for many days until the fever subsided and the rotten flesh fell away. He cleansed the wound every day, carefully cutting away dead tissue, urging the new flesh to come using the herbs and clay as he'd seen his grandmother mix.

One day, he returned to the cave to find Roaring sitting up. He was panting, and as ChaChuNee slowly approached, the cat bared his teeth and hissed. ChaChuNee spoke to him in his native tongue. 'No, Atakapa; do not fear, Maneater. I will do you no harm.' The cat stared silently and lay down. ChaChuNee scooped some broth from the kettle over the fire into a wooden bowl and carefully set it down in front of Roaring. The cat lapped the broth like a kitten.

As the days went by, Roaring allowed ChaChuNee to nurse him, ever cautious, but trusting. That is how ChaChuNee came to run in the woods and stay in the cave with the cat. There are tales from the people now that on still dark nights when the moon is right, you can see the two high on the ridge above the cave, staring at the stars.

Zane stirred from his nap just as Catherine shut the laptop. He looked at her and smiled.

"Was I out long?"

"No. Not really. I was working on a story. Are you hungry? How about I start dinner?" Catherine felt like she had experienced the moments in the cave. She could smell the musty odor of the rocks and feel the dampness of the stone. She could visualize the cat and she had a vivid vision in her mind of how ChaChuNee must have looked. It seemed strange and yet oddly familiar.

CHAPTER 13

Justin hadn't talked to his cousin, Catherine, since she left his father's house in Jensen Beach and returned to Highberry. There wasn't any reason to call her now. He would wait to call her and his brother, Waylon, after things settled down a bit. For right now, he was anxious to get on with his day. He inhaled deeply, backed the truck up to the boat trailer, got out, and moved the tongue over to align it with the hitch, watched it drop onto the ball, and slammed the lock into place. Once the chains were crisscrossed and attached and the lights were hooked up, he climbed back into the truck. He headed to his buddy's house. Curtis, who had been part of his life since elementary school, was waiting on the front porch with a cup of coffee in his hand.

"Mornin', you doing alright?" Curtis asked.

"Yes, I'm okay."

"Then let's do it."

They headed through Stuart and down toward Salerno, turning toward the river and Sandsprit Park. It was breaking daylight and there wasn't anyone else in the area when they backed down the ramp and launched the boat into the river. Justin carefully handed a box containing two bubble wrapped items to Curtis, telling him, "Put these in the empty console. I made room for them in there."

Curtis stayed with the boat at the dock while Justin parked the truck and trailer. The boat motor started right up and they backed the boat out into open water. Justin slowly pushed the throttle forward heading to the inlet and the open sea. They had picked a day with a low west wind, hoping it would be flat and smooth. They didn't speak as they cruised across the water and out toward the Gulf Stream.

As the sun began to sparkle and dance across the water, the ocean was crystal clear—more turquoise and green than Justin ever remembered. He took deep breaths, pulling in the salt spray. He thought about days when he, his father, and his brother had been able to go out in the boat together and fish. Their father had taught them everything they knew about fishing, and they had been successful at catching whatever fish they were seeking on any particular day. Everyone in Jensen Beach knew that if you were lucky enough to go fishing with any of the Kendale men, you would come home with dinner and plenty for the freezer. Back then, there was an abundance of fish of every kind off the coast and life had been really good. That was until they'd grown older and things became more complicated. When the boys were in their mid-teens, it was as if there were three fighting cocks in the house. Each of them had his own opinions about almost everything and there was always a great debate.

What was it that made them change so much? It would have been just as easy to accept the opinions of his father and brother and to see them as that—their opinions. What made men have to be right? His brother, Waylon, had been just as guilty. They had both pushed their father away. It had taken its toll on all of them. Somehow, his mother remained the equalizer who would diffuse the arguments. It couldn't have been easy for her to watch them turn on each other. In the wild, that's what happened, though. The young bucks are run off and become their own little herd until they grow and learn and come back to challenge the older bucks. The stronger wiser bucks maintain their dominance over the female deer, and in doing so, preserve the quality of the herd. It is survival of the fittest, but it didn't have to be that way with people.

Curtis bumped him on the shoulder and pointed to a huge cargo ship out to the east. When Justin was a child on the beach in Jensen, he had dreamed of being on one of those cargo ships. When he bought his first boat and made his way out into the open ocean, it gave him a thrill to get close enough to them to see the great mass of their hull. It still intrigued him today. He backed down the throttle and turned the boat to the north as Curtis nodded to him. They cut the motors.

Curtis asked him "Are you ready to do this?"

"As ready as I'll ever be."

Justin opened the console, pulled out the box, and removed the larger container. He carefully uncurled the bubble wrap, revealing the urn's beautiful blue and turquoise colors. Then he removed the smaller urn, which was in earth tones. Around the neck of it was a silver chain with a cross. He quietly stood there, first rubbing his father's urn and then his mother's. He flicked a tear from his cheek and looked at Curtis.

"I know, man. This is a really tough day for you, but it is for me too. I loved them and they were an important part of my life. I'm a better man for having known them." Curtis' body was visibly shaking. It was the first time the two men had ever hugged each other. They stood quietly, looking out across the sea.

Justin's lip began to quiver. He sucked in a breath and said, "Okay. Let's do it."

Curtis instinctively took Josie's urn and Justin picked up his father's. They moved to the side of the boat. They removed the lids and knelt with their shoulders touching and placed the urns into the water, close up against each other. Curtis looked at Justin and they let them go. Within seconds, the water filled the empty spaces and the ashes mixed with the sea water and began to come out of the urns, swirling together in a dance. The men looked at each other again and then down into the water. The cross on Justin's mother's urn was sparkling in the bright morning sunlight and began to flip up and down as the urn sank slowly down. Justin couldn't have wished for anything as moving or meaningful. It was what his parents had wanted. Justin slowly let the lids of the urns glide into the water too.

As a young man in World War II, his father had been sent to Europe. He was a medic and was very close to the front line. When they were able to escape the war, the men had spent time in a small village in England where Walton had met Josie. She hadn't hesitated for a moment when his father asked her to marry him and come to the United States.

His Uncle John, Walton's brother, had been sent to Europe too. He was a mechanic and worked on the planes. He was also an artist and one of the guys who painted the names and various emblems on the fighter and cargo planes. They had come home from the war very different people. But his father had coped with it more easily; partly because he felt bringing Josie home had been his reward.

"They must be so happy now. They wanted their ashes to go into the Gulf Stream so they could return together back to England," he told Curtis.

"It was a beautiful thing the way they loved each other. Even on the bad days, it was still good. It was beautiful how this happened here today."

Justin reached into the cooler and took out two bottles of beer.

"Mind if we just float for a while?"

"I've got all day," Curtis said.

CHAPTER 14

Catherine lit a small lavender candle and settled into her green chair in her office behind the pantry with her laptop. It was mid-afternoon and Zane had gone off to town to buy a part for the tractor. She inhaled slowly, deep into her lungs, removed all other thoughts from her mind, and began to click out the story on her laptop.

ChaChuNee had been on his vision quest and living in the cave with the cat, Roaring. When it was time for him to return to his tribe, ChaChuNee spoke to Roaring in his native tongue. The cat lay by the fire and listened intently, flattening his ears tight against his head as he rested his chin on his paws. He and ChaChuNee slept that night soundly in the comfort of the cave.

The Dream Walker came to ChaChuNee in the deep hours before dawn and spoke to his heart. "You must go slowly like the turtle when you return to the tribe," the voice said. "They will not eagerly accept what you bring to them, but in time, they will understand. You know you have completed your vision quest. Follow the guidance of your spirit song and the knowing that will flow through your blood."

ChaChuNee stirred and went back into a deep sleep. Out of the dark charged Roaring. The strong large cat hurled himself straight into his face. He felt his heart pounding just as the cat approached for the third time, then stopped, swiveled his ears back flat against his head, and snarled. Then the cat began to speak to him in a language that he had never heard, but he understood. The cat told him, "I have come into your vision quest as a test of your ability to blend the old and the new. You have passed this test by choosing to keep me alive. Through my life, my blood, flows all the mystery and knowing of your ancestors. Take this back with you to the tribe. Now go. You and I will forever be brothers. I will go high into the mountains in the summer when the people come and I will be safe. In the dead of winter, when the snow is so deep you can barely see any life at all, I will be here deep in the belly of the cave in its safety. Take what you have learned back to your people now because they need to know."

When ChaChuNee awoke, he was alone in the cave. He wished he had been able to say goodbye to his brother, the big cat, Roaring. It was the way it was, and he had to accept it. They had grown close and he would think of the cat in all of the days that were soon to come.

ChaChuNee gathered his few possessions, wrapped them in his deerskin, tying them securely with his rawhide laces, and slung them over his shoulder. It had been good these many months in the cave with the cat. Now it was time to return to his people.

When he left the cave, he stood at the entrance. Even after all this time, he looked in wonderment. The wooden box sat there with its lock still hanging. It stood ajar, and the entire box was brimming with aspen leaves as emerald as gemstones. Just behind the box was another area about three feet by four feet, piled high with more leaves. He knew it was good because summer would come and go and it would be a hard winter. The pack rats were at work, preparing for it and burying their supplies early.

When he had traveled a ways down the mountain, he turned and looked back toward the cave. He caught the movement of the tan hide he'd grown to know so well. It was Roaring. He watched him as he appeared high up on the rock ledge above the cave. They locked eyes. The large cat moved his head as if to nod him off and say goodbye. ChaChuNee did not wave or move. It was not their way. They had already said their goodbyes in the dream. Reluctantly, and with somewhat heavy steps, ChaChuNee left the sanctuary of the mountain and the spirit of the cave.

As he continued to journey down the mountain, he was left to his own thoughts and the fascination of the new quest he was about to begin. He walked often diagonally, making his way down through the steep terrain and then the prairie grasses. He let the seeds and kernels of the grass sift through his hand. He remembered another day when he had pulled those very grains and stuffed them in a pouch at his waist. He'd taken them back to camp and ground them. Those were many moons ago and in another life. He shuddered to think of it. He was glad to have this life, this time, for he had been a woman then.

The wild flowers were thick in the meadows. The bumble bees buzzed in and out as grasshoppers moved away from his feet. He was content with moving down from the high country because soon enough the snow would come. He had much to share with his people, but it would come in its own time.

~~~~~

The phone was ringing as Catherine dumped the load of clothes on the kitchen table. She answered the old wall phone on the third ring.

"Hello."

"Hey, Cuz."

She recognized Justin's voice. "Right back at you, Cuz. What are you doing?"

"I just called to let you know that I took my parents' urns out to the Gulf Stream this morning."

"Oh, you did?"

"Yes. Do you have a minute?"

"Of course," she said as she pulled the phone cord around the corner into the living room and sat on the arm of the chair.

"Cath, I'm so glad they asked me to do it this way. I had put it off as long as I could and I just couldn't stand seeing them sitting in those urns on their kitchen table anymore. The wind was coming from the west so I figured it would be pretty flat out there for us to make a run."

"Did someone go with you, Justin?"

"Yes, I took Curtis. He had offered right after Dad left. He pretty much knew what the plan was. He told me whenever I was ready."

"I've always liked Curtis." Catherine stuck the phone in the crook of her neck, walked back into the kitchen, and grabbed a pair of her jeans. She worked away on the pile, folding methodically as she listened to Justin.

"It couldn't have been any better. We placed the urns in the water at the same time and let them go. As
~~~~~

soon as they filled up with water, their ashes started swirling out and it was like a dance. I could hardly believe what I was seeing. The water spun them around in a circle. Mom's cross was sparkling in the bright sunlight, and the water was as turquoise as I've ever seen it. Her cross started flipping up and down as it was sinking deeper into the water. It was amazing. They would have been so pleased."

"I'm sure that they are."

"I think it was the right thing for them—to send them back across the sea to England. The urns will rest at the bottom. They wanted some sea creature to live in them."

"I know. He told me. Have you talked to Waylon yet? You have to tell him."

"No. I wanted to tell you first. I didn't know how I was going to handle it, but I'm okay."

"I'm very proud of you." She finished the last item from the pile, pulled out the kitchen chair, and sat at the round table.

"For what?"

"For what you did for them."

"It was too little too late. We should have behaved differently."

"We learn. It's tough, because we almost live our lives backwards. We should be born with all the knowledge, not have to learn it the hard way."

"It's true. I wish...."

Catherine cut him off. "Don't say it. You can't go back. It happened the way it was supposed to. That's all."

"It could have been better."

"You can make it better now. All of us can. We can choose to live our lives differently now for the people around us. You have your son."

"Yes, and I'm going to have a grandson."

"You are?"

"Yes, his girlfriend is pregnant. Matthew is about to be a dad."

"Well, congratulations. I think that's wonderful."

"Thank you. I guess I should tell you—Waylon and I are working out some details, but I think they are going to be living in the house—Mom and Dad's house. That's one of the things that pushed me to do this. We want to get the house ready for them and the baby."

"I think that's a wonderful decision. Now you will have the opportunity to do things differently."

"I want to tell you again how thankful we are that you came back to us when we needed you, when Dad needed you."

"It all worked out in the end."

"Yes, it did. Take care of yourself, Catherine."

"I will, and tell Waylon I said hello to him and Helene. And tell Lannie hello and I love you all."

"Will do. Talk to you soon."

It was done. Her Aunt Josie and Uncle Walton were on their way back across the ocean. She truly wanted to hang on to the idea that they would make it back to the shores of England and the place that had begun their story for them. Catherine put her hand over her heart and stood looking out the kitchen window, lost in thoughts of the little house and all the things it had brought into all of their lives.

<u>**CHAPTER 15**</u>

If anyone had told Buck Matthews that he would be attending classes in preparation for the birth of his two children, he would have knocked him on his ass, because whatever else they said after that would also be a lie.

He sat on the floor as best he could with his stiff leg stuck out to the side. He refused any special consideration just because he'd once been shot. He was toughing it out, although he wasn't very comfortable. Deb was nestled between his legs, her back up against his chest as they listened to the instructor. Buck wondered secretly when birthing children had become so damn complicated. In Montana, you were really up against it if you ran into problems because it could be hours before any professional help got to you, if at all. This was ridiculous, although, Deb was certainly no spring chicken so pushing out two babies might not be so easy. Plus, he didn't feel like he really had any choice. He'd just do it for everyone's sake. Besides, they were only a few of weeks from the due date and a light at the end of this tunnel. He really didn't like spending time with all these strangers anyway.

The phone was blinking when they entered the house. Buck pushed the button.

"Hello, Buck, it's your mother. Call me when you get in."

Buck dialed the phone. "Hey, Mom, what's

happening?"

"Everything is fine, dear. I'm just checking in with you."

"We are fine. How's Dad?"

"He's great. We've been finishing up the last of the calf branding. We had a good year."

"I'm glad to hear it."

"I might as well get to the point. Did you want me to come out there and help, well, I mean help Deb with the babies when they come?"

Buck understood her hesitation in what to call his new roommate. He'd run into that situation himself.

"I hadn't given that any thought. I could talk to Deb and call you back. We just came home from class and she went to lay down for a little bit."

"Well, with twins and all, I'm sure she's uncomfortable and it's got to be wearing. Then with delivering two, I just thought she might need some help, what with you working at the feed store during the day and all."

"That's thoughtful of you, Mom. We hadn't even talked about it."

"Well, discuss it with her and let me know. Your father can get along without me. We have the housekeeper and cook, so they will all be fine."

"The truth is, Mom, you'll be fine without all that work to do for a change, even if you are here helping with the babies."

It still sounded foreign to him to be talking about babies, but at the same time it was truly amazing. They finished their conversation and he promised to call her back as soon as he could. The time line for her to make arrangements was closing in. One thing for sure, the twins were coming and soon.

Deb came waddling down the hallway and out into the living room, looking a bit disheveled. Buck met her in the kitchen and pushed her red hair behind her ears and kissed her.

"Having a bit of a rough day, are we?"

She looked at him and shrugged her shoulders. She had never thought too much about carrying a baby, let alone twins. It was pretty uncomfortable. She couldn't lie on either side, and being flat on her back sometimes put a strain on everything. Even pushing pillows here, there and everywhere hadn't really helped today.

"I'm about ready to get this job done." She tried to smile.

"My mother called."

"I heard you talking on the phone." Deb was standing with her back arched, hands on her hips, looking very uncomfortable.

"She wants to know if you want her to come to help out. Would that be okay?"

"I thought my mother was coming, but she hasn't called in about a week."

He could hear in her voice that she was concerned.

"Why don't you call her today? Then we would know."

Deb sighed. "I'm a little afraid to call her."

"Why?"

"I don't know. I just have a feeling."

"Well, let's just call her and ask." He handed her the phone.

"I'm not sure I'm ready for this."

"It could be good."

"Or not!"

"Okay, then don't call." He was hoping for the opposite.

"What time is it? Oh, never mind, I'll just call her." Deb slowly dialed the phone. Buck walked down the hall and into the bathroom. She appreciated the privacy since she still felt uneasy with him listening. "Hello, Mom. It's me, Deb." The conversation didn't go the way she had hoped.

"No, Mom. I don't understand. I was counting on you this time. I understand that, but things have changed here."

Her mother had done it once again. She wasn't going to be there for her when she needed her. This time it didn't feel as bad. When she was raped as a young woman, she had tried to read her mother's face. Her mother hadn't looked directly at her. It had been her father who had gone crazy. He should have taken his anger out on the rapist, but instead, he attacked her, calling her unbelievable names. She never understood why her mother hadn't defended her. This time, she wasn't going to allow them to do it to her. She stood up as straight as she could and made a decision.

"Mom, I'll go to Plan B. It won't be a problem. You don't have to hide behind Dad or lie about anything this time. I get that he still feels the same way about me."

There was a long silence on the phone. Deb felt the urge to hang up, but she waited until her mother spoke again.

"It's not that at all, Deb. I didn't want to have to tell you this now, but your father is sick. He's not doing well, but he's not the one stopping me from coming. It's me. I don't know how to leave him like this." Deb hadn't been expecting this.

"What's wrong with him?" Her heart was racing.

"It's his circulation. He's not getting adequate blood supply to his legs, and now he's not able to walk. He didn't want me to tell you. He wants me to come take care of you and the babies. He's very happy about being a grandfather, and he wants you to be happy. He loves you, Deb. He has regrets about the past, but he's not able to express himself. He said he's very excited that his little girl is going to be a mother and that you will be very good at it because you won't make his mistakes."

Deb couldn't say anything as she tried to swallow the lump in her throat. Buck came up behind her and slid his arms around her, letting his hands settle on the top of her belly. Deb cradled the phone in the crook of her neck and held both of his hands under hers. She was shaking.

"Mom, it will be okay. Stay there with Dad. Buck's mother has offered to come from Montana, so we will arrange for that to happen. You don't have to feel bad about any of this. You can come when Dad gets better and the babies are a little older. Maybe then, he can come too. I'll still need you. Tell Daddy I do love him and to get better so he can see the babies too."

"I love you, daughter of ours."

"I love you too, Mom." The phone call hadn't turned out at all like she expected, but then nothing ever did. She turned around to face Buck and he kissed her on her forehead.

"Go ahead and call your mother and see when she's

able to come. I'm thinking it is going to be soon." She placed his hand on her tummy in time for him to feel a really strong thump. They looked into each other's eyes and smiled.

~~~~~

The thought of watching Buck and Deb's babies grow up made Catherine feel like she might have a chance at being sort of an aunt. At the same time, it made her feel conflicted about what had happened between her and James. There would never be any children in her life. Every time she had talked to James about getting pregnant, he had seemed eager and excited, but now there were questions creeping into her mind. She didn't want to blame James completely because they had certainly intended to find the perfect time to start a family. But then one thing had led to another, either with her changing jobs or his traveling with Robideaux Pharmaceutical, and before she knew it, they were both older, and then suddenly, he was gone. They had seriously discussed the idea of adoption as an option as the years rolled on. It made her sick to her stomach wondering whether he could have possibly been manipulating their situation by putting her off because he knew how dangerous his job had become. She wondered whether she would ever have answers.

In a flurry of dogs, Zane rushed in and reminded her it was nearly time to leave for the airport. With the impending dual births approaching, Zane and Catherine had offered to pick up Buck's mother at the airport. Deb would stay at the farm in order to be near the hospital and Buck, in case she went into labor.
~~~~~

They took Route 121 north of Highberry and headed toward Jacksonville.

"I'll sit in the back on the way home so Buck's mother can have the front seat," Catherine said.

"Good idea."

"When's the last time you saw her?"

"They flew down to Mexico once when Buck and I were bird hunting several years ago. His father shot with us for a few days. They continued their trip in a different part of Mexico, and we stayed on and finished the hunt. It was the only time I'd seen them since we left the ranches."

"Do you think you'll recognize her?"

"Buck gave me this recent picture." Zane pulled a snapshot out of his shirt pocket. Mrs. Matthews had white hair, a round pleasant face, and was sitting in a chair with knitting needles and yarn in her hands, her gold reading glasses perched on the end of her nose.

"She's a nice looking woman." Catherine stared at the snapshot for a few minutes. She could see Buck's rounded face, his twinkling eyes, and strong cheekbones in his mother's image.

"Very. She's also very strong."

"I guess you'd have to be in order to ranch in Montana."

"It's not just that. She's strong emotionally. She never questioned Buck's decision to run with me, even though they were close and she also never blamed me."

"That seems so sad, you two doing that."

"I'm sure it was, but she never complained."

"But then neither did your mother."

"My mother would never say a word. It's not in her

to do that. It's part of her heritage. They are taught to just take it."

"By 'they,' do you mean Native Americans?"

"Yes. Life on the reservation teaches them early to accept whatever comes your way."

"That's a tough way to live."

"It's the truth. They are fighting hard to change the standards on the rez, but it hasn't been easy over all these years. There's still a lot of unrest. Some families repeat the same patterns. They don't seem to be able to break themselves out of it."

"You'd think by now that the generations are far enough removed from what happened to them that they would be making improvements."

Catherine was enjoying the countryside as they drove north toward Jacksonville.

"I'm as baffled by it as anyone. I think that's why my mother married my father. It was a clean break from repeating any of it. She seldom went back to visit."

"It had to be very difficult for her to leave."

"Yes, but it also helped her understand why I fled. She knew how it felt to be persecuted, and she watched my own father do the same thing to me. He tried to keep me in check and in my place—in other words, completely control me. It's not too far off from the control the government has over us now."

"I'm not sure I know what you mean. Didn't your father want you to have a better life than he did?"

"I told you, he was a Wheeler. He felt everyone owed him something, because it was the wheelwrights who changed the entire West. He was very arrogant about it. He thought his way of thinking was the only way. He expected me to live under that shadow. I've always wondered whether my mother married the land more than the man."

"What do you mean?"

"The chance of a Native American woman like my mother owning thousands of acres of Montana land was highly unlikely. Don't you think she'd be more entranced with the idea of owning the ranch than she was in being married to a white man? It made me believe that she married the land."

"Well, how did they meet in the first place? That seems more unlikely."

"Apparently my father had to face the fact that he'd made a lot of mistakes with women. Rumor had it that none of the white women liked him very much. It was no secret that he was rough physically and verbally to the opposite sex—didn't have much use for them. He eventually gave up trying to date white women and started hanging out at bars. My mother was catching a ride to a nearby town with some friends and they stopped off at a bar where he happened to be. The people she was with ended up drinking too much and when the bartender asked them to leave, a brawl broke out. My mother hid in the corner, not knowing what to do. The guys were thrown out the front door, and they were so drunk that they piled into the car and took off, leaving her behind. The story is that my father gave her a ride back to wherever she was staying. I have no idea about the rest of how they ended up getting married."

"They never told you about it?"

"I heard most of this from other people. My parents never talked about anything and I never asked."

"It doesn't bother you?"

"Not any more. He's gone and she seems content with her life now."

Catherine stared out the window, watching the beautiful rolling land and the oak trees laden with moss fly by and feeling grateful for her own life.

~~~~~

Deb didn't want to get up. Her back was aching, her feet were swollen and she hadn't slept all that well. It took her two tries to roll over and sit up on the side of the bed. She dangled her feet over the side, swinging them back and forth just as she started feeling a little funny. That's when her water broke. Buck had just left for the feed store, and Zane and Catherine were on the way to pick up her children's grandmother. Now, the babies were about to come into the world a little bit early. She reached for the phone.

"Buck, you're going to have to come back to the house," she blurted.

"What? What's the matter?"

"It's time."

"It's time for what? Did my mother arrive? It's too early."

"No, Buck, it is too early. My water broke. The babies are coming. Please hurry."

Deb didn't get to say another thing, because he hung up on her. She dialed the doctor's number. She waddled into the bathroom, cleaned up, and struggled into a loose-fitting sundress for the trip to the hospital. She hoped that Buck hadn't gotten too far from the house, because the pain was beginning. She couldn't
~~~~~

believe she hadn't had any indication that this was going to happen today.

Deb pulled her little suitcase off the shelf in the closet, huffing and puffing, and set it on the bed. She couldn't get her feet into the shoes she wanted to wear, so she stuffed them into a pair of clogs. A sharp contraction made her grab her belly with both hands and grit her teeth. Buck better show up soon.

She heard the truck coming down the driveway and hurriedly grabbed the suitcase and headed out the front door. He met her at the top step and held onto her arms as she plopped down the three front steps.

"Listen; try not to hit any potholes on the way to the hospital or one of these kids might just fall out on the floorboard."

Buck shot her a look that made her giggle. He looked petrified.

"I'm only kidding. The contractions just started, but I don't want to take any chances. I'd rather be sitting in Alachua at the hospital than here alone and screaming. I'm telling you, if this gets bad, I'm asking for drugs."

"Darling, I don't care what you ask for as long as I don't have to do anything."

"What are you talking about? You have to help me breathe."

"Yes, I know that, but don't expect anything else from me."

"Don't worry, Daddy. The professionals will be there for me. You just get me there and now!"

~~~~~

In the early evening, Deb did a perfect job of
~~~~~

pushing first her daughter and then her son out into the world. She looked exhausted, but she was very happy when the nurse placed her newborn children into her arms. Buck couldn't stop fussing over the three of them. He was fascinated by their tiny little hands, feet, and their perfect sweet little faces. He leaned down and kissed her tenderly. "You did real good, honey. You really did. They are beautiful." He pulled out his cell phone and started taking pictures.

"Cut my head off because I have to look like crap," Deb said with a forced grin.

"Don't be silly," one of the nurses said. "There isn't anything more beautiful than a new mother holding her child. For you, it's a bonus. You are twice as beautiful."

Deb artificially smiled at them. "I'm not feeling so great. Could you maybe take the babies for a little while?"

"Are you in pain?" the nurse asked.

"Oh, no, I'm just feeling like I'm about to faint."

The nurse quickly checked her blood pressure.

"This happens sometimes. I'll get an order for a medication that will bring it back up and you'll be all right."

Buck felt like he was about to lose it. He was scared to death that something was going to happen to his.... He still didn't know what to call her. It would sound kind of stupid to call the mother of his two kids his girlfriend. He really needed to do something about this and soon. They better not let anything happen to the mother of his children.

"How long is it going to take for the medication to work? She's looking very pale," he asked in a panicked voice.

"It should be taking effect very shortly. Give it a chance."

He didn't want to give it a chance. He wanted her to be okay right now. Just then, Zane stuck his head in the door. Buck could see Catherine behind him and to her right stood Effie Matthews. He slipped quickly out the door and grabbed his mother. It took them a while to let go of each other. Her hair was almost white, her eyes still had their sparkle, but she seemed so much shorter. He hugged her again and started talking.

"Deb's blood pressure suddenly took a dive, but they gave her a shot. They say it should kick it up very soon. The babies are in there in these little beds. They are just beautiful. She did real good. Oh God, I hope she's going to be okay."

"We can wait until Deb's feeling better. It's okay," his mother said.

Buck couldn't stop looking at his mother because he was thinking if he had passed her on the street, he didn't know if he would have recognized her.

"I'm sure everything will be just fine," Zane told him. He pulled two cigars from his shirt pocket and handed one to Buck.

"We'll light these up first chance we get," Zane said as he waved his cigar around in the air. "We can go get some coffee. Leave you guys alone. What can we get you? Anything?"

The nurse was right. Within fifteen minutes, the color returned to Deb's face and she was able to hold the babies again. When Catherine, Zane, and Buck's mother were able to see them they told them the babies were more than beautiful and with Deb's blood pressure almost back to normal, Buck was beaming. All was well in their world.

It was getting late and Buck insisted on spending the rest of the night with his new family. He was happy when Zane and Catherine decided it would be easier to take Mrs. Matthews home with them, rather than drop her off at Buck's house, where she would be all alone. That way they could make sure she got breakfast in the morning, take her by the hospital, and later get her settled at Buck's house, even though she told Buck she didn't want anyone fussing over her.

Buck kissed his mother's cheek, told her goodnight and watched as she patted Deb on the arm and gazed lovingly at her two brand new grandchildren. He was tickled to see that Zane had his arm tightly around Catherine. This night couldn't have been any better.

~~~~~

Buck and Deb brought their newborn babies home from the hospital to the arms of their loving grandmother. Effie told Buck she couldn't believe the turn his life had taken and that Deb seemed to be a natural mother—nothing fazed her, except a little bit of fatigue due to lack of sleep, but for a new mother, she was quite adept at all the aspects of taking care of her children.

"My mother is quite taken by you," Buck told Deb.

"She keeps telling me how well I'm doing. I kind of surprised myself."

They were sitting side by side in matching rocking chairs in the nursery, each holding a baby.
~~~~~

Deb said, "I read that it makes it easier for babies if their mother is relaxed. I can't help but wonder if all this new autistic stuff these kids are experiencing isn't because of all the commotion people put their kids through. No one sits still with them anymore."

"I don't know what other people do. I'm just happy, Deb. I've never been this happy, and having you and my mother here taking care of my kids, well, who would have ever thunk it?" Buck got up and gently put his son in his crib. He walked over to Deb and took his sleeping daughter from her arms and placed her in the crib next to her brother."

"Are you sure that's okay? I mean should we do that?"

"They were together for almost nine months all snuggled in your belly. We'll just sit here and watch them for a while."

Buck sat down in the rocker, pulled it closer to the crib, and pulled Deb onto his lap. He ran his hands through her red soft hair and kissed her tenderly.

~~~~~

Zane and Catherine made a quick stop at Buck and Deb's on the way back from town to take a peek at the babies. They were down for a nap, so they all tiptoed in and then quietly snuck back out. Catherine felt that all too familiar pang around her heart.

"They are so sweet. You two must be very happy."

"We are, Catherine, and they are the best babies." Deb was beaming and Buck looked like his chest would burst with pride. It made Catherine think about James for just a split second. She quickly pushed the thought
~~~~~

out of her mind. She took a deep breath.

"What are their names?" Zane asked.

"Don't laugh. We had such a hard time. We named them Bobray and Diddie."

"Well then, at least you don't have to worry about there being other kids in their class with those names," Zane said.

Catherine was relieved to have something to distract her thoughts. She tried not to smirk, but the names seemed a bit silly.

"That's what we figured." Deb said. "While I was pregnant, we talked and talked about it, and we really couldn't decide. We didn't feel the need to name them after a grandparent so we decided to use the first letter of each of our given names."

"Best damn thing that ever happened to me for sure," Buck added. "We decided not to give them middle names either—just plain old Bobray and Diddie Matthews."

"Well, I don't know about plain, but this life sure looks good on you, Tuff," Zane smirked at him.

"God, I haven't heard that name in a while, but thanks. Say, didn't you tell me you were about ready to take off for Montana?"

"I'm not sure I'm going to be heading out soon, but don't you think it's about time?" Zane was hedging because of upsetting Catherine.

"Yes, and I'm really glad for you. I know your mother is going to be elated."

"I'm not telling her I'm coming and can't wait to see her face. You haven't spilled the beans, have you?"

"No, and I'll be sure to tell Mom not to either. When

you see your mother and Parker, tell them I send my love."

"I certainly will do that."

Catherine couldn't help it, but she felt a sense of fear at the thought of Zane leaving her. She didn't feel ready to be left alone on the farm.

"Catherine, while he's away, you know you can count on us."

"Thank you. I appreciate that, and don't worry; I'm certain I will call you."

They said their goodbyes and Buck and Deb stood waving in the driveway as Catherine and Zane drove out the lane.

Catherine wasn't happy about Zane leaving. She didn't want to be in the house alone, even if the dogs were there. She had started feeling edgy. She had a shaky feeling way down in her gut, like something was about to happen. She had known feelings like that ever since she was a child. It was similar to when she first crossed paths with Celia Fenmore, her half-sister. She had intuitively felt something toward Celia's daughter, Olivia. The feeling was similar to that, but this time, it didn't feel like it was going to have a good outcome.

CHAPTER 16

James felt relieved now that they were in Arianne's apartment in New York City. No one had given him a second glance. The surgery on his face had seriously transformed him. It was very strange peering into the mirror because he simply didn't recognize his reflection. Even when he touched his nose, his face, it didn't feel like his skin. The sensation felt strange, like his hands were touching something foreign, almost plastic. He hated it. He wanted to go home and have everything be normal, but he didn't have a home anymore. Worse, New York made him miss Catherine even more. He wanted to go to her favorite bakery and buy her cheese cake and burst into the apartment with it. He wanted to sweep her up in his arms and smell her hair and look into her beautiful face.

"Arianne, where the hell is the shaving cream?" he shouted.

"You don't have to yell, James. It is on the edge of the tub. I shaved my legs. Sorry."

"Can't you put anything back where it belongs?" he barked.

"I got distracted."

"Well, straighten up."

He hated people who couldn't put things back where they belonged. He couldn't believe that a woman could be so haphazard. It was simple—if you take it out, put it back. There was a place for everything and everything in its place. How hard was that? He knew he was growing increasingly impatient with her, but honestly, a dog was easier to train.

"Did you pick up my suit from the cleaners?"

"Not yet."

"Well, what the hell were you doing all day yesterday?"

"I did a spa day."

"Well, good for you; now could you make a point to pick it up today?"

"Sure James."

He walked right past her and out the front door of the apartment. He had to do something about all of this, but he didn't know what. He did know exactly where to go to get a phone that couldn't be traced, and once he had the damn thing charged, he was going to get some answers.

~~~~~

Arianne was tired of playing house with him. She was also tired of pretending that James' behavior was acceptable. It was time to do something about their living arrangements. She had been there for him when he needed her, but this had grown ridiculous. She was tired of babysitting an angry man who didn't want to be living the life he ended up with. It wasn't her fault he got himself into this situation. She had nothing to do with his decisions. Even though he had been played by the guys involved in the plot, he had done a great thing. The end result was what should have mattered to him, but he was stuck on losing Catherine. He would never get his life on track as long as he was this angry. There was
~~~~~

no way she was going to continue in this non-existent relationship with him. He was using her. She knew perfectly well that he wasn't thinking about her anymore when he was romping on top of her. It had grown tedious. She had to tell him. He wouldn't be happy, but she wanted her life back. She'd never been the kind of girl who could stay put for very long or with one man for that matter.

He would have to find his own place. She needed to be a big girl, and he needed to put on his big boy pants and get out. She would handle whatever stupid tantrum he threw. She was certain she could get louder and more dramatic than he was used to with Catherine. The shit was about to hit the fan.

~~~~~

James pulled a small piece of paper from his pocket and slowly dialed the number. He stopped breathing as soon as she answered the phone. He listened to her voice, heard her apprehension, and then he pushed the button and slammed his fist into the wall behind where he was standing. He didn't say a word. He was living his worst nightmare.

He realized now that the decisions he'd made had been selfish. He hadn't thought it through, but then they would have played him no matter what. How in the hell was he going to explain this to her? Even if Catherine listened, he couldn't just move back in with her. What if it somehow put her in danger? He was screwed and he knew it. Still, he just wanted a moment with her. He needed to look into her eyes and say it—*"I'm sorry. I didn't know it was going to end like this."*
~~~~~

Could she forgive him? Would she? He had no idea about anything anymore. Almost worse than not seeing Catherine was his not having anything to do. The boredom was driving him crazy.

He would have given anything to have his old life and their apartment back, but, more importantly, he longed to hold Catherine in his arms. He had dreamt about her lying in the bed with him, her head on his shoulder. He would wake up alone or with Arianne. It wasn't fair and it definitely wasn't working. He felt like he was caught in a constant nightmare from which he would never wake up.

He reluctantly walked past the doorman, rode the elevator to Arianne's floor and slid the card in her door. He waited a long time for her to return to her apartment and when she did, he was sitting on the couch, staring into space.

Arianne leaned down in front of him and asked, "Is everything okay, James?"

He didn't answer. He just gave her this blank look.

She said it again, "James, are you okay?"

He stood up, smoothed his pants, and pushed her out of the way. He had been drinking. He turned back around, picked her up, and carried her into the bedroom. She didn't resist. She knew better because she'd learned that she couldn't reason with him when he was like this. She tried to ignore his mood and enjoy what she sometimes craved from him, but he was rough. Still, she didn't try to stop him. She was as intoxicated by him at times as he was with his liquor and she knew it. She allowed him to use her one last time.

In the morning, she waited until he stirred, and

then she rolled over and stared into his eyes.

"What?" he asked

"James, I care about you a lot; you know that, but this has got to end. I can't do this anymore."

"I know."

"You have to move on and you can't do that with me. And, you can't stay here anymore. I have to get my life under control again. I feel so bad for you."

Arianne was propped up on her elbow, her hand behind her head, looking down at him.

"I know."

"James, would you please quit saying that you know. You make me feel guilty."

"Don't."

He rolled over on his side so he was facing her.

"Don't what?" she asked.

"Don't feel guilty. I made the decisions. I'm responsible for the consequences."

"You don't deserve this."

"I know."

"James."

"I know all of it, Arianne. I've thought about it every day since I figured out what they were going to do with me, with us. I just wish I could have told her. She might have understood."

"James. You did what was best in that moment."

"I don't know anymore."

"It's been fun. I mean, you and I were always good in bed."

She ran her fingers over his face tenderly.

"Don't say any more," he said and took her hands and pushed them away.

"No. I mean we always had that connection. Chemistry—whatever you want to call it. We were just hot."

"I told you not to say it."

"Well, we have to stop it. We have to stop it now. It's not good for either one of us."

"I know."

"James."

"Arianne, I want my life back. I want to go back to that night here in your apartment when she walked in."

"Honey, it would be nice to turn the clock back, but we can't."

He grabbed her by her hair and pulled her on top of him and kissed her as hard as he'd ever kissed her.

"James."

"Just shut up, Arianne."

~~~~~

She watched him pack his clothes and take his things from her bathroom. Her entire body ached, but it seemed a small price for her to pay after what had happened to him. She had been the only thing she could give to him that would make him feel better, and she had given him everything she had to give. She had stayed with him in that godforsaken town in that stupid small cabin for months and months. She had put up with his moods and his crazy sex-capades. She had been afraid of what he might do if she hadn't been there for him. She had convinced herself it was what she needed to do, but now she was done. She knew he was trying to make her into someone she wasn't. She could never be Catherine. Now, it was acutely clear to her that
~~~~~

she needed to let him go.

"James, I feel so bad. Where will you go? What will you do?"

"I don't know. I'll figure something out."

"Promise me you won't do anything crazy. Promise me you will keep in touch with me."

He didn't want to promise anyone anything. He had promised to do a job for the government and look where it had gotten him. He had promised Catherine that he would honor her, but look how he had messed that up. He had promised himself that he would.... None of it mattered anymore. His entire life had been shattered. He didn't know how to go back and fix anything. He could only move forward. "I'll be in touch."

"James."

"Please, Arianne, I'll be okay."

"No you won't."

"It doesn't matter." He walked out of the bedroom with her right behind him.

"It matters to me."

"You say that, but you need to get your life back. You want that. At least you'll be able to now."

"I know, James, but it just isn't right."

"Nothing is right anymore, Arianne. Please. Let it go. Watch me walk out the door. That's all. Then don't worry about me anymore. You've done more than enough. Don't think for one moment that I don't understand what you've given up for me."

"I care about you, James."

"Well, you need to stop it. You did enough."

He slid his hand behind her neck and pulled her head into him and kissed her so hard she cut her lower lip on her teeth. She didn't make a sound. He turned on his heels, grabbed the handle of his suitcase, picked up his overnighter, slung it over his shoulder, and strode out the apartment door without even a glance over his shoulder.

Arianne let out a long sigh and silently thanked God that this would be over. She couldn't have lasted another day. She walked into her bathroom, turned on the faucet, and poured Epsom salts and lavender soap into the tub. She let her silk crème-colored gown fall off her shoulders to the floor and slid into the hot water as soon as the tub was full. For the first time in her life, she didn't feel good about who she was. She had been sleeping with someone else's husband—Catherine's husband. Worse, she had been sleeping with a man everyone thought was dead. She scrubbed and scrubbed every part of her body and then pulled a pillow under her neck, closed her eyes, and soaked in the tub until the water turned cold.

CHAPTER 17

Catherine and Zane finished the night chores and headed from the barn toward the house. She stopped in the dark and placed her hand over one eye and then the other.

"What the heck are you doing?" Zane asked.

"To tell you the truth, I think I can see more clearly since I moved to the ranch."

"Catherine, I'm sure you can."

"But, Zane, how is that possible? Is it the air or the food or my imagination?"

"It's none of the above."

"How can that be?"

"Here's what I know. People who live in the city experience a kind of moon blindness. Their eyes become so accustomed to constant exposure to light that at night they can't see very well. Now that you are out at night in almost total darkness, your eyes are going back to the way they were intended to function."

"Well, it makes sense. I swore I could see in the dark as a kid. I just thought not being able to see after dark now was part of aging."

"I'm sure that's possible, but I don't think it's probable."

"Why is that?" Catherine asked as they walked slowly towards the house.

"I had a hard time with the bright lights when I had to live in the Washington, D.C. area for training. It bugged me, so I'd keep most of the lights off in our hotel room. Buck hated it, but we compromised by him keeping the television on all night."

"That's kind of funny."

He didn't answer her. They were walking back from the barn on one of the darkest nights she had ever seen. Catherine loved to stand and stare at the stars. They appeared so close that she felt like she could almost touch them, and there were so many of them. She was surprised at how many clusters she could still identify. Zane helped her with others. It made her feel infinitely small.

"I can't believe I spent so much time missing all of this. My life became over-scheduled and involved. I'd much rather be staring at the stars than at a television or a computer screen."

"I never got sucked into that. Buck was the techno guy. I'd sit outside and listen to the night every chance I got."

"I did that as a little girl in Jensen Beach. I would lean my face against the window screen at night in my bedroom and listen to the sounds, until the mosquito population found me. I have no idea how we lived without air-conditioning, but it honestly didn't seem that hot."

"First of all, it probably wasn't as hot, and second, it's whatever you get used to."

"Well, I'm certainly getting used to this. I hope it lasts forever."

She leaned her back against Zane and he folded her into his arms tight against his chest.

~~~~~

The next morning, Catherine was breathless as she flew through the back door with all the dogs. They were excited, greeting Zane, jumping around him, some of them barking.

"The locusts are calling early this morning. I bet the heat is going to bring a thunderstorm later this afternoon. I can't tell you how wonderful it is to hear a mockingbird singing, and I saw a beautiful male cardinal in the brush by the house just now. I'm in heaven."

"I'm glad it makes you so happy." Zane was washing his hands at the kitchen sink.

"It does. I feel like I can finally take a deep breath. The air is clear after that nice rain last night and the humidity is down."

"I know. The horses were really enjoying themselves this morning bolting around."

"We are so lucky."

"Yes, we are."

She wrapped her arms around his waist and looked up into his face. She loved his rugged look, which reminded her of Robert Redford in his younger days. His salt and pepper hair was always perfectly combed. She loved feeling his muscular build too. She loved everything about him, even the way he smelled.

"Thank you," he said.

She had been lost in her thoughts of him.

"For what?"

"Just thank you."

They kissed softly and he carefully pushed her hair
~~~~~

away from her eyes. She felt like she had been reborn. First, the house had placed its loving arms around her, and then somehow, Zane had come into her life. It made everything she had been through seem less painful. Still, there was a nagging feeling she couldn't shake. She found herself spending too much time thinking about James. Things were beginning to bother her again; plus, there were the clues she had somehow overlooked during her busy life in New York. There was that time James had cut their trip short with no real explanation after she had seen him knock some man down in the parking lot of the hotel. Why hadn't she confronted him? Why hadn't she demanded that he explain to her what was going on? She would never have that opportunity now. Who was that man and what were they arguing about? Had he lied to her about that trip? How could she have become that naïve? She had pushed it out of her mind. Were there other things that she missed? Had she been in denial? She thought she was too intelligent to have missed all of it, and yet he had completely deceived her.

At least she had stopped waking up wondering where she was. She knew perfectly well where she was and who was sleeping in her bed. She and Zane hadn't talked about taking their relationship further. They both seemed content with it the way it was for now. She didn't know how she felt about marriage anymore. He had made no demands of her, gave her money for his food, paid for Trouble's expenses even when she protested. He offered to pay half of the utilities, but that made it seem like he was a roommate and she didn't like how that made her feel. She wanted their relationship to be more than jumping in the sack with the guy who was renting space from her or eating meals with her. She wanted to feel exactly like she did. She was in love with him.

She did feel disappointed that she allowed her mind to keep going over what happened with James. What bothered her most lately were the questions concerning the relationship between James and Arianne. They had known a lot about each other—almost too much. She understood that they had been involved before her, but there had been looks and nudges that indicated they knew each other a whole lot more than they admitted. She had caught them talking when they didn't know she could hear them. Arianne had said, "I'm telling you, she hasn't got a clue about how involved you are with this." James had responded, "I have tried very hard not to show the amount of stress I'm under. They have me over a barrel." Catherine had thought it was about his work. Now she was wondering whether it was about the government controlling him and what he did with that destructive drug. She wasn't sure whether knowing more about it would alter the course of her life. Maybe none of that mattered anymore.

~~~~~

Catherine was sitting at the kitchen table, bent over a notebook.

"What are you working so hard on?" Zane asked.

"Let's say a bunch of characters, just for grins."

"What kind of characters? Are you writing your book?"

"Not exactly, I was thinking about how all of our
~~~~~

lives interplay with each other and I started putting together sort of a family tree. Mind if I ask you some questions?"

"Fire away." He pulled out one of the kitchen chairs and sat next to her.

She tapped her teeth with the eraser of her pencil. "I scratched this out a few weeks ago. Okay, here we go." She asked, "So what's your mother's name?"

"Her given name is Maggie White Calf, but my father called her Coot."

As Zane spoke, Catherine began jotting down notes.

"Why did he call her that?"

"He said it was because she was small of stature and her hair was dark like the little ducks that sometimes came to the creek. Some people didn't like him calling her that because it sounded demeaning."

"How did she feel about it?"

"I think my mother became somewhat numb to him."

"What do you mean?"

"She didn't show any emotion or respond to him most of the time."

"Coping skills; she created her own coping skills."

"Exactly," Zane said as he scooted his chair back. "Do you want something to drink?" He poured them each a glass of iced tea and joined her back at the kitchen table.

"What's next?" he asked.

"Father's name?"

"Foster Thomas Wheeler."

"Sounds like a good strong name."

"It was. Do you know anything about the Wheelers

and their role in what happened in the West?"

"Not really."

"I'm sure you can search for this on line. Look up the wheelwrights."

"Okay. Wheel as in Wheeler? The wheelwrights? Seems interesting." She made several notes, including an asterisk with a circle around it so she wouldn't miss it.

"I'm sure you will enjoy the research."

"What about Buck? What about his family?"

"Names?"

"Yes."

"I'm not sure about how accurate this is, because it's what we called them. His mother is Effie Matthews. Don't know anything else about that. His father I only knew as Roan. I'm not sure if that's his given name or what."

"I like that name. Where do you think that came from?"

"It could just be a family name, but it is also a color of a horse. The hairs are two colors blended together. Red and white or blue and white."

"Blue?"

"Yes. The darker hair mixes with the white and gives the horse a blue hue."

"Do you think they named him Roan or it's his nickname?" Catherine had scribbled all the names on the pad in front of her.

"Don't know. Why this sudden interest in their backgrounds?"

"I'm just curious. You're right. I can do searches so easily on the Internet. I think it will be fun, and I want to play around with my writing too. I plan to research my family as well. I wonder how far back I'll be able to go."

Zane thought for a minute and then said, "You can probably go back to whenever the first census was taken. I think they also have information on the Native Americans when they moved them to the reservations. I'm sure that could prove to be very interesting to you. Do you know that many of them used symbols to sign their names when the government forced them to sign?"

"That's interesting."

"Well, think about it. You have groups of people who spoke similar languages, but were from different tribes. They learned sign language so they could communicate with each other. They didn't have the written word, and then the government was asking them to sign their names on a piece of paper. Take Eagle Calf. He drew a stick figure of an eagle and then a calf. Eagle Calf. Do you get it?"

"Yes, I do, now. I never had an occasion to think about it before. It seems like it will be very interesting. So you think your mother goes back to a white calf?"

"Not a cow like you are imagining—a buffalo calf. I'm certain her lineage goes back in some way to Buffalo Woman, but the name got twisted around into White Calf. It most likely has to do with White Buffalo Woman and the sacred white buffalo calf. Did you know there was one born recently? It is very sacred and spiritual to have a white buffalo calf born on your land."

"This seems like it is going to get a lot bigger than I thought."

"Or not. You can make it whatever you want. You

don't have to do anything with any of it if you don't want to. Just see what happens."

"I will."

Catherine typed in the words "White Buffalo Woman" and waited for the computer to list the search results. *"A spiritual being in Lakota tradition who passed the Buffalo Calf Pipe to the people along with sacred rites. Also White Buffalo Calf Woman, White Buffalo Calf Maiden, Ptehincalassanwin."* She searched for "Buffalo Calf Pipe." *"The sacred pipe of the Lakota."*

She couldn't wait to delve deeper into the history she knew so little about.

Her fingers slid over the keys as she began to type the names that Zane had given her into her laptop.

Zane Wheeler – Mother - Maggie White Calf
Father - Foster Thomas Wheeler
Siblings – None ?

Buck Mathews – Mother - Effie Mathews
Father - Roan Mathews
Siblings - ?
Deb Albom – Children: Bobray & Diddie

Catherine DeLong – Mother - Elizabeth Howell
Step-Father - Hamilton Wesley Howell
Siblings - Sister - Constance Kendale (KiKi)
Father - John Kendale (deceased)
Half-Sister – Celia – Celia's Husband ?
Niece - Olivia

Uncle Walton Kendale/Aunt Josie
Children: Waylon and Justin – Cousins

~~~~~

Catherine felt like she always had a story buzzing around in her head— she had some pages scratched out, a brief outline saved, and ideas about some characters. Now that her life had taken such a drastic turn, she was thinking more seriously about writing. She had checked out some web pages and ordered several books on writing. She finished reading one and was nearly finished with a second. She was happy to be thinking about something positive for a change. It felt like a force was pushing her in a definitive direction.

The last chapter of the second book was entitled "Going Home." It was from Natalie Goldberg's book, *Writing Down the Bones—Freeing the Writer Within.* Natalie said, "It is very important to go home if you want your work to be whole. You don't have to move in with your parents again or collect a weekly allowance, but you must claim where you come from and look deep into it. Come to honor and embrace it, or at least accept it."

Catherine felt like that was exactly where she was right at this very moment. It was ironic and spooky. She didn't have an answer to why she had stayed away from her Uncle Walton or her hometown for so long. He never went anywhere, almost never on a vacation or anything, so she could have popped in at any moment and he would have been there. He had loved her unconditionally, but she had put parameters on herself that had not allowed her to go back there, at least, not until he had needed her. After his son, Waylon, phoned her, she knew she had to go. She was certain it was comparable to the feelings Zane was having about
~~~~~

returning home to his mother after such a long time away. She understood, even though she didn't want him to go.

~~~~~

The skies became dark as a thunderstorm blew in. Zane ran out to bring the horses into the barn before the rain. Alachua County was famous for its lightning strikes so there was no sense taking chances. He told her, "Catherine, stay right where you are. I'll get them in. Not to worry." He was shouting to her as he pulled on a rain parka and flipped on his hat. She looked up long enough to see him blur out the back porch door with all the dogs following except Friskie. "I'll let them out now in case the rain settles in. No sense fighting the mud."

She nodded and kept staring at the computer screen. As soon as he was out the door, she spoke out loud. "What the heck?" She knew she hadn't put any pictures on her laptop because she hadn't taken any. It shook her to the core. She didn't remember ever seeing the file before. Within a few minutes, Zane burst through the back porch door with all the dogs. Friskie had stayed right next to Catherine on her chair. Her constant shadow, he stood up and leaned out as Zane ran his hand over the little dog's head.

"This storm looks wicked. You might lose your signal or power for a while."

"I'm getting ready to sign off anyway. I want to take Friskie out before it starts."

"You better hurry. Are you okay?"

Catherine wasn't quite sure what to say. She leaned back in her chair and looked up at him.
~~~~~

"Something strange is going on here, Zane."

"Like what?"

"I'm certain I didn't have any pictures on this laptop, and now there's a file called 'pictures' on here?"

"Well, you know I'm fairly illiterate when it comes to this stuff."

"No, you are not." She clicked on "turn off" and closed her laptop.

"Well, almost. I just don't know about how things get where they do on that thing."

"I know enough to keep me out of trouble, but this has me baffled. I don't know how this got there." Catherine stood up and stretched and headed to the utility room to get Friskie's leash.

"Did you open it? What's in it?" Zane asked as he walked behind her.

She didn't know if she should tell him because they had promised not to keep any more secrets from each other.

"Okay, I'll tell you. It's a picture of James and me."

"Do you remember the picture? I mean, when it was taken?"

"I do. It's the last picture taken of us before…" She stopped in mid-sentence.

Zane didn't know what to say, but he didn't have to because Catherine started talking again.

"We never printed that picture or did anything with it. I mean, I don't remember ever getting it printed. It was in James' camera—the camera I bought for him right before he…"

"I'm sure there's a simple explanation," he cut her off.

"I don't think so. It is very upsetting and feels like someone is messing with me. I'm very suspicious. I can't help it. I simply don't understand a lot of things that happened."

"Don't you have some kind of fire wall or scanner on that thing?"

"I do."

"Then how is that possible?"

"I don't know because I paid a lot of money to feel safe on my laptop. I don't understand."

"Me either." Zane was shaking his head.

A clap of thunder reminded her that she needed to get Friskie outside before the impending rain. She picked him up and headed out the back door. She made it back into the house just as the power went off.

~~~~~

It was several hours before the lights came back on and Zane hurried out the back door to throw night hay, fill water buckets, and turn off the barn lights. The dogs raced around in the drizzling rain.

"Hurry up, guys, before you all get completely soaked," he called to them.

It didn't really matter to them, but he was trying to get them in before it started pouring again. He was keyed up. He didn't know what to make of the photo appearing on her laptop. She was right. What in the world would anyone gain by hacking her computer and posting a picture of her and her dead husband? What was bothering him the most was that the picture was the last one of them before James' little accident. He had no answer, but he knew someone who might. First thing
~~~~~

in the morning, he would head into town and straight to a certain friend's feed store.

Catherine had already turned off most of the lights and gone upstairs when he came in the back door. He turned off all the remaining lights, except for a night light in the kitchen, and headed up the stairs. "Son of a fucking bitch," he whispered under his breath as he started up the stairs.

When he slid into bed with Catherine, she said, "I love how you do that."

"Do what?"

"Slide in and fit perfectly up against me. You make me feel safe and tonight I really need to feel safe."

"I understand, honey, and I promise you that picture is nothing to worry about. It's probably some kind of a computer glitch. I'm sure there's an explanation. We will figure it out."

"I hope so."

Zane reached over her to the night stand to turn off the light and he whispered in her ear, "At least I know something that can make you forget about it tonight," just as the room went dark.

CHAPTER 18

She hadn't felt him leave and awoke to an empty bed and the sound of his truck starting. She jumped up and looked out the bedroom window in time to see him pulling out of the driveway. Now, there was no real reason for her to get up. She was certain he had done the chores. The bed was nice and cozy as she pulled up the covers. Friskie hopped out of his little bed and popped into bed with her. She raised the top coverlet and he slid in between it and the sheet and curled up against her side. "You are the cutest," she said as she patted his little body. He was a comfort to her this morning.

The phone startled her out of a deep sleep. She grabbed it from the night stand and said, "Hello" in a throaty dry voice. No one replied.

"Hello. Hello." She thought she could hear someone breathing. "Is someone there? Can you hear me? If you can hear me, please speak."

Nothing happened. She quietly placed the phone on the cradle. Zane never called her. In fact, no one really called her. Once in awhile, Buck would call Zane, but mostly, she handled her business on the Internet now that she had service. It was a whole lot easier to send her step-father, Hamilton, or her attorney e-mails than it was to place a phone call. Scanning or using attachments had made her life much easier for forwarding documents. She just didn't know who could be calling her. She picked up the phone and dialed her caller ID number, which was of no use. The phone number had been blocked. It made her feel uneasy. She had that nagging feeling back in her stomach again and she didn't like it.

"Why is this happening now?" she asked out loud. She was sick of thinking about the mess James had left behind.

~~~~~

Zane sat in the truck, waiting for Buck to open the feed store. The minute Buck turned the key in the lock, Zane was behind him, pushing him through the front door. Buck was startled and tried to push back and spin around until he realized it was Zane.

"What the fuck are you doing?"

"Just get inside. I need to talk to you." Zane pushed him into the store.

"About what? And stop pushing me."

"You know what. Why in the hell did you do it?" Zane had Buck's shirt in his hands.

"Do what? And, let go of my shirt. I don't know what you are talking about. Settle down."

"Don't you tell me to settle down. You were the only one who had access to her computer, and you told me you were doing one thing and you did something else?"

"What exactly are you accusing me of?" Buck asked.

"You put that photo of her and James on her computer. What the hell is that about? Why are you trying to mess with her?"

"I have no idea what you are talking about and I didn't put any picture in her computer."
~~~~~

"You were the only other person to have access to it."

"Maybe. Is she using the Internet?" Buck mused.

"Yes."

"Well, bingo. There you go. Don't go accusing me of something I know nothing about."

"Why would anyone else be messing with her?" Zane wanted answers.

"I have no idea."

"What the hell are they going to gain by doing it?" Zane asked.

"I don't know. What's it a picture of?"

"She says it's the last picture taken of them, her and James, before he was killed. She says the picture was never taken off his camera. That it was on James' camera."

"Well, do you believe her?"

"Of course I believe her. Why would she make that up?"

"I don't know. If I've learned one thing, Zane, it is that things aren't always what they seem."

"Well, someone wanted her to see that picture for some reason."

"Who?"

"You tell me. You're the one who still wants to be involved with them. You're still buddy-buddy with Bill Brannan."

"I am not. I was just available when they needed me."

"You were very conveniently available. Tell me, what do you owe them?"

"I can't simply walk away. It was my life."

"It was my life too, but now I'm done."

"Okay, so what do you think is going on?"

"I think someone wants to keep things stirred up, and I don't know why. I hope it's not that son-of-a-pain in my ass attorney she fired; Roger what's his name."

"Well, what's in it for him?"

"I'm sure he'd like to make it look like I was involved so she won't trust me."

"And then what?"

"Well, she gets upset with me, kicks me out, and he makes a move on her again."

"I don't think she'd let him do that, Zane. Do you?"

"I don't know. I don't think so. She really didn't like anything about Roger."

"So stop worrying."

"It's not that. I just have a weird feeling about this whole James situation and so does she. I watch her and she's always thinking about it. You can tell by her body language, and she gets that faraway look in her eye. What if it is him, Buck?"

"Seems like you don't have any choice but to wait it out."

"Can someone trace how that picture got on her computer?"

"Probably not anyone in this area. That's a bit sophisticated."

"You mean on a tech...."

A customer opened the door, ending their conversation. Zane quickly shook Buck's hand and turned and walked out. He didn't have a clue what to do next. The last thing he wanted her to know right now was that James was alive.

~~~~~

"Where the heck did you go?" Catherine asked.

"To town to get something sweet for your breakfast." He handed her a white bag. Catherine looked inside and then set it on the kitchen counter.

"Apple fritters with cinnamon and sugar. I love it. That was sweet of you."

"Well, you had a bit of a rough go last night so I figured."

"You are going to completely spoil me."

"Yes, I hope so." He leaned in and kissed her. "I also asked Buck about your computer, but he doesn't have any ideas on how that photo got on there either. I thought maybe he could figure it out."

"I think someone hacked my computer. I changed my passwords, but there's nothing else I can do. And I have to tell you, someone called this morning while you were gone and I thought I heard them breathing, but they wouldn't answer me."

"I hate this, honey. I want to protect you from all of it, but I feel like I'm failing."

"You are not. It has nothing to do with you."

"It has everything to do with you, though."

"It's okay. I'm a big girl. I'll figure it out. We will figure it out."

"How? I'm impatient. I want it fixed now."

"I'm not sure yet how we do that."

"I like the word yet," Zane said.

"I thought I was beyond all of this and then here it is again. I don't understand what this is about. Is someone trying to scare me? Is someone trying to tell me
~~~~~

something? I have no idea. I want to go ride. I can't do this today. It's too gorgeous outside and I want to go riding and not think about any of this."

"That sounds good to me. I threw hay before I left for town and I'll go give them their grain right now. We'll have our breakfast, and by the time we get out there and we groom and tack up, it will be perfect timing."

"Thank you, and, Zane, not a word about all this today. I'm shelving it for now."

"Not a problem."

As soon as they finished breakfast, Zane headed out the back door with some of the dogs with him. Champ stayed behind with Catherine and so did Friskie. They sensed when she was edgy. She quickly made her way up the stairs to change into another pair of jeans that fit better. She couldn't wait to be riding her horse in the peacefulness of the woods.

<p style="text-align:center">~~~~~</p>

Zane and Catherine rode up through the meadow and into the pine forest. She always rode her gelding. This time, Zane decided to tack up her bay mare for himself instead of Trouble, his stallion. "This little mare is coming along much faster than I expected. She's got a good mind and she never hesitates about anything."

"I'm really glad to hear that. I liked her from the minute I saw her, but I had no idea how she would turn out."

"No, she's doing well. I'm happy with her. Say, I want to show you something, but we have to go across some downed trees. It will be good for both of them."

Catherine had been riding almost every day and felt

fairly confident with Sundy now. "That's fine. I'll just follow you."

"Let him pick his way through here," Zane told her as he gave his horse more rein.

They rode out into the meadow, skirting the edge of the forest and then up to a stand of old pecan trees. There was a fence around them and a bit of underbrush growing up inside the fence. Zane pulled two sets of hobbles out of his saddle bag and put them on their horses. He had halters over their bridles so he unbuckled the reins, stuck them inside the saddlebags, and turned the horses loose to graze.

"We won't be long and they'll be fine," he told Catherine. "I've had these hobbles on them in the stalls so they are used to them and I have them both in grazing bits."

He held her hand, telling Catherine where to place her foot in the fence to balance and swing over. Zane followed and guided her down to the edge of a sink hole. He stepped down a narrow path, turned around to face her, and held out his hands.

"Are you serious? Is it really safe to go down in there?" she asked.

"Do you think you are safe anywhere?"

"You always do that. You answer a question with a question."

"Well?"

"Never mind."

She took his hands, made it down over the first large rock, and then followed him down a steep, narrower path. At the bottom of the hole, she gasped. Once her eyes adjusted to the darkness, there in front of her was crystal clear deep aqua water surrounded by beautiful ancient boulders.

"Do you want to go in?" Zane asked.

"Now? In the water?"

"Yes, now, in the water." He was grinning at her.

"We don't have swimming suits."

"And?"

"Well, you know. We're going to...."

"Yeah?"

Catherine had never done anything like this in her life, and Zane could see her hesitation.

"Who do you think is going to find us down here? Don't you own this property?"

"Yes."

"Well then?"

She looked around for a place to sit. He placed his shirt on a large rock. It didn't take Zane long to figure out that the quicker he got her boots off, the faster they'd be in the water. Once they'd undressed, they held onto each other and stepped off the ledge. The water was frigid and took her breath away for a second, so she held tight to Zane. He had one hand on the ledge and the other arm around her.

"I've got you. Just relax," he said softly. He could see by her face that she was trying not to freak out.

"What if something happens and they never find us in here?"

"Will you please stop it. The horses won't get far and someone will find us eventually. And, besides, what do you think is going to happen? This sink hole has probably been here for hundreds of years. Just take a breath."

She looked up at him and he let go of the ledge. He placed both hands on her waist, lifting her up above him. She had felt strange in the cold water with his warm body against her. He pushed her up higher out of the water and then turned her loose. As she dropped down into the water, he dove and disappeared. She let out a scream as he came up behind her.

"You are freaking me out," she said, but she didn't finish the sentence because he had grabbed her around her waist and was pulling her out into the middle of the small body of water. He lay back, floating, with her floating above him.

"There isn't anything in here but us is there?" she asked.

"No. The water is too cold. Nothing could live in here. Would you just relax?"

Catherine floated down until their bodies were touching and his head was next to hers. If she looked straight up through the trees overhead, the sunlight filtered through their leaves, creating sparkles on the water that reflected on their faces. Their skin was shriveled by the time they got out of the water. Zane watched as she attempted to dry off and he began wiping her down with his shirt. He helped her struggle with the dampness to get her jeans back on.

"You had to pick your tightest pair of jeans," he teased.

"They are better for riding."

He was behind her as they made their way up the steep rocks, and he said, "About those jeans—that's not all they're good for."

She stopped abruptly on the path and he ran into

her. She pretended she was going to kick him. It made her feel good to hear him laughing. The bright sunlight blinded them for a few seconds when they first stepped out of the rocks. They walked back into the field and found their horses safely grazing. It only took a few minutes for Zane to put the reins back on their bridles and remove the hobbles.

They rode back to the house without saying a word. There was nothing they could say that would make that morning more perfect for either of them.

CHAPTER 19

When Buck and Zane ran away in the middle of the night from their lives on their ranches, they left behind those they loved and their own heritages. Now, retirement had flung them both into lives they had never expected. The United States Intelligence Community had quickly become their new family and kept them mentally and physically away from their own realities. Buck knew it had been good for them, but it had also been bad for them. At the end of their careers, they were honored by being commissioned to create the finest state of the art training facility in the country. They had the final say on the majority of the plans. Their retirement ceremony took place right there in Langley, Virginia. A plaque on the wall dedicated the building to Zane Wheeler and Buck Matthews, declaring them "American heroes."

Buck figured they would find a little town, hang out while getting their heads back on straight, and then head to Montana and home. He never expected Zane to desert him. When Buck headed south to Florida, on a whim, he found a realtor, and before he knew it, he had signed on the dotted line, not once, but twice. He was the proud owner of All Around Feed Store and another little eighty-acre spread down the road a piece that he liked to call Overall Ranch. Both of his acquisitions were in Highberry, Florida. He had a little sign made of a guy in overalls with a piece of hay hanging out of his lips. It was silly, but it made him smile every time he turned into his driveway. He was crazy about the fact that his gate opened automatically and was operated by a solar panel.

As members of the CIA, he and Zane worked closely with other agencies to collect, analyze, and produce sensitive information to support national security. They participated heavily in counterintelligence activities and executed covert operations, approved or not, by the President. They were familiar with the people closest to the President, the National Security Council, Secretary of State, Secretary of Defense, and all the other executive branches.

He and Zane had worked hard from the first day they walked through the CIA doors. They were completely devoted to their work. There had been nothing in their lives holding them back so they were free to go anywhere, any time. They also had the attitudes required to accomplish any task set before them. They quickly moved up the ladder by spending countless off-duty hours studying and then devising complex and often intensely dangerous plans.

When they finally walked away from their careers, neither one of them knew exactly what they were going to do. They had both accidentally fallen into where they were now. No one was more surprised than they were that they were currently residing in the same town. Suddenly, all the years of calculating every move they made came to a screeching halt and they were simply attempting to live a "normal" life.

~~~~~
~~~~~

Buck picked up the phone and dialed Bill Brannan's number.

"What's up?" Bill asked.

"You tell me what the hell is going on. I thought we were done with all this." Buck was agitated.

"What do you mean, Buck?"

"It's the James DeLong case. I thought it was closed, but it is rearing its ugly head again. What do you know about it?"

"Nothing. I don't know a thing."

"Well, Zane came into the feed store today and reamed me. Seems a photograph popped up on Catherine DeLong's computer and he's not too damn happy about it."

"A photograph of what?" Bill asked.

"Just happens to be the last photo taken of Catherine and her husband, James, before he supposedly died. What do you make of that?"

"Shit. I have no idea how that happened or why."

Buck believed him. "Me either. Who the hell would be doing this?"

"It makes no sense to me either."

"Only thing it would accomplish is messing with her brain. I can't figure out any other motive. Unless..."

Bill interrupted him. "Don't blame me. I have no idea where the hell he is. You don't think he's behind this, do you? Why would he do it? And I have no way of finding out."

"What do you mean you can't find out?" Buck was puzzled.

"They gave James complete immunity. Once they release him, they have no control over his whereabouts or what he does."

"Are you serious? Why would they do that?"

"They probably figured that James is well aware of the potential danger to himself and his wife, and knowing his history, they didn't think they'd have to worry about him."

"Well, what the hell would he gain by sending her the picture? Unless...Bill, you don't suppose that it's his way of letting her know he's still alive?" Buck was bewildered.

"I don't know how Catherine would make the connection."

"I don't either, but are you sure you don't know what he's up to?"

"I'm almost certain they have turned them loose. I'm telling you, we covered every angle with Catherine, including his funeral. I don't think she would figure it out. He was with Arianne, you know. They gave him a new identity and sent them on their way. No one will recognize him. His facial features have been completely altered. You know that. They are free to move about as they please."

"You mean no one is tailing them?"

"Apparently they felt there was no need. At least, it wasn't obvious to us that there was any need. They had them isolated, re-programming him. You know the drill."

"They kept him isolated until now, but don't feel the need to tail him?" Buck was disgusted with the whole set-up.

"Buck, listen; we can't watch every Tom, Dick, or Harry who works for the federal government. James came through with everything he promised, and they must have felt pretty secure in letting him go. They didn't expect him to contact her. We'll have to play the 'wait and see' game for right now. What else can we do? James hasn't really violated any laws."

"I understand that, but.... Oh, what the fuck."

"Right, you simply have to wait it out."

"Well, thanks for nothing."

"You're welcome. Good luck man."

Buck hung up the phone and stared out the front window of the feed store. It did get his adrenalin pumping when he had something besides babies and the feed store to think about; not that he wasn't elated with his life.

Deb seemed perfectly content in his rambling country home with her two new babies. He was proud that he had an innate ability to get his kids to go to sleep. He didn't mind feeding, rocking, or burping the babies, but he wasn't too good at getting the diapers on right. Still, if that was his worst offense, then everyone in the house would have to be okay with it! He had tried to be attentive to Deb's needs, often stopping on his way home after he closed the store to bring whatever she requested. He liked the role of being a father and was toying with the idea of being a husband. He just wasn't ready to let go of his old life completely yet.

~~~~~

Buck enjoyed having his mother visit them. They spent evenings getting reacquainted and catching up on all the years after he left Montana. His mother seemed happy. They were in the living room after dinner. Deb had put the babies down for the night and they were
~~~~~

enjoying the quiet of the house.

"Buck, it has been a long time since you've been home," his mother said, as she worked on her cross-stitch.

"I know."

She continued, "And your father and I aren't getting any younger."

"None of us are, Mom. That's for sure."

"You know the ranch is doing well. The money you invested in it took us to a different level than when you were there with us. We've been able to upgrade the equipment, and the new ranch manager is very talented with the breeding stock. Things are going quite well for all of us, and we are better able to support the people who live and work on the ranch."

"That's really wonderful, Ma. I'm really glad for you and Dad."

"Well, here's what I'm getting at. I'm just going to come out and ask you. Do you have any plans to return and run the ranch?"

Buck sat silently for a while. Deb quickly excused herself to check on the babies, giving Buck a chance to speak to his mother alone.

"Mom, I don't want to upset you and Dad, but that's just not something I've thought too much about."

"That's okay, son. I know your life was hectic before."

"But I also know this is probably something that you and Dad had hoped for." Buck uncrossed his legs, leaned forward, and picked up his coffee cup from the coffee table.

"Well, yes. When you were younger, but now you

have your children and one of them might...."

"That's a possibility. It's just that..."

She interrupted him. "Honey, you don't have to give me a reason. It's okay to say 'No.'"

"Well, I don't want to say 'No' for forever. Not necessarily forever, Ma."

"You don't have to, Buck. Here's what I'm trying to say—your father and I have spent our entire married lives on that ranch, and maybe it would do us some good to take a break before it's too late. We had talked briefly about this, and I was thinking about it when I was flying here. I think maybe this would be a good place for us to try for a while."

Buck didn't really know what to think because this was so unexpected. He couldn't imagine their ranch without his parents. At the same time, he understood what his mother was saying.

"Mom, I will support whatever you and Dad decide. None of it has to be permanent. With the money I still have, you can do whatever you want to do. You can stay with us or we can find a place here—whatever you and Dad want." He stood up, set his cup on the table, walked over, and leaned down and kissed his mother on the top of her head. "Just do whatever you want. It's okay with me. You can stay with us. Dad can fly in tomorrow, if you want. We'll work it out as we go. I'm okay as long as you two are happy." He left his mother sitting there and walked down the hall to check on Deb and his children.

~~~~~~

Buck was glad to see his buddy, Zane, coming
~~~~~~

through the feed store door. He nodded at him. Zane nodded back and asked, "Hey, Tuff, how ya doing?"

"Good. And you?"

"I'm fine, but that mare of Catherine's tried to eat grass on the wrong side of the fence and skinned her head, so I need something to keep the flies off of her."

Buck walked over to the middle counter and handed Zane a pink jar.

"How bad is it?"

"Not bad. She just took the skin off the top of her head and ear."

"This stuff works because it has fly repellent in it and it helps the hair grow back. I sell a lot of it."

"That'll do. Oh, Catherine wanted me to ask how the babies are doing."

"Great. They are great. In fact, I wanted to talk to you. My mother is going to stay with us, and Dad is actually going to join her for a while."

Zane raised his right eyebrow. "You've got to be kidding?"

"Yeah, I never thought much about it, but Mom was telling me that they've spent their entire married life on that ranch. She said they want to try something different before it's too late."

"Did that come as a complete surprise to you?"

"It did at first, but I'm actually okay with it. I haven't talked to Deb too much about it, but I think it will be all right. Ma is a big help with the twins."

"I can see where she would be, but are you sure about this?"

Buck sat down on one of the stools behind the counter while Zane remained standing, leaning on the counter.

"Hell, Zane, none of us are getting any younger. I think it would be an opportunity for us to get reacquainted, and I know they will love spending time with their grand-kids. That's a bonus."

"I know what you mean. Your dad's not going to be too happy without some livestock for him to tend to."

"I'm not so sure. I think we will have to wait and see what he wants to do."

"Well, good luck with all of that, buddy."

"Yeah, I'll keep you posted. I'm sure Dad will want to see you."

"It's been a long, long time."

"How well I know."

"Well, I better get back to the ranch."

Zane pulled some cash out of his pocket and tried to hand it to Buck.

"I can't take your money. I have strict instructions from Catherine to put everything on her bill."

"Don't tell her. Better yet, pretend it's for Trouble."

Buck took the money from Zane and gave him his change.

"Take care, Buck, and kiss those young'uns for me."

Zane stuck out his hand to shake Buck's, but Buck came from behind the counter and pulled him in, slapped him on the back, and gave him a hug.

"Hey, man, I'm really happy for you guys."

"Thanks, Zane. I'm happy for all of us."

Buck hadn't said a damn thing to Zane about what Bill Brannan had told him about Deb. He had decided that some things were better left alone.

CHAPTER 20

Parker Iron Crow pulled the pickup into the front yard in a cloud of dust. The young man sitting on the seat next to him hadn't said a word on the long ride from the reservation. He had been released from White Buffalo Detention Center earlier that day. The facility was under investigation by the United States Government and it was forcibly being closed. All juveniles were to be placed elsewhere by that afternoon. Parker had heard about one particular boy and told Maggie that he was going to get him. He wasn't a blood relative, but Parker knew his story.

Parker told her, "He's had it tough ever since he was born. His father's been in and out of prison, and his mother's family wasn't pleased with her choice of men. Her father is on the Tribal Council and fighting to change the future for the youth on the reservation, but he couldn't accept his own daughter's mistakes. His family had a hard time providing the best environment for any of them. The boy didn't have a chance."

Maggie White Calf hadn't voiced any objection. She had simply nodded while he spoke, kissed Parker on the cheek, and whispered, "Go get him." She worked in the kitchen all that afternoon, making a special dinner for the boy's first night on the ranch.

Many boys had come to them over the last several years. Some of them had been obedient, grateful. Others had been rebellious, pushing every button, testing their patience, and making them wonder. Through it all, there had been enough successes that the tribe began supporting them with allotments for each boy. She had never stopped missing her own son, not for one moment. When Foster passed away, Parker had talked to her about taking in the young men. It seemed the obvious thing to do with the ranch.

They decided to accept only boys because boys are generally the ones who lead the girls down the wrong path. If they could redirect the boys, they could change the outcome for the families. They wanted to give them better morals, teach them options to make a living, and instill a desire in them to give back to their tribe and community. It was no easy task.

There were a lot of photos around the house of the many activities the boys participated in. There were also pictures the boys sent to them after they left the ranch and attempted to find another life. They would bump into some of them from time to time in town or at various activities—the rodeo, the fair, in a restaurant, or at the movies. It was always interesting to hear their stories.

Some of them loved the ranch and the horses as much as Zane had. It made his long absence a little easier. They would see glimmers of him, especially when the boys would take off from the house, galloping their horses toward the mountains. It helped to fill both of their empty hearts.

Parker invested a lot of time and energy into each of the boys. It had been good to share his ceremonies with them and pass on that part of his and their heritage. Because of his belief that we are all related, it felt very natural for them to open the ranch to the spirit of these boys. It altered the course of all of their lives. It was all good.

~~~~~

This last boy had been a handful and they were grateful they had taken him on solo. He would be with Parker practically 24/7 and watched over by the other ranch hands. There would be no interference from any other boys. Parker understood him beyond what others might have seen. He was descended from Two Guns White Calf, a Blackfeet Chief.

One day in a fit of anger, the boy had said, "You expect me to listen to you and yet you live among these white people who have stolen our lands. You help them with their cattle, cattle which have taken the grazing rights away from our buffalo. Then you want me to obey you like you have some authority over me when you are acting like a white man. You and this woman of yours, this Maggie whoever, how dare she call herself White Calf?"

Parker wasn't about to allow John Two Guns White Calf to talk to him in that manner, but it did reveal John's level of thinking.

"Who do you think you are speaking to? I am your elder and you are being very disrespectful. You can argue your point, but my point is that we are no different than you. In fact, Maggie White Calf is more entitled to this land than you may think. And as for me, you don't even know a thing about me because you've never taken the time to ask. You are too self-involved to think from where I have come."
~~~~~

To Parker's surprise, John quit arguing and sat right down there in the dirt with his legs crossed beneath each other.

"I'm all ears," he defiantly said, as he crossed his arms as well.

"I have no time for this now," said Parker. "You will have to wait. Now, get up from there and finish your chores."

John didn't say a word, but he did get up and walk into the barn.

"And when you are done, make yourself presentable before you come to Maggie White Calf's table," Parker called to him as he walked away.

John didn't look back, but he did show up for dinner. The ranch hands, Parker and Maggie chatted as they always did about occurrences on the ranch, the weather reports, and the news. Meanwhile, John quietly ate his food. When everyone was finished, he helped clear the table and carried the dishes to the kitchen.

"May I help you with the dishes tonight, Miss Maggie?" he asked politely.

"That would be very nice, John."

"And could I ask you a few questions about your being a White Calf?"

Parker winked at Maggie and slipped out the back screen door, leaving the two of them alone in the kitchen.

~~~~~

"That kid had no idea who he was messing with," Parker said in an irritated tone.

Maggie dried her hands and placed the towel on the
~~~~~

counter. "Well, maybe he does a little better now."

"He is so arrogant and self-assured. It comes to him naturally and he does present a good argument. His great-grandfather was just like that."

"And how do you know this?" Maggie asked.

"It was no secret about John Two Guns White Calf. He claimed that it was his profile on the Indian head nickel. He used that to become the publicity spokesman for the railroad up at Glacier. He was an emissary for his people as their chief and he went after the United States Government concerning their unmet treaty agreements and the monies owed the Indians. Plus, he headed the secret Mad Dog Society. He was arrogant, but the people listened to him."

"And what did the Mad Dog Society do?" Maggie asked.

"They were attempting to preserve the Blackfeet Heritage, including the traditional dances."

"You mean like the Sun Dance?"

"Yes, exactly. The government was actually a little afraid of him. They didn't want him to go back on any kind of warpath."

"I think I remember hearing about this." Maggie poured them each a cup of hot tea and joined Parker at the kitchen table.

"Two Guns did great things for his people and was quite famous. He even traveled to Washington, D.C. to collect monies owed to the Blackfeet. When they refused to give him the monies, he told them he was going to stay until he got the money, even if he had to die like his father Chief White Calf, who died in the President's private chamber, fighting for tribal claims."

"And what happened?" Maggie was truly interested.

"Actually, two Chief White Calfs died in Washington D.C. fighting for the rights of their people. The first died in 1903, but his people were able to keep a million acres and their 16,000 head of cattle. John Two Guns White Calf died in 1934, but he was the one who was handed the check due the Blackfeet tribe from the government."

"I guess you've done your research. So, now are you fighting for this boy, because of what the Chief White Calfs did for all of us?"

"Yes, and because of you."

"Me? Why me?" She sounded surprised.

"Well, Maggie White Calf, do you not know where you came from either?"

"Of course I do, but I've been far removed from it for so long. I don't think about it that much anymore."

"I wish I could believe that."

"So you actually think John and I are related?"

"No. I know you are. You have to be."

"But, Parker, does it really matter?"

"What really matters is that we are preserving him, whether he realizes the blood that he came from or not. Hopefully when he digests it all, he will understand that he was born for greatness as well. We have to teach him that he doesn't have to be the result of what has happened to him. That he can rise above it just as his ancestors did. Maybe he was never told these stories."

"Well, you have the perfect opportunity, Parker."

"And so do you. You have the perfect opportunity to admit who you are too and stop hiding behind the shadow of a ghost."

Maggie picked up the towel from the counter and

walked out to the laundry room. It had been easier not to think about it.

~~~~~

John didn't want to be so arrogant. He didn't know exactly what to do since he'd been removed from the detention center and placed on this ranch. He had heard stories about his ancestors, but he didn't really understand what the fuss was all about. This man had taken him away from the rez, his family, his home, and his friends. He didn't know a single person on the ranch, and from the beginning, all he wanted to do was run. But, judging from the long truck ride, he knew it would take him several days to find a road, if he could find one at all. Besides, the food wasn't so bad here, and the room they'd put him in was unlike anything he'd ever seen. The bed felt like he was sleeping on a cloud, and he was the only one in it. He even had an indoor bathroom all to himself with running water, towels, and soap. He wondered, though, what was going to happen when it was time for school to start. They'd have to send him home for sure then.

In the meantime, he had been given new clothes and a pair of boots. The old man had asked him if he knew how to ride a horse and when he'd nodded, Parker had simply motioned for him to follow to the barn where he'd pointed to a horse and tack. No one helped him with any of it, and when he'd tried to get on the horse, the saddle slipped halfway down the horse's belly. He managed to get his foot out of the stirrup and catch his balance. That old man walked over, adjusted the saddle and girth, helped him get on and then got on his own horse,
~~~~~

and they rode up into the mountains. They had been on those horses all day, only stopping once to relieve themselves and to drink some water from a creek. The old man hadn't said a word to him all day. They arrived back at the barn and removed the saddles just in time for the call for dinner. John had to admit, he had a lot of trouble making it up the three front steps because his legs were painful. His feet had been completely numb most of the afternoon. After that, he decided to pay closer attention to that old man and what he was saying and doing.

CHAPTER 21

It seemed as if the moment Catherine began to feel content with her new life, Zane started talking about leaving for Montana. It made her apprehensive to think about his going and her being left alone. Everything about their lives had become so perfect. It wasn't that she didn't completely understand why he wanted to go. He had been away for a long, long time, too long, and she couldn't even imagine how happy his mother would be to see him. And, of course, he would get to see his old friend, Iron Crow. She could never get that man's whole name in the right order. It confused her.

She had reluctantly given Zane a list of flights and was waiting for him to make up his mind about the dates. She hadn't mentioned it to him because the longer he put it off, the longer he'd be with her. She didn't want to think about it, but what if he didn't come back? Logically, she knew, he had to, because he was leaving his horse, Trouble, with her. The phone rang and abruptly brought her back from her thoughts as she rushed to the kitchen.

"Hello."

No one said a thing, but she could hear someone breathing.

"Hello, is anyone there? Hello. I know you are there. Can you hear me?"

Silence. She softly placed the phone on the cradle. That was the second time it had happened. Zane was in the barn so she knew it couldn't have been him. This was really starting to bother her. She didn't want to admit it, but it was actually scaring her.

Zane came through the back door, hung his hat on the hook, washed his hands at the kitchen sink, and kissed her on the cheek.

"Did you need me to feed the dogs?"

"Sure. That would be a big help while I finish up in here." Catherine knew he didn't mind feeding them one bit.

"I'm always surprised that they get along at feeding time. Were they always this way?"

"Yes, I never had a problem."

"I think that's unusual. In the wild, they would have a pecking order."

"Do you think they understand that they were saved? I mean I've heard that dogs who are rescued understand how lucky they are. Do you think they know?"

Catherine closed the blind in the kitchen window and turned on the light above the sink.

"I'm not passing any kind of judgment, but I'd have to say that I think they get it."

"I think so too. They all made it so easy for me when I brought them home."

He put their bowls at the appropriate spots and walked to the kitchen table, pulled out a chair, and sat down.

"Did you have a nice afternoon?" he asked.

"I did, but I got another strange phone call. When I picked it up, I swore I could hear someone breathing, but no one would answer me. That's the second time."

"I'm sure it's nothing. People dial the wrong number all the time."

"I just wish they would admit it and say something."

"I know."

"I try not to let it bother me, but I think it's rude."

"It is rude, but what if it's not a person at all. Maybe it's a computer."

"Thank you, but I swear I heard someone breathing."

Catherine placed a huge plate of food in front of him.

"Wow. That looks fantastic and so do you."

He grabbed her around the waist and pulled her onto his lap and kissed her.

"You are amazing," he said.

She struggled back to her feet as he steadied her and said, "Go get your dinner."

"I will," she said as she moved into the kitchen and filled a plate for herself. "And don't you think I cooked this just for you," she teased because she knew that chicken fried steak, mashed potatoes, and green beans was Zane's favorite dinner too.

~~~~~

She was confident Zane would be happy with the airline routes she found for him. It wasn't what she wanted, but she certainly understood his desire to go home. His leaving Trouble was her security blanket because it made her feel like he would come back. She unplugged the laptop and carried it out onto the porch.

Zane had told her the most interesting story the other day about a time when he was a teenager, riding
~~~~~

his horse on the ranch, and he stopped to drink from a stream. She wanted to get her ideas about his story on her computer while it was still fresh in her mind.

ChaChuNee had been walking all morning when he came to a stream. It was deeper than usual and he knelt down to take a drink. He scooped the cool water into his hand and drank, thanking Mother Earth for its abundance and its blessings. He stared into the reflection in the deeper pool and was startled, for what he saw was not his reflection, but that of a woman. She was carrying something. He turned around and there she stood. She said not a word, but tried to hand him a bundle. He thought it was a baby and he reached for it. Just as he was about to take it into his hands, the bundle and the woman disappeared.

She had been so beautiful that he had become breathless the whole time she was standing there. He turned full circle looking for her, lost his footing on a rock and nearly fell backwards into the creek.

She had been wearing a deerskin dress, beaded down the front, her black hair was braided, and she wore feathers and beads at the ends. The feathers moved in the wind.

'Why did she want to give me her baby,' he wondered.

It was several days before ChaChuNee walked into the camp of his people. They were glad to have him back among them. He went directly to the Medicine Man, who was sitting outside his tepee near a small fire. The Medicine Man greeted ChaChuNee and they began to converse about ChaChuNee's vision quest. The Medicine

Man listened quietly, looking intently into ChaChuNee's eyes. ChaChuNee told him of the message from the cat and the cave. The blending of the people is the same as the beads; the beads come off your fingers in a beautiful pattern, so it is with the people.

The Medicine Man told him he was going to embark on a great adventure. He told him not to hurry the process, but to honor the path.

ChaChuNee then told the Medicine Man about the reflection in the water and how he had turned and saw the woman. He told him she had tried to give him her baby.

The Medicine Man chuckled his deep belly laugh and then he spoke, "That was not her baby. It was the Sacred Medicine Bag. Her name is Maya and her grave is up on the hill. She was buried standing, facing the East with her arms outstretched to protect all of her people. You have been called to be great among your people. You have been called at the time when the old must blend with the new. Mountain Lion medicine is a very difficult totem for you because it targets you for the problems of others. It is about leadership. You must learn to balance this power and be careful about what you intend to do with it. You will be responsible to know when to push the cubs out of the cave. You must not think that you are the king of the mountain. You are the peace keeper. First and foremost, you must always tell the truth. Refuse to hide in the cave. Roar with conviction, roar with laughter, but remember to balance the medicine."

ChaChuNee appreciated the words of the Medicine Man and the truth of them. It was a great gift, but a responsibility. He could only hope that the choices he made for his people would be as successful as what he had been able to do for Roaring, the cat.

ChaChuNee also knew that in this life there were no failures, only lessons to be learned. The Medicine Man picked up the old turtle rattle, shook it four times at ChaChuNee, blew smoke into the air from his pipe, and fanned it toward him. He began to chant a deep melodious chant and ChaChuNee turned to walk away.

The old man called to him: "Go, wise man now and share what you have come to know."

This is the story of ChaChuNee. This is all that I will tell you today. Tomorrow, in the morning, look to the East and to the sun for it will bring you hope.

CHAPTER 22

Zane was in deep conversation explaining to Catherine about the Carlisle School and the Government Indian Policies. She had been doing research on her computer when he came in from the barn. She was standing in the kitchen with her hands on her hips visibly upset after listening to what Zane had just said.

"I don't understand why the white people felt so compelled to remove the children from the reservations. Why?" she asked him.

"It is difficult to understand their thinking. The Reservation Boarding School system was a war in disguise declared against the Native Americans. The intention was to eliminate the enemy. They called it the "Manifest Destiny." It was a philosophy that enabled the white people to believe that they had a divine right to take possession of all the land and the fruits thereof. Let me give you an example. There was this little girl named Molly, who had been taken from her reservation and adopted by two teachers. She was Blackfeet and should have remained on the reservation with her people, but the whites were attempting to integrate their belief system into the Native American population by forcing them to give up the children so they could educate them in their white ways. When the two teachers offered to adopt a small native girl, it seemed like a better opportunity for her."

He continued, "Never mind that this child would be confused, would probably think that her parents didn't want her, and be thrust into an entirely different life than she had ever known. It infuriates me that they thought this was okay. Let's just say that another country came over here and began to kidnap our kids and say they were going to educate them in the ways of their country, not ours, and you had absolutely nothing to say about it. They could just take your kids and you had to stand there and let them do it. Well, that's exactly what the United States Government did to the Native American people. And guess what? It didn't work."

Catherine chose not to speak because she was too upset about this information. As she contemplated all of it, she knew exactly how she was going to continue the story of Charging Bear. As soon as she finished her chores, she headed to her computer.

ChaChuNee left the medicine man and walked to the tepee of his mother. It had been five years since his father's burial ceremony. His heart was heavy, but pounding fast as he had longed for his mother's voice and even the smell of her. He opened the flap and entered quietly. She was sitting with a small child in front of her, braiding her long black hair. When she looked up, his mother's smile covered her entire face. Her son was home from his vision quest and soon the people would know of his journey.

She quickly lay down the hairbrush and jumped up, leaving the startled little girl and rushed with her arms wide to embrace him. He realized now why he had missed her so much. They held each other closely and breathed as one. When she moved back to hold him at arm's length, she looked into his eyes and said, "It was good. I can feel it. The knowing has come into you."

They held each other for a moment longer with their eyes. It was good to be home to the tepee of his mother and the circle of his people.

"But who is the little one here?" he asked as he peered over his mother's shoulder at the little black-haired girl looking back at him with huge and beautiful eyes.

"She is one of the little lost ones. Her mother is only seventeen. She has no way to care for her. They will come for her soon. They say it is the only way to save these children from this life."

ChaChuNee knew it was not the way the tribe wanted to treat their children, but the younger ones were being tempted and confused by life on the reservation, and they were doing things that led them in the wrong way.

"This little one has been chosen. Her new parents are both teachers at the big town, and this child will have all that she needs and more than she wants."

"I know it has come to this, but we must continue to blend the old ways with the new. How long does she have with you?"

"Maybe two weeks."

"Then, my mother, you must teach her. Teach her much so that she will take this knowledge with her. One day she will yearn for these learnings again and she will come back to us, to her people."

"We talk about her as though she does not hear us."

His mother turned to her. "This is my son, Charging Bear, but I call him ChaChuNee. He was once the same size as you, and I brushed and braided his hair. He didn't sit still like you, though. I will tell this to you now so you will understand. Once you were known as Brightest Star, but soon you will be known by another name. You will be called Molly."

ChaChuNee knelt down in front of this little girl who was staring up at him and carefully and slowly took her little hands in his. Her touch was as gentle and soft as a rabbit's fur.

"Brightest Star, soon to be called Molly, you are a special little girl. You are as beautiful as the largest star in the sky from which you were named. You are more precious than the shiniest stone in the riverbed or the bluebird song. You will go and live among another people. They will give you what we cannot, but know this—you will never be forgotten, and one day you will find your way back home. Then you will know the circle of the journey and the wisdom of the Creator. Don't be afraid because your path is already chosen and your journey has already begun."

He gathered the child into his arms and up onto his lap. ChaChuNee knew the power of the gift he'd been given. He watched a tear slide quietly down his mother's cheek as she smiled at him and the little girl.

CHAPTER 23

Catherine sat thinking about the words she'd written on the pages she held on her lap. It was risky having someone read her work. She'd never felt apprehensive when she'd written the newsletter every month for The Missing Link Foundation. It wasn't that difficult, but this was different. The newsletter had been just that; news about what they were accomplishing and upcoming events. Creative writing required some fact, but mostly imagination. It made her feel vulnerable. She didn't know what he would think. What if it were too simplistic, juvenile? She'd taken courses in college and apparently learned her craft. The first magazine she had applied to hired her. She had loved her job until James had suggested that she create her own business. That's when the Foundation was developed. But this was an entirely different venue—one she had never contemplated before. Still, she wanted to write.

Thoughts of James crept in again for no reason and gave her that sick feeling in the pit of her stomach. She hated it because she usually felt that way when something was about to happen. She couldn't explain it. Maybe it was pure intuition, but she strongly felt like something was going to happen and soon. She wanted them to arrest the person responsible for his murder, but she thought it was going to be something more than that. She felt vulnerable, and with Zane planning his departure, she didn't know how she was going to handle whatever it turned out to be. She tried not to let herself think about the possibility that the person who killed James might be looking for her.

Zane came in from afternoon chores and sat in the chair next to her on the porch. Lately, it had been an afternoon rendezvous for them. They would chat about what they'd been doing or what they planned to do together.

"What have we got here?" he asked

"Something I've been working on. I created some short stories from what you told me about growing up on your ranch. I'm a little nervous, but I'd like to know what you think. I just printed them out."

"Hand them over. I'll read them right now."

"Are you sure?" She was nervous.

"Of course I am. Give them to me."

Catherine handed the pages over to him, but she was worried.

"I'll go get busy with a few things in the kitchen while you read."

She pared potatoes and carrots, made two individual dinner salads, cleaned up a few dishes, and dried her hands. She walked back out onto the porch. Zane was sitting with the pages on his lap.

"Well, what's the verdict?"

"I like it. I really do. I'm very surprised at how you took a few facts that I gave you and wove them into such an interesting story. Where did you get all the other information from?"

"Oh, the Internet is my lifeline, but you do know, Zane Wheeler, that you are a very good storyteller. You make it appear very vividly in my mind. I can see every scene so well that it isn't that difficult to put it on paper.”

“Right.” He sounded surprised by her comment.

“No, I'm serious. You do. You tell a very convincing story.”

“Convincing? It sounds like you don't believe me.”

Catherine knew that he loved to mess with her. She grabbed the pages from his lap and headed back to the kitchen. She was giggling. “It's okay. You don't have to like my writing.” She knew he would respond.

“No, Catherine, I really do like it, seriously.” He got up and followed her into the kitchen.

“I'll take it. The first review is always the hardest they say. It's just that I don't know where to go from here.”

There it was—her first review and from someone who loved her.

“You have the unique luxury of not needing to go anywhere with it. You can set it aside and write about something else. Or, you can go back to it later when you are so inspired.”

“Inspired or when you tell me some more of your stories?”

“No, I mean inspired. You will know when the time is right to go back to it.”

“And how do you know this?” she asked.

“I just know.”

Catherine giggled again. “Now you sound like ChaChuNee.” She didn't have the slightest idea how to go forward with the next story anyway. The important thing was that she had put what he'd told her so far down on paper, but with his planning to leave, that process would come to a screeching halt. She didn't want to think about any of it.

~~~~~

Zane knew some questions have no answers. He also thought that must be how Catherine felt. She certainly had unanswered questions about James. He was reading *The Lucifer Effect* again about how a simple demonstration had such an effect on the behavior of individuals. It turned out to be a powerful illustration of the toxic impact of bad systems and bad situations causing people to behave in pathological ways often alien to how they would normally behave. It paralleled what had happened to James. Here was a man working hard to create medications that helped people when he stumbled upon a combination that would do the opposite. His decision to share that knowledge not only ultimately ruined his life but that of Catherine and other people involved. James had been seduced by the idea of the project's importance. He must have felt some sense of power from being in control of such a perverse substance, only then to become completely powerless against the people he trusted with it.

Experiencing the loss of his personal identity, being subjected to continual control, and then being completely deprived of his privacy, must have made James feel utterly helpless. The situational forces were constantly impinging upon him, and he most likely had become resigned to his circumstances.

Buck had informed him that James and Arianne had been kept under round-the-clock surveillance with rules and dehumanizing processes. The behavioral
~~~~~

interactions between the two of them and the guards were to be somewhat scripted in order to create the outcome that the government wanted. By the time the two of them were released, they would be programmed to have submissive uncritical attitudes. It would take a pretty strong personality to maintain his identity under such perverse scrutiny. The boundaries would become blurred between the old role James was attempting to maintain and the new role they were training him to perform. The new role would make him dramatically different from whom he had been, including his identity and appearance.

Zane knew there was no telling what James would be like when he gained his freedom. He had been highly regarded at Robideaux Pharmaceutical, but he was never going to be able to go back to that position. If James were as smart as most people believed he was, he might have been completely capable of playing multiple roles, including out-maneuvering the authorities by compartmentalizing the conflicting aspects of their "brainwashing" techniques. If James pulled it off, he could come out of their process somewhat unscathed. For better or worse, James was alive and possibly quite well.

The very worst scenario would occur if James tried to solve his debacle with Catherine. Zane had to admit that the two unexplained phone calls were worrisome. James had to be conflicted between his recent behavioral decisions and his belief system. He had a good reason to feel dissonance. It had been his job as a "good soldier" to protect the country he loved, and he had answered the call by a powerful authority to act.

The rewards had been contrary to what he believed was going to happen. It just proved that sensible individuals can be deceived into engaging in irrational actions, including immoral acts.

Zane was certain James must have had second thoughts about what he had done. What exactly had James been seeking by providing the means to destroy someone else's life, whether or not they were the "enemy"? What made him decide to do it? Who was actually responsible for the outcome? How did he become so radically transformed?

Even after millions of years of evolution, people still have the fundamental need to belong. They need consistency and rationality in order to give their lives meaning and direction. However, given the right set of circumstances, humans can also be swayed into perverse behavior by such things as grudges, revenge, and even rumination over trauma that may have happened years ago. James had come from a difficult background. He had been abandoned by his single parent and raised in foster care. He had excelled because his last foster family, who then adopted him, was involved in scientific discoveries, which led him down the path to the job with Robideaux. It was his curiosity and inquisitive nature that motivated his research and may have been his motivator in the sinister plot.

James certainly wouldn't see anything immoral about taking out some of the "heads" of countries who were determined to destroy everything he believed in. Zane realized James was no more accountable for his actions than he and Buck had been when they did their deeds of complicity. How could he sit in judgment over her husband? Now all of them were living lives that they had never expected, but the biggest loser did seem to be James. There was no one looking out for him. No one saw his life as sacred, but rather equated everything based on what was most important and foremost—national security.

Zane wondered whether all this would make sense to Catherine, if or when she discovered that James hadn't been the body in the car in the ravine. If she understood the ultimate price her husband had paid for everyone, would she be able to process it in such a way that allowed all of them to continue the lives they now enjoyed? No one could answer that question but Catherine. There was no way to know what he should do, either. Tell her, not tell her? Who knew? He had no training whatsoever in this type of psycho-babble. Meanwhile, there would be no glory days for James. Even though he had accomplished a great thing, he would most likely remain a total unknown in the interest of protecting his safety, as well as that of the government officials who had "helped" him with his project. After all, his research had been necessary for the country's well-being and he had become the powerless one in the end. It had to suck.

Hopefully, they had debriefed James properly. They had certainly manipulated him through the "moral" issues, so he would understand the enduring value of his work for the general public. What good did that do him when no one would ever know? Keeping him in a confined setting and feeding him only what they wanted him to know wasn't genius. They simply attempted to reprogram his brain, basically telling him what to believe. Now, the big question, "Had they been successful?" Only time would tell. Meanwhile, Zane wanted to keep a close eye on Catherine, but that kind of threw a monkey wrench into his leaving for Montana.

~~~~~

"I'm not sure how I feel about leaving you when you are feeling so nervous about these two phone calls." Zane had pulled her onto his lap on the porch love seat.

"Zane, you know how much you want to go home."

"I do, but I want you to have some peace of mind and confidence here."

"I don't know if that is ever going to happen. My whole life is so different now."

"I understand. I want to tell you that everything is going to be fine."

"Want to?" she asked.

"There aren't any guarantees. You never know what tomorrow will bring."

"That's not very reassuring." She made a face at him.

"You know what I mean. You see it in the paper or on the news every day. All the stories about this happened and that happened. There's a car accident, a weird happening. Like today, they found some news intern's body at the bottom of an elevator shaft. No one is sure how he got there or what the heck that's about."

"Zane, you aren't making me feel any better about this. You have to go to Montana, and I know you have to go in the summer. The weather is so bad once it starts to snow."
~~~~~

"Oh, it's not about me and the weather. It's about you and the chores being easier with the summer grass for the horses."

"Oh, I hadn't thought about that."

"Since they stay out in the pasture longer this time of year, and the dogs are easier, everything would be better for you. And, I think I found someone to help."

"You did?"

"Yes, Dr. Grant said she's willing to share her helper. She's a young woman, so I knew you'd feel better about that. Plus, she's right down the street. The gal actually lives in Dr. Grant's guest house."

"That would be convenient."

"And Dr. Grant said if you need anything at all, just let her know and she can either help out or she'll find someone for whatever it is. And you've always got Buck."

"That does sound better. So, you are going through with it? Did you pick a date?"

"Yes, I think I have to. I need to go, but I don't want to leave you here. I'm completely torn."

She knew he meant it.

"Zane, don't worry. I'll be fine."

He kissed her tenderly.

"I know you will, but I'm really going to miss you."

"Well, I'm going to be counting the days, so don't you stay away too long."

"I've got to go home to make amends with my mother. You know that."

"And to see Parker what's his name."

"Yes, to see Iron Crow and the ranch. Plus, I have some things I need to say to my father."

"Your father? I thought he was..."

"I'm sure he's up on the hill in the family cemetery. It's time."

~~~~~

It should have been simple, but she felt sick to her stomach. She would not be happy living in this house alone without him. At least she had the dogs. They wouldn't let anyone into the house, but she just didn't know how she was going to sleep without him. In her heart, she knew he had to visit his mother, but her head was telling another story.

"I'm going to call Dr. Grant and make arrangements for that gal to come over so I can meet her. I want to be sure that she's the right one to help me before we get too close to your departure date." She was attempting to be brave.

"I'm sure you will like her just fine; after all, I don't think Marcia Grant would have someone working for her that you couldn't trust. You know that because she's a doctor, she has to be gone a lot and needs someone dependable for her own animals."

"I know. I'm just nervous about new people."

"It will all work out. Make a list like you did with me of all the chores you want her to do. I'll help you with it."

"I will."

"Okay then, can you just relax?"

"It's a lot of changes."

"Yes, but the good thing is that it is only temporary."

The truth was that she had lost her confidence again. She hadn't felt like this since the last day in the apartment in New York. It felt like that moment when she wanted to blink and have everything the way it used
~~~~~

to be. Now, she had grown accustomed to having him in and out of the house all day long—grown used to his breathing in the night, his occasional snoring. She didn't mind carrying his dirty clothes downstairs in the hamper because they smelled of him. Now, all of that was going away. Temporarily or not, it scared her. She didn't like not knowing what was going to happen, and they had a nice schedule. She always knew what they were going to do. Suddenly, the "they" was going to disappear.

"I think I'm going to hate it."

"I think I am going to love it when I get back."

She wanted to strangle him, but it would be bittersweet. She could picture herself running out the front door as his truck came down the drive. She would run into his arms and he would kiss her.

"Hello. Where did you just go?"

She could feel her face flush.

"I was just thinking about how I am going to do this without you."

"I'll be back before you know it."

"You won't be back soon enough."

"But I will be back."

~~~~~

She had everything planned so it wouldn't be so hard to say goodbye to him. She had met Dr. Marcia Grant's gal and she liked her. Lauren Bartlett was in her mid twenties, raised in Alachua County with horses in her backyard. All the dogs seemed to like her. It appeared to be good. Lauren would arrive at Catherine's every morning as soon as she was finished with Dr.
~~~~~

Grant's horses and barn. She could stay and help Catherine in the middle of the day with whatever chores she needed, but she had to be back at Dr. Grant's later in the afternoon to bring those horses in and hose them off and feed them. If a storm blew in, she would have to hightail it down the road, but she would come back as quickly as she could and finish up. It was an ideal situation.

Zane seemed comfortable with all of it. He told Catherine he liked Lauren from the get-go. She knew horses. She was easy with the dogs and even Sweetie, the cat, liked her. She wasn't afraid of work as they had her help with the stalls to check her out. She had pitched right in with throwing hay and had asked the right questions. She seemed confident she could handle it.

Catherine knew that once he'd made up his mind to go, Zane was getting itchy to be on his way. He'd started packing his duffle bag, cleaned up his good boots, pressed a line down the center of each leg of his favorite jeans, and spray starched his purple shirt and had it hanging on the back of the guest room door. She could tell he was excited.

Before she could blink, it was the night before he would head out from Jacksonville International. They hadn't said much all afternoon, and now they were seated at the dinner table. Catherine was barely eating, picking at her food.

"I know this is hard for you, love, but I really have to go."

"I know you do. I want you to. I think it is important."

"So, do you want to talk about what's so difficult for you that you can't eat?"

"In my head, I know it is the right thing for you, but my heart is breaking. I'm worried that something will happen and you won't come back."

"You know you have a safety valve."

"What?" She had only half-heard him.

"I'm leaving my horse. I have to come back for him," he teased.

"I wish I believed that."

"You can. You know he's my BFF."

"I can't believe you just said that."

"What?"

"BFF. I didn't even know you knew what that meant."

"I don't exactly. I saw something in the newspaper or somewhere."

"You can't make me laugh."

"Yes, I can."

"No you can't. I won't smile or be happy about this."

"I'll make you."

"You can't."

"Oh, yes I can."

He launched from his chair, knocking it over backwards, dogs scattering as he scooped her up and took her in the living room where he threw her onto the couch. He pounced on her so fast she hadn't even had a chance to try to get away. She had grabbed his hands and started to fight him.

"Oh, no you don't. No, I'm not going to laugh no matter what. I won't." She tried to fight him.

Zane pulled up her shirt and started to tickle her.

"That's not fair and you know it." She tried not to laugh.

They had slowly rolled off onto the floor, and the rest was a blur with them eventually making their way up the stairs. She heard him slip out to walk the dogs and throw night hay. He made sure the alarm was set, and it seemed like she had just dozed off when they were both startled awake by the buzzer going off at four-thirty. It seemed a cruel end to their perfect night.

She was standing at the front door in her robe when he pulled out of the long driveway. It seemed impossible that the night had gone that fast. She walked into the kitchen and cleared the plates that still contained uneaten food from their dinner, scraping it into the trash. She was going to be completely miserable without him.

CHAPTER 24

The only thing missing from their lives right now was his father, Roan Mathews.

"Did you get a hold of him?" Buck asked his mother.

"Yes, I did, and he said he's coming next week."

"Honestly?"

"Yes, he says he's coming."

Buck was amazed that his mother had persuaded his father to fly to Florida. Even though he and his mother had spent several evenings discussing it, he was skeptical that it would happen. He was sure his father's decision had been more to please his mother than anything else. One thing his father had taught him as a young boy was that if Mama wasn't happy, no one on the ranch was going to be happy either.

"That's pretty amazing," he told her.

Buck's parents had moved to the ranch on their wedding day, and they had been there ever since. He simply didn't know what his father was going to do without any chores or livestock to tend to. His mother told him, "He will be just fine. He needs a change of scenery, and I know he will be excited to catch up with you and meet his new grandbabies. Land sakes, if he gets bored, he can go to the feed store with you."

Effie had settled in like syrup on a stack of pancakes. She said that Highberry was like living inside a movie, what with moss hanging from the beautiful oak trees and them swaying in the Southern breeze.

Buck was excited about his father's arrival. It would be good to spend quality time with him. He wasn't quite ready to load up with livestock, though. It had been nice without any responsibilities, except for Deb and his kids. He liked the peace and calm when he came home from the feed store. The babies were thriving and Deb had taken to motherhood. They were enjoying evenings after dinner in the great room, rocking the babies or with Grandma sitting nearby either doing cross-stitch or knitting. He could sit out on the front porch in the dark after the twins were asleep and actually feel the quiet for the first time in his life.

His mother came out the screen door and sat next to him on a rocker in the dark.

"Life sure has turned out different than you expected, hasn't it, son?"

"Yes, ma'am, it sure has." He swallowed hard. "You never said a word to me about us leaving—me and Zane. You simply met me with open arms every time I came home, no matter what."

"Ranch life is hard. I have lived it every day. As much as I wanted you to stay, I also understood why you had to go, especially because of Zane leaving. It was the hardest thing to do, letting you two go, but I knew it was the best thing for both of you."

"Well, I don't know about it being the best thing, but it certainly altered the course of all our lives."

"That and that time you won the lottery. Now that was some life changer." She chuckled as she rocked back and forth, the old boards squeaking under the rungs of her chair. They sat there quietly enjoying the sounds of the night.

CHAPTER 25

Zane walked out of the airport with his duffel bag over his shoulder, pulling his suitcase behind him, and headed toward the rental car lot. The size of the airport in Great Falls hadn't changed much, except that the terminal had been upgraded and there was now an upstairs restaurant. He was hoping for a nice lunch before he started the drive to the ranch, but not with all those people. Plus all the years of flying from one airport to the next had cured him of airport food.

The car rental guy had handed him a map. He was certain of the way home, but took it anyway. The ranch was off of Route 89 northwest of Great Falls. He would pick up Route 200 and then scoot over to Route 21 and right to the ranch's main entrance. Part of their land backed up to Glacier National Park and he was anxious to see the mountains.

He threw his bags on the passenger seat of the pickup and climbed in. A short drive from the airport, he found a rustic-looking restaurant where he was sure he'd get a good meal. He felt excited, but nervous about surprising his mother. He couldn't imagine she'd be anywhere but on the ranch at this time of the year with calving and foaling. After eating, he cleaned up a little in the bathroom and stood peering at himself in the mirror. His mother wouldn't recognize him. As he ran a comb through his graying hair, he barely recognized himself.

The long straight road and the constant hum of the

engine put him into a form of melancholy as he thought about what he'd done with his life. The ranch had offered him so much that was real and, yes, meaningful, and he had chosen a divisive life instead. His work had been full of adventure, invigorating to him for quite a long time, but then it turned into something mean and disdainful. They used a top secret "nominations" process to designate terrorists for kill or capture. Technology had changed everything and the state of the world altered the thinking of many at the top. They had their "kill list," and he and Buck, along with other operatives, had been methodically and obediently systematically doing their jobs.

He recalled recently how the drug debacle involving Catherine's husband, James, had actually come as a surprise to them at one of the "Terror Tuesday" meetings. Until then, they hadn't been aware of that aspect of the Clandestine Service. Their assignment had been under executive order and involved taking no one alive, eliminating the problems with holding new prisoners at Guantanamo. At that meeting, they first learned how key people were being taken out in a devious way by making it look like a stroke.

In addition, the drone strikes in several countries were killing machines. They had been named TADS, for Terrorist Attack Disruption Strikes. Although the strikes had eviscerated Al-Qaeda, the drones didn't see the children. The part that had disgusted him the most was the method of counting the civilian casualties. Any military-age male in a strike zone was counted as a combatant. It wasn't right because most of those kids were innocent.

That's when things began to unravel for him. It reminded him of the brutality on the reservations. They had called the slaughter of Native Americans collateral damage. At the Tuesday meetings, there had been too many reported casualties and ineffective explanations as far as he was concerned. When Buck sustained the almost fatal gunshot, they had both endured enough. Worse for him was the fact that all the futuristic gadgets hadn't done a thing to protect the one thing needing protection—the children.

In some ways, he felt like he had failed himself, and worse, his mother. The roles that officers of the Clandestine Service had to undertake involved lying and cheating—essentially everything his mother taught him not to do. They had become the "sneaky guys" in order to fulfill their job requirements. At the end of the day, he was the one who made the decisions. He had been involved in all sorts of espionage and undercover work, which had involved human elements. Now, with all the technology, it was too easy for someone to track you, listen to you, or see you. It was like the future flashed before him at the same moment the assailant fired the shot into Buck. He suddenly couldn't do it any more. He was done. The very things that had seduced him into the work and had been somewhat irresistible had sent him far from it and longing to go back to his past.

He shook his head as he realized he was getting very close to the turn off to Route 21. The new roads had made the drive mesmerizing, and the absence of traffic made it easy for him to drift off into his memories. He was very close to the ranch and whatever was about to happen. He suddenly felt as keyed up as he had the night he'd taken off with Buck so many years ago. The enlightened prince who had gone out to conquer the enemy had become an ordinary man again and was going home.

CHAPTER 26

Catherine was disturbed by the fact that she hadn't heard a word from Zane. She wanted to believe no news was good news, but she had expected him to call to keep her posted about his whereabouts. She hadn't spoken to anyone except Lauren Bartlett when she arrived to help with the barn chores that morning. She was tempted to call Buck, but she didn't have a good enough reason. She wanted to be sure Zane had made it to the ranch and to know how things had gone for him. Patience was not her virtue; besides, she really missed him.

It was early July and hot. The horses had been waiting at the gate every time she and Lauren went to bring them in. They were hosing down two of them when Lauren asked her whether she gave any thought to leaving them out at night.

"I don't think I could sleep. It would worry me with them out all night. I'd dream up all sorts of things that could happen to them."

"Well, Miss Catherine, you have a lot of grass and your pastures are behind your house away from the road. I really think they would be all right."

"I'm not sure about it. I know it's so darn hot, but I feel like we should all go to bed at the same time."

"You wouldn't have to come down here to the barn alone at night then, you know."

"I have the dogs." Catherine didn't want to be reminded about all this.

"I know you do, but I'm just thinking...."

"I'm fine. Really, I am. I'm doing just fine." She wasn't just fine. She hadn't realized how much she depended on Zane. There were a lot of details in a day with all the animals. Lauren was a huge help, but she and Zane had a nice pace going for them, and now she couldn't even ride.

"Lauren, do you ride?" she asked, in an attempt to change the subject, but also solve her dilemma.

"Well, yes, ma'am, I do. I run barrels."

"I see. That must be a lot of fun for you and your horse."

"Yes, ma'am, my boy and I both love to go really fast and he's really good at it."

Catherine wasn't sure that would be the right thing to do—asking Lauren to come ride. She certainly didn't want to be riding any faster than a lope.

"Did you need me to ride one of these guys for you, Miss Catherine?"

"I'm not certain any of them could go fast enough for you."

Lauren was laughing. "Oh, ma'am, you don't have to worry about that. My daddy would whoop me for sure if he thought I ruined one of your horses for you. He already warned me to understand that you had these fancy horses, and if I got an opportunity, I was to behave like a lady. He really thinks I'm some kind of hellion. He just says that on account of he can't admit that he wanted me to be a boy. He has to live with me being a little wild and act like he's okay with me as a girl."

"Do you honestly think that?"

"No. I know it. But, Miss Catherine, my daddy taught me how to ride his good horses too, so you don't have to worry. I know how to ride slow and easy too."

Catherine wasn't sure what she wanted to do, but she sure felt desperate to speak to Zane.

~~~~~

She hadn't been in the house very long after the afternoon chores when the phone rang. She felt nervous about answering, but at the same time, she hoped it was Zane. The caller ID said, "Unknown Name." She picked it up anyway.

"Hello."

"Catherine, hello, it's Celia Fenmore. Am I bothering you?"

"Bothering me? Oh, no, not at all. I just came in as a matter of fact."

"I was thinking about you today and decided I would call. Is everything okay?"

"Yes, sort of." Catherine hesitated to tell her the truth.

"Sort of?"

"Yes. It's just that someone has been calling my phone and not saying anything and I was a little worried about answering it right now."

"I'm sorry. That has to be annoying." Celia sounded sincere.

"It does rattle me a bit."

"I imagine, but maybe I can get your mind off it for a while. I have something I want to ask."

"Okay, go ahead."

"It's this thing about us discovering that we are half-
~~~~~

sisters. I wondered if you've had time to think about it and what you believe we should do."

"What exactly do you mean? I'm not sure I'm following you," Catherine asked.

"I guess I'm questioning if you told your mother and your sister and if you did, what was their reaction?"

"No. I haven't said a word to anyone, really. Not family members anyway. It is going to sound strange, but I haven't talked to my family."

"I've only talked to my grandmother about this. My mother has already passed away. I haven't said a thing to my husband and I haven't told my daughter, Olivia, even though she seems to be very tuned in to you."

"Do you think it's strange that we've both kept it to ourselves?" Catherine asked.

"No. Not really. I think this is very personal and I'm wondering about the advantages and disadvantages of telling anyone. Do you have an opinion on that?"

"I'd have to give it some thought. My family doesn't really discuss things." Catherine couldn't even remember the last time she'd spoken to her mother or her sister.

"I have my grandmother. She was well aware of the whole story. She kept it from me, because she said she wanted to protect me."

"Celia, maybe knowing only matters to us. It wouldn't change anything for anyone if they knew. I think if we lived closer to each other, it would make a greater difference. If I were able to spend time with Olivia, then I would want her to know I was her aunt."

"I know it would be confusing to her at first. It seems our father didn't make the best decisions, but he must have had some good genes to have produced two smart women like us." She giggled.

Catherine couldn't help it. She began to laugh too. "I know. You're right. It is ridiculous how we found out about each other, and now that we did, it's just as ridiculous trying to figure out what to do about it. I didn't know that much about him after my mother divorced him, and my memories of him are very limited."

"I didn't even know who he was."

"Celia, I'm okay with waiting until we are certain of what the outcome might be before we decide what to do. It doesn't make sense to confuse Olivia right now."

"Yes, and I'm okay with that too."

"It's very nice talking to you, Celia. It's good to hear your voice. Please call me anytime."

"And, the same to you. Take good care of yourself, Catherine."

"Yes, you too. Good night."

Catherine hadn't spent much time thinking about finding her half-sister while she was staying at her Uncle Walton's house in Jensen Beach, Florida. Following his death, she had felt vulnerable. Once she arrived back at her ranch in Highberry, she had become extremely ill with a virus and exhaustion. During her recovery, she and Zane had fallen into their unexpected relationship. Other than the recent phone call from her cousin, Justin, she hadn't spoken to any other family members. She knew she had been isolating herself, but she honestly didn't feel like dealing with any of it.

~~~~~
~~~~~

Lauren was scheduled to help her seven days a week. Catherine felt guilty about needing that much assistance, but she honestly would have been totally alone 24/7, except for when she traveled to town for supplies. Buck delivered feed and hay once a week and said he didn't mind bringing anything else she needed, but sometimes, she needed to leave the property. She knew Zane must have asked him to keep an eye on her. That's why she was surprised when she saw a small blue car coming down the driveway. It made her stomach tighten, wondering who it could be. She stood in front of the house waiting. As the car slowed and stopped, Catherine could see that it was a woman driving. It wasn't until Effie got out of the car that Catherine realized it was Buck's mother.

"Hello, Catherine. I hope you don't mind my stopping over for a spell. I borrowed Deb's car."

"Oh, no, Mrs. Matthews, how are you?"

"I asked Buck how to get here. I know you've been alone and thought you might want some company."

"That is so sweet. Won't you come in? Let me run around to the back and I'll come through the front door and let you in."

"I can follow you right around, dear. My legs are still working."

"Okay. Are you sure?"

"Yes. Of course, I'm sure."

They made their way around the house and in through the back porch door. Catherine was careful with the dogs so they didn't overpower Mrs. Mathews. "We can sit at the kitchen table or in the living room. Which would you prefer? And, would you like something to drink?"

"Right here at the table is fine; reminds me of home, and yes, I'll have a little water. That would be nice."

They sat at the table, talking about the weather, how the babies were doing, and how nice it was for Zane to be with his mother after so many years.

"I'm waiting to hear from him," Catherine told her. "He hasn't called me and I'm anxious to find out how things went."

"Well, he'll probably have to call you from the landline because our cell phones don't always work out there."

"He warned me. He said sometimes you have to drive to a certain spot and wait for a satellite to go over. I thought he was teasing me."

"Oh, no, it is true. I really appreciate being able to come over here. I'm getting a little stir crazy being in the house all the time. Even though it's nice with the babies, I was in need of a little change of scenery, if you know what I mean."

"Do you like horses?"

"Of course, I do. We still use them on the ranch for working the cows, although I'm not able to ride much lately because my hip has been acting up. I'm not ready to ride that all terrain vehicle chasing cows, though."

"Would you like to go down to the barn? The horses are already in."

"That would be nice."

Mrs. Matthews followed Catherine out the door as all the dogs piled outside, except for Friskie. He stayed obediently at the back door, looking through the bottom glass.

"This is a nice barn, my dear. You must be so pleased."

It was concrete with four stalls, two on each side. The wash rack was at the end of the barn. There was a feed room on one side and the tack room on the other. The aisle was wide enough to run a tractor through.

"Yes, I am. Zane and I have been riding every day and it made me really appreciate the barn."

"Are all of them Arabians?"

"Yes, they are. Did you know Zane ended up with Trouble? He's the black Arabian stallion in the end stall. He rescued him."

Mrs. Matthews tried to pet his neck, but Trouble was pushy. She gently moved his head over to the side and looked over the stall door.

"He has nice conformation, but I'm surprised Zane wanted an Arab."

"He picked him up at an auction. He said he was in very poor shape."

"It seems like he hasn't missed a meal lately."

"Oh, no, he's doing great. You should see Zane ride him."

"I'd like that. That boy could always sit a horse. We have a few Arabians on our ranch we use to work the cows. They are great at cutting out a sick one or finding a calf separated in a thicket, and they can go all day. Are you planning to breed your mares?"

Catherine opened the feed room door, filled a small cart with hay, and gave each horse a small amount. "That was the plan, but now I'm not so sure. After studying the bloodlines and all, it seems like a huge decision. You are controlling the outcome, but you can't always predict what will happen. It kind of scares me."

"I know what you mean. We have an expert on our ranch, and all he does is study our cattle for the best genetic outcomes. We want to produce cattle that are well proportioned and produce the best beef. We hold back certain cows because they are such good producers. It is a lot of work. Buck has really helped us with financial support. It has moved us into a level we never imagined. In fact, my husband and I are, for the first time ever, thinking about leaving the ranch for a while."

"You mean moving? Living somewhere else?"

"Well, I'm already here and all that has to happen is for my husband to join me. The nice thing is that if we don't like it, we can always go home. We have housing for our employees, so our house can just sit and wait for us."

"I had no idea."

"We actually didn't either. It sort of happened over the last few months, what with Buck buying the farm here and now with the grandbabies."

"Well, I wish you lots of luck, Mrs. Matthews. It will be a big change for you and your husband, but it will be nice to have you here."

"Yes, I'm actually looking forward to something different. We have lived on that ranch our entire married life." Effie glanced at her watch. "Dear me, look at the time. I better get back. I'm sure you have lots to do what with Zane being gone and all."

"I have this young woman helping me, but it does get lonely and I so appreciate your visit."

"I'll just have to do this again then."

"That would be great."

Catherine and Mrs. Matthews walked from the barn past the house and into the front yard to the car. Catherine stood waving goodbye until Mrs. Matthews pulled out of the driveway.

CHAPTER 27

Maggie White Calf was at the kitchen window watching the dust plume off in the distance created by a truck flying down their road. She couldn't imagine who would be coming to visit on this hot July afternoon. The ranch hands had finished lunch and were off taking what they jokingly called a siesta before finishing up whatever chores needed to be done. She had been out in the garden rescuing more of the vegetables that were suffering from the lack of any precipitation. There were reports of fires farther north caused by lightning strikes and one that was the result of some fool's target practice. A neighboring ranch had been almost completely destroyed. They had saved the house, but the barn was burned to the ground with sheep inside. She could only hope that this wasn't one of the neighbors with more bad news, but she didn't recognize the truck as it came through the last cattle guard and into the yard.

Maggie walked onto the front porch, holding a dish towel in one hand and shading her eyes from the sun with the other. The man jumped out of the truck, leaving the door open, and strode in long ground-covering strides toward her. She didn't recognize him and was startled when he flew up the steps and grabbed her. It wasn't until she was looking straight into his face and heard his voice that she realized who he was.

"Oh my Lord, Zane, is it really you?"

He picked her up, spun her around in a circle so fast her legs swung out behind her. She could scarcely believe how tall and strong he was. He put her down and she couldn't speak for a few seconds.

"I wanted to surprise you. I hope I didn't give you a heart attack." He was beaming.

"You nearly did because I had no idea what man would come in here and grab me like that."

"I didn't want to tell you ahead of time. Plus, I just made the decision to come. I figured you wouldn't know me. I barely recognize myself."

"I would always know you once I could look into those eyes."

She wrung the towel in her hands.

"Oh my, Zane, I can't believe you are here. Come in. Leave your things in the truck. We'll get them in a minute. Just come in out of this heat and dust."

They walked through the front door into the great room, Zane holding onto her hand as she walked in front of him. He didn't want to let go of her. Not for a minute. Not yet, but she let go of him, turned and stood looking up into his eyes.

"I am liking that smile," he said.

"What?"

"I don't remember you ever smiling like this. I like it. You look so different. You look happy."

"I must look much different to you, what with my graying hair and sagging face, but yes, I am happy. Come. Let's go to the kitchen. Let me get you something."

"You don't have to get me anything. Just seeing you and being here is enough."

She watched as he looked around the room. Although she knew some things looked different to him, she had tried to keep it nearly the same. Some of the pieces of furniture had changed, but the art work on the walls and, of course, the structure of it hadn't changed.

"It's good to be home, Mama."

"It's good to have you here, my son."

"I have so much to tell you and so many things I need to say."

"You don't have to say anything, Zane. It's just good for you to be here."

"No, I do. I have a lot to tell you."

"We will talk, but for now, just come into the kitchen. You have me so rattled; I don't know what I was doing."

"I hope you were making fry bread."

She laughed. "You and your fry bread; you always drove me crazy."

"I know I did."

They looked at each other and laughed. He swooped her into his arms and hugged her. "Mama, we do have so much to catch up on."

"And we will. Now, come with me."

There was a gray-haired man sitting at the end of the table cutting corn off the cob. He had a bushel basket next to his chair and was working away.

"Who was that in the truck?" he asked before he looked up and saw the man standing behind Maggie.

"Someone came to see us," she said.

Parker Iron Crow nearly knocked over the bushel of corn as he pushed the chair back and wiped his hands on his jeans. He grabbed Zane, slapped him on the back and gave him a bear hug. He had recognized him in an instant.

"It is good to have you home."

"It is good to be here as well, Iron Crow."

All three of them continued looking at each other for several seconds.

"Sit you two."

His mother motioned for them to sit at the table.

"What can I get for the both of you?"

"I'll have whatever he has," Parker said and winked at Zane.

"And what would you like, Zane?"

"Honestly, Mama, I'd like some of our water."

"Then that is what you shall have." She gave each of them water from the tap and Zane quickly swallowed the entire glass, drinking steadily but slowly.

"I have waited a long time for that."

She filled his glass again.

"I don't know what kept me away so long. I should have come home before this."

"You did what was right for you, Zane. Let it be. Now, let us enjoy each other. I will be busy making you your fry bread, and we will be busy listening to you. Tell us. Tell us about you now and tell us about this woman, Catherine. Tell us."

"Oh, God, I never called her. I was so excited about getting here and surprising you, I completely forgot to...."

"Here, son, right here is the phone. Call her. Parker and I will be right back. Just use the phone."

"You don't have to go."

Maggie motioned for Parker to follow her and they

went out onto the back porch.

~~~~~

"When do you want to tell him?" Parker said softly as he sat down on the bench. Maggie stood in front of him.

"I think we should tell him soon, but not just yet."

"I know what you mean. We should give him a little while to settle in. Get his bearings. He's had a long trip. His life has changed so much."

"I know, but he has to learn the truth."

"I'm not too worried. I think he's had an idea something was always wrong."

She had kept her secret long enough. She would tell her son after dinner tonight. It would change everything for all of them.

"If he looks, let's say so mature to us, how old must we look?" Iron Crow's eyes were twinkling. They both laughed.

"Oh, Iron Crow, you know we are old. We can feel it clear into our bones."

"Yes, but we are young in our hearts."

"So you say."

Zane opened the back door.

"Catherine must be out doing chores. I left her a message. At least she knows I'm alive."

The screen door slammed behind him as he stepped outside. Iron Crow looked up at Maggie.

"Some things never change," he said smiling at her.

"What?" Zane asked.

His mother grinned at him.

"You have always let that screen door slam, ever
~~~~~

since you could first walk."

He squeezed his mother's shoulder.

"It's really good to be home," Zane said as he looked across the dry parched land

~~~~~

Catherine saw the light blinking as soon as she stepped into the kitchen. She pushed the button on the phone, eager to hear the message. "Hey, Catherine, it's Zane. I have arrived at our ranch. I'm fine. I'm sorry, but I just got here and I'm calling from the land line. I'll try and call you later."

It was a relief to hear his voice. At least she knew he was safe. Now, she would have to wait until later to hear about his trip. Everything had been okay until this afternoon when she discovered a cut on her gelding's leg located right above the knee. There was no evidence of how Sundy had done it. She put Blood Stop on it after calling Buck to find out what to do. It would have been so much easier if Zane had been there. She was worried about it getting infected. She would wait for Lauren to figure out how to dress it. It didn't appear to need stitches, but the flies had been all over it. She wished she would have caught Zane's call so she could have asked him what to do. She had used a pink salve that was on the shelf that said it included a pesticide. Still, she worried about doing the right thing.

She busied herself by gathering a load of clothes from upstairs, started the washer, and then began to clean up the house. She hadn't realized how much time they spent with each other, making decisions for the day, interacting with the dogs or working the horses.
~~~~~

She was anxious for him to get back and he hadn't even been gone that long.

Sometimes it felt like she and James were another lifetime ago. It was getting harder to pull up memories like the sound of James' voice or other details about him. She had found one of his shirts in her drawer the other day and pulled it to her face and smelled it. Either it had been in the drawer too long or.... It didn't take her back to those old feelings that she once had. On the other hand, there were shirts and jeans left in Zane's hamper, and just the scent of his dirty clothes made her miss him even more.

Zane's leaving had made it difficult for her to ride. She was scared to do it alone. What if something happened? She felt like the horses were watching her, waiting for her to do something with them. She and Zane had been taking daily rides and she hated losing that momentum. She wanted to ask him about Lauren when he called tonight. She could call Buck and ask him, but he didn't know that much about her horses. She wished she had thought to discuss this with Zane before he left, but they had both been preoccupied with his leaving and it had come upon them suddenly. She also wanted to tell him about the conversation she'd had with Mrs. Matthews. She couldn't wait to talk to him.

~~~~~

Zane practically pounced on the plate of fry bread as soon as his mother set it in the middle of the kitchen table.

"It's hot. I just took it out of the oven. Be careful," Maggie said.
~~~~~

He was tearing off a piece of it and shoving it in his mouth as he mumbled around the dough. "I have been waiting for this moment for a long, long time."

"And so have we."

He smiled, barely chewing the bread, and swallowing hard. "I can't tell you how good it is to be here with you and hear you laugh, Mama."

"It is so good, son, to have you home."

Parker had a look of contentment on his face. The lines around his eyes had deepened and his face was more weathered, but he looked amazingly well.

"Iron Crow, you are looking good, my man."

"As are you."

"So what have you been doing all these years, my friend, to look so well? The ranch looks like it's in pretty good shape considering the lack of rain."

"We have been lucky. We had a few storms blow through the high country. The ranch takes care of me. You know."

"What about the horses?"

"They are running up on the ridge where we used to go. It is still green up there near the mountains. We can take a ride in the morning."

"That would be good."

"That would be very good. It will be as it used to be."

Zane watched Maggie give Iron Crow a look. He couldn't help but wonder what was going on between the two of them.

"So what are you two up to?" he asked.

His mother answered, "It's been difficult keeping the ranch going. We are worried about the fires, the lack of grass, beef prices."

"That's not exactly what I meant."

"Oh? Then what?" she asked.

He knew she wasn't going to give him an ounce of information. Some things with them hadn't changed. There had always been a hidden undercurrent, sometimes as if they had a secret silent language. He had seen it many times as a child. They would give each other a certain look, a glance, a gesture. He had never fully comprehended it. Now he was seeing it, feeling it again.

"Is there something I need to know?"

Just then, the back porch door opened abruptly and a tall, young man with long black hair came in. He nodded to Iron Crow, said hello to Maggie, and then looked at Zane.

"John, this is my son, Zane Wheeler. Zane, this is John Two Guns White Calf."

Zane reached out his hand to John, but he was looking at his mother.

"White Calf?" he asked. He was relieved to learn that although his mother and this boy carried the same last name, they were only distantly related. For a few seconds, when he'd heard the boy's name, he wondered whether his mother had kept some bigger secret from him. When she explained that she and Parker had taken in this young man after the detention center was forcibly closed, his heart settled.

John told Zane it had been an adjustment when he came to the ranch. Zane understood how he might have felt trapped, but that running away would have presented its own set of challenges. John admitted that the parched land and the distance from the paved road to the house made him have his doubts about making it safely out. He had decided not to run.

"This is the first time I am hearing this story out loud," Iron Crow told them. "Although, I had suspected you were thinking this, John."

"I think you knew I was like a scared rabbit, but I also knew you were hoping my thoughts of the predators and the elements would keep me here. You are a wise man and I have learned to respect you, although I'm sure there were times when you might have wanted me to flee."

"I'll admit it, John; sometimes Maggie and I talked late into the night trying to figure out our best approach, but the struggle has been worth it to see you now."

"If I haven't said it enough, thank you for all that you have done for me."

"Well, John, we are expecting great things from you still. We should tell you, Zane, John is not our first young man. You will see the pictures and we will surely talk about our tales when we have a chance to relax in the great room after dinner. Speaking of which, Maggie, is there anything we can do to help with the evening meal?"

"No, Parker, thank you. I think I have it under control. We'll have some of that fresh corn you've been working so hard on. Zane, do you want to freshen up? You know where your room is. I'm sure you can find it still."

Parker said, "Come and I'll help you with your things from the truck. You can help too, John."

They made their way out the front door and helped

Zane bring his things into the house. He had his duffle bag, one suitcase and his hat, which Parker stuck on his head. Zane smiled as he watched Parker skip up the front steps. The old man still had a spring in his walk and it truly was good to be here with him again. More importantly, it was good to be home with his mother.

CHAPTER 28

James Robert Campbell walked down the long corridor, boarded the plane, and sat in his first class seat. After flying from LaGuardia, he would change planes in Washington, D.C. and then fly straight to Jacksonville, Florida. He had made arrangements to pick up a rental car there. He had no idea what the next few days would bring, but he had nothing to lose. Not one person had given him a second look. No one had any idea he had been James DeLong in his other life. He had to do this for himself and for her—no one else. He didn't care how long it took; he would find a way to see Catherine.

As soon as the plane lifted off the runway in Washington, he began re-studying the map. He knew exactly which roads to take to Highberry. He knew he'd be staying at an old motel on 441 west of town, and he knew no one would recognize him. He had to see her and explain everything to her—and to be sure she was okay. He had become obsessed with thoughts of what he would say to Catherine, rehearsing the scenes over and over in his mind. He wanted more than anything to tell her exactly what had happened—to make things right with her.

There were times when he thought it would be better if he had a job to occupy his mind, but he didn't have a clue what he would do. It wasn't like he wanted to go back to work for a pharmaceutical company. That had gone completely wrong for him. He could work in computer technology, but that had brought him into all this conflict in the first place.

Arianne had become his angel in the cabin in the woods for a while, but during all those months, he had constantly plotted a way to seize an opportunity to speak with his wife. He knew he had to do it. What he wanted most of all was to tell Catherine the entire story—all of it—how he had never intended for it to turn out this way. How he felt horrible about what had happened to her on an emotional level and in her trusting him. He needed to explain that he didn't have any choice once he made the commitment to the government. He would tell her how much she meant to him and that he would never forgive himself for what he had done to her innocent loving heart. Tell her how she had given him life again after all that he had missed as a young man and that he had most certainly taken her for granted. He knew she would be shocked—he wasn't certain how she would react when she discovered he was still alive.

And even worse yet, what would she think when she saw what they had done to his face? Any part of it might destroy her all over again. He didn't recognize himself when he looked in the mirror, and he worried how she would deal with it. Oh, my God! He didn't know if he could do this, but he had to. He had become an emotional wreck. He hadn't felt this way since he had been abandoned as a child and placed in foster care. He felt that old sense of panic, as if his life were spiraling out of control. At night, he would wake up in a sweat, grabbing the sides of the bed, because he was falling—

falling into a deep dark pit. He wanted everything to go back the way it was supposed to be. He wanted to wake up in their New York apartment and roll over and find Catherine next to him in their bed. He had prayed for a normal happy life long ago when he had been in strange people's houses in the dead dark of night. When Catherine came into his life, his prayers had been answered, but then his miscalculated choices had sent her away. He had begun to pray even harder now, but he knew deep inside nothing was ever going to be like it used to be. He couldn't stop his hands from shaking as the heaviness in his chest tightened even more.

~~~~~

James threw his bags in the back of the dark blue Lincoln Navigator and drove straight from Jacksonville International Airport south on Interstate 10 to Lake City. He easily located the plaza he had scoped out on the Internet before he left New York. He walked briskly into Cowboy's Western Wear and purchased a couple pair of jeans, a few shirts, a belt, and boots. Soon he was back on Interstate 75, heading south to Highberry.

He checked into the small Country Motel just west of town. It was clean, but the building was archaic, painted a rusty orange color. It was definitely old Florida, but he didn't care. All he needed was a temporary roof over his head and a place to sleep.

He would have to be patient until his path crossed with Catherine's. He would frequent the grocery store, the only gas station in town, and he was certain she would eventually show up at the feed store of that bastard, Buck Matthews. In the meantime, he wanted to
~~~~~

check on an old friend. He plopped down on the low sagging bed, adjusted the pillow behind his neck, and dialed his cell phone. Roger Halvesord answered on the third ring.

"So Rog, how the hell are you?"

"Who is this?"

"Who do you think it is?"

"James, is that you?"

"Of course, it's me. What are you doing?" He enjoyed playing him.

"I'm doing fine."

"Really? I asked you what you are doing and you tell me how you are doing. How is it possible that you say fine when I heard you had to take a job with a law firm in order to save your ass?"

"What are you talking about? Who told you that?" Roger asked in a strained voice.

"Never mind; I just know. That's all."

"It was in my best interest to join a more lucrative practice. My office manager graduated from law school and moved on. It's just too damn hard to train someone. This way, I share the office staff and lease my space, lowering my overhead. I'm sure you get it."

James loved that Roger was babbling. He knew he wasn't going to tell him that his life had completely fallen into the proverbial shitter. Roger would never admit that he had to downsize his practice, sell his fancy sports car, and rent space at a bona fide law firm in order to have any clients; that he had gone after Catherine, failing miserably at that as well. No, Roger wanted his best buddy, old friend, to think that everything in his life was perfect.

James answered Roger gruffly, "I get it all right. I heard through the grapevine that you were making the moves on my wife. What do you have to say about that?"

"James, think about it. Didn't you ask me to take care of her? I thought you'd be okay with me looking after her."

"Looking after her or going after her? There's a thin line, if I ever saw one. Did you get a little confused about boundaries? Did you think for even a moment that she might not be the least bit interested in you?"

"James, she was very distressed and then she became extremely ill. She wasn't thinking clearly. I was only trying to protect her, take care of her. Wouldn't you rather have her be with me than this nobody that she's decided to shack up with?"

"Hey, watch it! She's not ...."

Roger cut him off. "James, face it. She's got that cowboy living with her. You're kidding yourself! They are riding high, and my pun is intended."

James clenched his jaw and it began to twitch. He squeezed the phone tighter. "Roger, you stupid son-of-a-bitch! Of course, I knew she was upset and I know about the cowboy. I'm expecting her to be equally upset when she finds out I'm alive. And, I expect she will be upset with you too when she finds out the truth about what you knew."

"Yeah, but I'm not the one who lied to her and doesn't even look like the man she married, and what is she supposed to do—run into your loving arms? She won't even know who you are when she sees you. But I did hear that they did a really great job on your face."

"Wow, Roger. You of all people should know how

much she loved me. She will still love me, and she won't care what I look like."

"Good for you if you want to believe that, but there's one slight problem. She thought you were dead and she's moved on."

"I just need to talk to her, to explain."

Beads of perspiration formed on James' forehead and he flicked them off with his index finger. The damn window air-conditioner was grinding away, but it was hot in his small motel room.

"You are about to commit double suicide. Let me clarify this for you. She thinks you're dead, but wait, you're alive. You don't get it. Now, if you blow your cover and they find out, someone may actually want to kill you, only this time you really will be dead. You were dead, but this time you really will be dead. Don't you get that? What about putting her in danger? Have you thought about that?"

"Stop it?" James had heard enough. He sat up on the side of the squeaky bed.

"No. You have to stop this. You can't have any contact with her whatsoever. You will put all of us back in jeopardy, but especially yourself and Catherine. I'm surprised the government is letting you get anywhere near her."

"Actually, this is none of the government's business. They don't care about me anymore. They told me I can do whatever I want."

"James, don't kid yourself. That sort of lip service is just that. You can't believe a word they say."

"Well, Roger, you were the first one who believed what they said, and then I believed what you told me.

But guess what? I'm not so stupid now that I wouldn't know if someone was tailing me. Have you been here? Of course, you have. It's like the middle of nowhere. I'm trying to resolve what your bright ideas did for us. I have to talk to Catherine. I have to stand in front of her, look into her eyes, and tell her. Then it's up to her."

"You mean you are there where Catherine lives? Then here's my final question: Do you love her enough to let her go? Do you? Think about her for once in your life."

"I love her. I have never stopped loving her from the moment I met her."

"Then you know what you have to do. I'm telling you, James, you have to let her go."

"You were wrong about the outcome of this project, and I'm betting you are going to be wrong about her." James was completely frustrated with Roger.

"I don't think you are going to get the outcome you want, James."

"I don't think you are going to get the outcome you want either, Roger."

James pushed the button on his phone and threw a pillow across the room.

His mother's cooking was more delicious than anything that had crossed Zane's lips since the night he ran away from the ranch and the disappointments of his childhood. Just the aroma made him salivate. Being back in that environment gave him a remarkable peace deep inside his core.

The kitchen was large with old wooden planking on the floor worn from the many weary feet that had trod across it. The kitchen cabinets looked exactly the same as they had when he was a small boy, sitting at the table, swinging his legs back and forth because his feet didn't quite reach the floor. Floods of memories drifted in and out of his mind.

His father had placed heavy demands on all of them. Foster Thomas Wheeler had this misguided idea that he not only owned the ranch, but also any breathing being that lived there, including his wife and son. Everyone and everything had to adhere to his iron fisted rules. It was his "God damned birthright." They had devised ways of working around him, but Foster made every effort to stay one-step ahead of everyone. He was ruthless with people and animals alike. He saw everything as what he could get from it, rather than what he could give to it. Plus, he had a deep sense of entitlement. He was "a Wheeler, for Christ sakes, descended from the wheelwrights. The West would have been nothing without the...." Zane had heard his father's viewpoint on it hundreds of times.

His mother tapped him on the shoulder and brought him out of his deep thoughts.

She had quietly cleared away all the dishes and stacked them on the sink.

"Let's move into the great room. I'll bring in coffee. Would you like a cup?"

As his mother made her way to the cupboard to gather the mugs, he felt a deep sense of the familiarity with the way she moved across the floor, the sound of the wooden boards, and even the soft familiar scent of her. How many times had she gone to that same cupboard?

"That would be very nice," he said.

John excused himself from the table, saying he had things to do and headed upstairs to his room. Zane and Iron Crow settled into the flowered arm chairs just as Maggie came out of the kitchen with a tray of coffee mugs and cookies.

"Do you need milk or sugar?"

"No thanks, Mama. I take it black." Zane realized that was one of the many things his mother didn't know about him. He had caused her to miss so much of his life and he had missed so much of hers and Iron Crows.

"You must be getting tired. You've had a long day," she said.

"I'm still excited about being here, but it will hit me soon. Don't they say the second day is the worst for jet lag?"

"You would know more about that, Zane. You are the world traveler."

"Yes, I guess I would," he said and smiled at her.

"So, Zane, how are you handling your retirement?" Parker asked.

"It started out a bit aimlessly, but then I accidentally met Catherine. It was out of her need that we became acquainted. I think you already know that I took care of her farm and animals while she went through a tough time with her uncle. He was quite ill before he passed away."

"I'm sure she was glad to have you there while she went through that loss and then her recovery," Parker said and set his coffee cup on the table between their chairs.

"It was the only thing I could do. I couldn't just walk out on her. She had been through so much. First she lost her husband and then her uncle."

Zane stared at the beautiful woven rug, lost for a moment in a memory of being with Catherine.

Iron Crow said, "Your mother was happy that you found such a place to rest. For so many years, you have been involved in your work. It seemed it would be good for you to sit still for a while."

"Yes, it was a perfect rest for Trouble too."

"Ah, yes, your horse!"

"Yes, my horse. He's quite the character."

Parker yawned softly and said, "I'm thinking maybe it won't be long before I'll be putting myself to bed."

Zane saw his mother's expression as she searched Parker's face and then she softly said, "No, Parker, you should stay for a little while. Zane, there are some things we need to talk to you about, Parker and I. We all need to talk."

Zane sat intently waiting. It took a moment before

his mother began her story.

"This is going to take you quite by surprise when we tell you."

"Tell me what?"

"There's no easy way to say this, except to finally tell you the truth."

"Tell me the truth about what?"

Maggie took in a deep breath and swallowed hard as Parker got up from his chair. He sat next to her on the edge of the couch. They were sitting directly across from Zane. His mother began.

"You know I was raised on the Blackfeet reservation. Things had become a bit difficult for me. My family was upset because I was running with what they thought were terrible people. One night, I was in a bar and there was a brawl. The people I was with were thrown out of the place and they were so intoxicated that they left me behind in the bar. I was a long way from home and some men in there were giving me a bad time. That's when Foster Wheeler rescued me by offering to give me a ride back to my home. I knew he'd had a few drinks and I was a little afraid of him, but the situation in the bar was worse, so I climbed into his truck. On the way to the rez, he presented me with a proposal."

"And what was that?" Zane asked as he straightened in his chair.

"Everyone pretty much knew about Foster Thomas Wheeler. I knew of him, and I was surprised to suddenly be riding in his truck. He was the largest property owner in the area other than the Blackfeet Tribe. He told me that he was fed up with the women he had been dating. That's what he said. He wanted someone who was young, attractive, who would be obedient, take care of his house and give him children. There was just one problem."

Maggie took Parker's hand and they looked at each other. Parker began gently rubbing her arm. Zane was watching them, wondering what was about to be said.

"The man you knew as your father was actually unable to have children. He had been furious about it. He couldn't understand how it could happen to him when he was such a strong, virile man. He had gone to some fancy doctors who ran tests on him and there was no doubt that he was sterile. He told me that no one could ever know that he was what he called 'shooting blanks.' It had been caused by a secondary infection he had after coming down with the mumps when he was in his early twenties. He said if I came to live on the ranch, he would make sure I had a better life, but I had to produce a son. He told me that I should pick myself some young buck, and when I knew that I was pregnant, he would come and get me and lay claim to the child."

"And are you telling me that is what you did?"

"No, not exactly. I already knew Parker. He was a bit older than me, and my family didn't approve of me seeing him. Part of my rebellion was because of that, and that night in the bar, I was actually on my way to see him. When Foster offered me the opportunity, I went as quickly as I could to talk to Parker. His family had connections to the Wheelers and so we concocted a plan. Parker found a way to work as a ranch hand for Foster. It was shortly after that I discovered that I was already pregnant. Foster forbade me to ever reveal the identity of the father of my child. In fact, he himself didn't want to know. My family wasn't happy that I was marrying Foster, but they knew that I would be taken care of."

Zane's head felt like it was in a vice. He was attempting to process what he had just heard.

"So, you are telling me that all these years the two of you have kept this secret from me and from him? All that time, the two of you were my biological parents and you let me go through all that bullshit with that son of a bitch?"

Zane pushed himself up out of his chair and began pacing back and forth. He stopped in front of the fireplace and turned to face them.

"How could you let him? Why would you do that for him?" His shoulders slouched forward and he felt like that small boy again standing there in the great room.

"Zane, I know this is difficult, but I was young and we protected you as much as we could." His mother tried to stand up, but Parker held her firmly by the arm.

"That bastard made me miserable. He made you miserable," Zane replied sternly.

"That man made it possible for me to give you life, and look what you did with it. You used that life to defend your country against great enemies. Foster, in his own way, taught you many things including tenacity."

"My life could have been very different. I ran away from here because of him." Zane was trying hard not to sound bitter.

"We couldn't have lived on this ranch or owned this land without him or you, for that matter."

"Oh, so you sacrificed your child for the land?" Zane asked.

"No. I'm not saying that. I always wanted a child, but because of you, we could all have a better life. The land was a bonus. You were the one who made the decision to leave. We made the decision to stay."

"I wish it were that simple."

Parker finally spoke. "There was a bigger picture. Look at what has happened to all of us. None of us planned the lives that we received, but look what we have done with them. There are no accidents in life. Only what we make of the things that happen to us."

"So, Iron Crow, let me ask you this: When my so-called father was off working the ranch or away on business, were you two sneaking around behind his back?"

Maggie and Parker looked at each other lovingly and then Parker answered him.

"Zane, we are human. We had our moments, but we also had our dignity. We deeply loved each other, but most important, we always loved you. We did what was best for you and all of us. We suffered when you ran away, yes, but we understood that it was the best for you. We always wanted what was best for you, but most of all, we wanted to be able to give you a better life."

"You gave me a life, but you also put me through hell. It was all a lie. All of it with him was a lie."

"We are none of us in hell now," Maggie said softly.

Zane looked at Parker, who was looking at Maggie.

"Mama, you two make it sound like it should all be okay. It was never okay what he did to you. And I couldn't protect you from him."

Maggie spoke softly, "You were a little boy and then you became a young man. You and the ranch were all that we had, and that is all that we have now. Parker and I never wished Foster ill will or for him to be dead, but his passing opened a lot of doors for all of us. The ranch is now ours and it will be yours."

"I don't care about the ranch," Zane said in a muffled voice.

"You say this now and I do understand how difficult this is for you," his mother reassured him.

Zane started pacing again, but he stopped right in front of them. "Mama, you taught me to always be truthful and to do the right thing and my entire childhood was spent with that miserable man and trying to please him, and all the time all of you were living this lie. Then I went out into the world and...." Zane was shaking his head.

Parker spoke up. "We were each living our own truth. We would never have had any of this without Foster. He made sacrifices as well, but he became very bitter about it, and he took it out on the people closest to him and the animals. We protected them and you as much as we could."

"He had no right to take it out on my mother or me. He had no right to be that way."

Maggie told him, "He was what he was, but he gave all of us a great opportunity. You were worth it, Zane. Just look at what you did for the country, how you saved Buck's life, and look at what you have done for this woman, Catherine."

"So that makes all of this okay?" He was looking back and forth between them.

"No, you make all of this okay. We are all okay, because you lived." His mother smiled softly at him.

"This is just nuts. I have to take a while to digest this." Zane smoothed his jeans down the front of his legs, stretched out his back, and headed to the stairs. "I don't get it. I don't get why that man would have allowed all of us to live in this house, his house, together, when the whole time the two of you were actually my parents."

Parker had stood up and was standing in the middle of the great room. He said, "I'm not sure he ever knew that I was your father, Zane. He never said a word to me about it—never."

Maggie walked over and stood next to Parker. "Foster was a proud man. He saw his inability to have a child as his failure."

"He was a failure as a father," Zane said.

Parker said, "But Zane, you didn't fail."

"I'm not sure I succeeded either. I'm not sure about anything anymore. It's as if the entire world has gone crazy. I'm going to bed. I'll talk to you two in the morning."

He left them standing there together in the middle of the room.

~~~~~

Zane couldn't believe what he had been told. He made his way up the old wooden stairs, worn down in the middle by hundreds of footfalls. He walked down the hall and opened the door to his room. His bags were just inside the door where he and Iron Crow had left them. He was surprised to find the room virtually the same as when he left so many years ago. It was clean, orderly,
~~~~~

and all of his things were where he had left them. He opened the closet door. It was completely empty of his clothes, but there were a few familiar boxes up on the shelf. He closed the door and lay down on the bed, folding his arms up under the pillow supporting his head.

What in the world had his mother been thinking, taking up with one man while carrying the baby of another? Her story shook him to the core. Every part of his being was shaken. On the one hand, he had never been attached to Foster Thomas Wheeler in the way a son should have been. He simply couldn't get close to him, but now Foster's attitude toward him made a whole lot more sense. On the other hand, Parker Iron Crow had been a constant even before he had been able to toddle out the front door and into the yard. He had a remembrance of being little and Parker had scooped him up and it seemed like from that moment on had kept a watchful eye on him. Now all the time Parker had spent stalking him, protecting him, guiding him also made a lot more sense. He had been teaching his own son the ways of his people and the land. The glances he had seen between Parker and his mother were now revealed as part of the secrets they kept not only from him, but from his so-called father. What a convoluted web they had woven over so many years. He couldn't help but wonder whether Foster had known the truth all along and that was part of why that man had been so miserable—a man who wanted to control every situation. It must have driven Foster nuts and constantly been eating at his gut.

Zane didn't quite know how to feel about all this. He

needed time to process it. He could understand how his mother had wanted to leave the reservation, but why would she choose this rocky road? It seemed a huge personal sacrifice to leave her family. None of her family members seemed to have actually benefited from her move, at least as far as he could figure, and certainly not while Foster had been alive. It was easier to comprehend why she picked Parker Iron Crow. He was one of the finest men you could ever meet, and he had certainly kept Zane from getting into all sorts of trouble on the ranch. It was all slowly sinking in.

His so-called father had been such a miserable man, clearly bitter, and now Zane had all the clues as to the cause. How difficult it must have been to be so powerful and feel so powerless. He could imagine the pent-up frustration that man must have felt. He wondered also about Parker and Maggie. How had his parents been engaged in this on going relationship all along right under his nose? How in the hell had they kept it from Foster, and why hadn't there been any other children? It was mind boggling and he wondered whether he would ever figure out all the pieces.

CHAPTER 30

There wasn't one thing James understood about Highberry. It looked like a scene from an old movie. The buildings in the main section of town were worn and weary. The sidewalks were narrow and the road through town was a slow moving two lane where you often had to stop because someone was backing out of a parking space in front of an old storefront. There was a café that was in constant motion with people coming and going. There was also a hardware store, a beauty salon, a furniture store, some sort of women's shop and that asshole Buck's feed store. Mixed in between were old houses that needed paint and their yards tidied. Only a few appeared to have been renovated.

He wondered what kind of people moved to this type of area and whether they were happy with their decision. On a side street, he discovered an ancient movie theater. He couldn't even imagine sitting in the worn dirty seats and viewing a movie on the mediocre screen. There was a small sewing shop that also repaired sewing machines. He didn't even know people used such things anymore. What in the world did they sew? Why not just toss it and buy something new? There was a small engine repair shop. It completely surprised him that a town like this could survive. He had no idea why someone as intelligent and educated as Catherine would want to live here. It made no sense to him. It seemed boring since there wasn't really anything to do.

He felt completely disjointed living in the old motel and eating every meal out, but it did get him into the rhythm of the town. He was observing, waiting, trying to figure out how to connect with Catherine. He couldn't just show up at her place. He was spending time sitting at the café where he could look out the window and see All Around Feed Store. He watched Buck and his customers coming and going. He refused to call her live-in by his name or anything else because the whole damn thing infuriated him. Some other man was living with his wife. How in the hell had he allowed this to happen? How did he let it happen to her? And the worst part was that he was almost certain he wasn't going to be able to fix it, but he had to try.

Finally, after a lot of hours spent watching, waiting, he saw her. She had driven right past him and he had quickly attempted to make a U-turn. She was gone by the time he pulled back on the road, headed north out of town. If his hunch were correct, she was heading to the only grocery store, so he pulled into the parking lot and searched for her vehicle. When he found it, he parked nearby and waited.

She took his breath away when she came out of the store pushing the filled grocery cart with her hair bouncing the way he loved it. She opened the rear hatch and slowly and methodically placed the bags in the back. He watched as she pushed the empty cart back to the front of the store. That was so like her. He wanted to jump out and run up to her and spill his guts, but he wouldn't do it to her. Not in the middle of a public place like this.

Catherine slowly backed out and drove away. He waited a few seconds and then fell in line two cars behind her. He would follow her, the entire time wishing he was in the car with her, talking to her, going home with her. It was making him crazy. He was obsessed with trying to figure out when to make his move.

Unaware that he was following her, Catherine headed south on Route 232. He had to admit that the scenery was peaceful. Much of the route had large oak trees hanging over the roadways, their limbs intermingling and creating a canopy. In the open spaces, beautiful pastures spotted with horses or cows were framed with a clear blue sky. Some had beautiful rolling hills with white board fences. Others had wire fencing and round bales of hay. It was a vastly different scene from the busy hubbub of New York City. It had helped him decompress somewhat in this not so fast-paced community. The people he came in contact with moved a lot slower than what he was accustomed to.

As they approached the entrance to her farm, he was the only vehicle behind her. When her right tail light began to blink, he had to fight pulling in right behind her and following her down the tree-lined drive. What the Samuel Hill was he going to do? He couldn't stand this. He had to talk to her and soon.

~~~~~

Catherine drove the car around back and unloaded the groceries through the back porch door to make it easier. She had three steps to tromp up, but then she could go straight into the kitchen and utility room with everything. The dogs greeted her, tails wagging, barking.
~~~~~

She let them go outside, except for Friskie, who was following her back and forth.

She hated cooking for one person because it wasn't much fun eating alone. She planned to invite Mrs. Matthews over for dinner. It didn't get dark until after eight, so she could cook early. She would also invite Lauren and Dr. Grant. They were right down the street and might like to come by after their hard day. She didn't like being alone one bit and she really missed Zane.

~~~~~

James was falling apart. He felt edgy, shaky inside, like his guts were going to explode. He hated being this close to Catherine and not being able to say one word to her. He had to figure out a way to get to her. He didn't know what the hell he was going to do. He was feeling completely uncomfortable in these clothes too. Walking around in boots bothered his feet and he had low back pain, most likely from the miserable bed. He had never felt so uncomfortable in his own skin. Worse, he was still having problems when he looked in the mirror. He didn't even recognize himself. He saw a strange face staring back at him. He was completely alone with no one in his corner now that he and Arianne had parted ways. He understood how Arianne felt. She was a free spirit and he knew that from the moment he met her. He had completely disrupted her life. He had been damn lucky to have her for all those months in that miserable cabin in the woods. If she hadn't been there, he most certainly would have gone insane. She had given him a reason to believe he could get to the other side of all
~~~~~

this, but reality was setting in.

No one knows what death looks like until you experience it, and his own convoluted, fabricated death had turned out to be the worst day of his life. He made the wrong decision by protecting Catherine from his truth. When he had the chance to stand in front of her, looking into her eyes, he could only hope that she would listen and accept what he had to tell her. What would have happened if he had just said it before? "Catherine, I created a product that, when given to humans, mimics a stroke, and I am going to allow it to be used to knock off a bunch of people who are a threat to the United States."

He could only imagine what her face would have looked like. She would have looked into his eyes and she would have questioned him. She would have spent a lot of her energy thinking about it, until she came to some conclusion. But, he hadn't taken that chance. He knew she would have been put at risk had anyone found out that he was the perpetrator who created the drug. He knew it had to be this way. In spite of his perfect life, he had wanted more. He had certainly received more money. Now, the money had no purpose other than to take care of her. It was the bonus at the end of a miserable journey and he was glad that he was, at the very least, able to arrange for the remainder of Catherine's life to be easier from a financial standpoint.

Meanwhile, he wondered what purpose his life held for him. Sometimes he thought death would have been easier. On the worst days, he actually wished he had been in the car at the bottom of the ravine. He would never be okay with himself until he could tell her he was sorry. All he wanted was to tell her that he hadn't intended for it to end like this. That he thought he was protecting her.

Their love had delivered him to places he had never even dreamed of. When he was with her, everything felt okay in the world. From the moment he met Catherine at Arianne's apartment, he had been smitten. When they had fallen into bed together and he had made love to her, he knew. He couldn't explain it. Catherine was the complete package. Even now, the thought of her moved him deep inside. He could taste her, smell her. He wanted desperately to feel her skin, kiss her neck, to be tight against her.

"Oh, God, my God, where the hell are you?" he shouted. "You are killing me? What the hell did I do to deserve this?"

He had found what he thought was God one night as a little boy in a dirty bed in one of the many foster homes. He had been scared to death of the man who owned the house. He and his wife had been intensely mean and the house was filthy. They were using the children to fill their pockets with money. He had made himself very small and quiet and didn't do a thing to bring any attention toward him. He lay in the dark every night, silently praying. He knew that people prayed to God, and he heard people say that their prayers were answered and so he prayed. It was on a Friday. He remembered it vividly because the mean man's wife had given him a brown paper bag and told him to gather his things. He hadn't needed a large bag as he dutifully put his few items into it. The woman had ordered him to sit on the couch in the living room, and there he sat, quietly clutching the bag to his chest. He watched out the window as a car parked out front. That was the day that he moved into the last foster home. Eventually, those people adopted him. He had been eight years old and all he had in the world were two pairs of pants, two shirts, three pair of underwear, his shoes, a toothbrush, and a comb.

His adoptive parents educated him both socially and educationally completely preparing him for entry into college. Through a lot of hard work, he had transformed himself into someone a woman like Catherine would actually give a second glance.

Recently, he had started praying again. He said a simple prayer. "God, just give me a few minutes to explain myself to her, and then I will do whatever she wants. I promise. Just give me a chance. Please and thank you." He felt child like when he said the words, but kept at it. This morning, he added, "And, please, dear Lord, help me figure out a way for me not to scare her." In the meantime, he was attempting to listen to the voice inside him that would tell him what he was actually supposed say.

CHAPTER 31

It was a perfectly clear day in Montana. The sky was deep blue, with a few clouds gathering on the horizon. Everyone on the ranch was up early, seated at the table in the kitchen. Maggie was rushing around finishing final touches on the robust breakfast she prepared for the ranch hands. Zane walked in from the great room, nodded at the men at the table, and said hello to Parker and John. He walked over to the stove and kissed his mother on the cheek.

"Boy, it has been a long time since I smelled these wonderful smells in the morning. It can't get any better than this. Coffee and bacon make you feel alive."

His mother giggled. "And I have your fry bread ready to go in the pan."

Zane kissed her again and whispered, "There really is no place like home."

He pulled out a chair as Parker began to introduce him to the ranch hands.

"This is Maggie's son, Zane Wheeler. He has come home from a long journey."

Zane nodded to Parker and slid down into the chair. He had no idea what to say to anyone. He had barely begun digesting his news from last night. This new truth meant that he wasn't actually a Wheeler at all. Did it mean he should change his last name to Iron Crow? Nothing made any sense at the moment. Serving bowls were passed, his plate filled up and his mouth was full of his mother's cooking, making it easy for him to keep quiet.

"Zane and I are going to ride out and check on the remuda this morning. I'll be riding Blue, and Zane will take the buckskin gelding."

Parker was speaking directly to a man seated next to him at the table. The older man nodded. The others continued eating their breakfast. As soon as they'd finished their meal, they thanked his mother and made their way out the back door to finish up the morning chores.

"You'd think by now you'd have some help," Zane said as he picked up several plates and silverware and carried them to the counter.

"I'm not going to have someone else in my kitchen," she scolded.

"I thought you'd be tired of it. Wouldn't you like to sit at the table and be served?"

"Heavens no. Me at the table with a bunch of men? No thank you."

"You are comical."

"I'm glad you think so. Oh, Zane, it is so good to have you home."

She wrapped her arms around his waist and gave him a hug.

"Yes, it is good to be here, but we need to sit and talk further about this news you have given me, along with some other things. Is he up on the hill?"

She nodded.

"I thought I was coming here to give him a piece of my mind, but now I'm not sure what to say to him."

Parker came into the kitchen with a pair of deerskin

gloves and handed them to Zane.

"Am I interrupting anything?"

"No, Parker, not anything that can't wait," Maggie said.

"Well, okay then. Zane, you ready to head out?"

"You bet. Mother, we will have time to sit and talk a bit later."

She followed them to the front door and watched as they mounted up and headed toward the mountains.

"Parker, don't you bring him back sleeping in that saddle like he was so many years ago," she called after them.

Zane turned and looked at her over his shoulder as Parker took off his hat and waved it at her. "See you in time for supper, Mama."

Parker settled his hat down on his head and they squeezed their horses into a lope, spewing dust up behind them.

~~~~~

Zane felt good in the warm sunlight with the rhythmic squeaking of the leather beneath him. Even with the drought and the dust, it was good to be in the wide open spaces of the ranch.

"Are you going to be able to walk tonight when we get back?" Parker chided him.

"Iron Crow, don't you even start on me. I'm not some greenhorn. Besides, I have been in the saddle, you know. Catherine has a couple horses I've been training and I have my stallion, Trouble."

"Ah, yes, the Arabians. You call those things horses?"
~~~~~

Zane knew that twinkle in Parker's eye. It was very familiar.

"Parker, you know darn good and well that all these horses on the ranch have some Arabian blood. They were crossbred with those Spanish horses. You plan to pick on them or on me?"

"Neither. Just checking how much you remember. That little bay mare I used to ride had a lot of that spunk and fire in her and she had a pretty little head to boot."

"Yes, she was a refined little mare and she'd go all day long for you."

"That she did." Parker was grinning from ear to ear.

They settled into a nice pace and Zane began to relax and take it all in. When they reached the edge of the tree line, the scenery became green and the air cleared of its heaviness and dust. They rode in silence for quite a while.

"So where do we go from here, Parker?"

"I guess that's up to you."

"I seriously don't understand how you could have kept something as important as that from me all these years."

"Everything I've ever done has been for your mother and for you."

"It couldn't have been easy, Parker. I understand that."

"The needs of many outweigh the needs of one. It wasn't about me. To me, there was no other choice. We all did what we had to do. It was important to your mother to leave the reservation. She wanted more for her life and yours. She had a different dream."

"You don't think living with that man was a hardship for her?" Zane raised his eyebrows and looked sternly at Parker.

"He wasn't always mean to her."

"I'm having trouble comprehending how he could live that lie all those years. And I don't understand you either. How could you let him do it? Not to mention, all of you having to live the lie every day."

"Foster had a completely warped image of himself. He was all wrapped up in how he appeared to the people in the community. Even if no one else did, he held himself in the highest regard and to him what he controlled outweighed everything else."

"He didn't need to control my mother."

"In the beginning, as a young woman, she didn't know any better, but it didn't take her long to figure it out. Your mother is a very clever woman, and eventually, she got everything she ever wanted. When Foster died, the ranch passed to her."

"Well, bravo for her. I guess she got her dream, but the whole time her life was a complete lie."

"No, not exactly. It was her truth. Don't you think some people knew something wasn't right? She had people who supported her and she made her own choices."

Parker turned his horse up a narrow trail and Zane had to follow single file behind him.

"Just because some people surmised something, it didn't make any of it right."

"What is right, Zane? People do what they have to do to survive. From the little bit I know about what you were up to all these years, you had to step over that line many times. You weren't raised learning how to kill people. You did what you had to do because you signed up for it. Your mother did the same thing."

"I can see a little of what you are saying, but then, didn't she use him to get the ranch?"

"What else was he going to do with all this? It had to go to someone when he died. Maybe this was the best thing for him too. He didn't care whose kid you were, really. What he cared about was that people thought he had a kid. You just happened to be that kid. Your mother protected all of this for you."

"It seems so messed up."

"I'm sure this sort of thing happens more often than we want to know. Tell me that you always walked in truth. People talk about a rat in the wood-pile. Well, I guess you could sort of call me that rat."

"I don't even know how to wrap my mind around that, and I certainly wouldn't call you a rat."

They rode down the other side of the ridge and came to a creek. They dismounted and let the horses take a long drink of the cool clear water. Zane took his hat off and smacked it on his knee to shake off the dust.

Parker walked his horse over to him and stood looking into his face. "I understand this came as a complete surprise to you, totally out of the blue. You came home to set things right with your mother and you planned to say some words to your father, and now you find out he wasn't your father at all. It's a lot to accept. Just know that your mother and I always had your best interest in our hearts. There was nothing we did that we didn't think about how it would affect you."

"It's going to take a while to redirect my thoughts on

all of this."

"I understand."

"I'm not sure you do, Parker."

"Well, then let me say this—I will have an open heart and a steady shoulder if you want to lean on me, son."

He knew every inch of Parker Iron Crow's face, the way he moved his hands, and the way he walked. He had watched him closely during all his childhood years, and he couldn't imagine how he hadn't realized how much they were alike.

~~~~~

They were riding in an area that Zane knew well. It was the canyon where every spring he and Iron Crow caught the horses. They worked their way quietly up the ridge and found the herd standing below them at the water hole.

"Damn, Parker. They are looking good considering the drought."

There were horses of every color, mares with weanlings and yearlings, and one very sturdy blue roan standing with its nose stuck in the air, staring straight up at them.

"We've been pretty lucky. This higher elevation is getting some precipitation and the grass has been okay."

"That's a nice looking horse, that blue. Say, I have to ask. Have you been up to the cave lately?"

"No. There hasn't been a reason to go. We had a young man who was interested in the cave and I did take him, but it has been a few years ago. Why? Were you thinking we needed to pay it a visit?"
~~~~~

"I guess I'm a little curious. You know I had quite an experience when I was in there with you. I never forgot it. I've been telling Catherine about it, and she's very good at putting it on paper."

"This woman sounds intriguing."

"She is. She is very beautiful, intelligent, and it is a damn shame her life took such an unexpected turn."

"But it sounds like you were in exactly the right spot at the right time. Your mother told me you have been helping her."

"Well, it started out that way. I was taking care of her farm while she went to care for her uncle for a few days. It turned out to be several months once she discovered he was terminally ill."

"But it seems that it was okay for both of you in the end, wasn't it?" Parker asked.

The herd nervously circled, stirring up a cloud of dust. Parker turned his horse and began the descent down the ridge. Zane braced himself in his stirrups because it was steeper than he remembered as a child.

"While she was away, we started talking on the phone out of necessity. She would call to check on her animals. I was doing some things for her in the house and I discovered quite a bit about her from her scrapbooks and other items. She is a caring person who ran a foundation that assisted children. She abruptly gave it all up when her husband died."

"Her husband died?"

"Well, not exactly. First, they told her that he had been killed in an automobile accident, but then she found out that he had been murdered. She doesn't know that he's actually alive. It was all a convoluted means to protect them both."

"It sounds complicated. Protect them from what?"

"It is complicated. He was involved with this government deal. It's a messy long story. Technically, I'm not sure if she's still married to him, since he's not dead. Right now, I'm trying to decide whether to tell her the truth or keep it to myself. The glitch is that they have turned her husband loose from protective custody, and I think he's trying to make contact with her."

"What makes you think that?" Parker asked.

"The last photo of them together before his so-called accident suddenly popped up in a file on her laptop."

"How does that happen?"

"I'm not sure; plus she's getting mysterious phone calls where no one says a thing, but she thinks she can hear someone breathing."

Parker shot him a look and asked, "And you left her there alone?"

"Not completely. Buck isn't too far from her, and there's someone helping her every day with barn chores. Lauren comes and goes."

Zane eased deeper into the seat of the saddle and adjusted it back to center. They skirted a group of trees and then headed back on a different trail. The scent of pine was thick in the air. It felt good to have the sun on his face, the wide blue sky above, and the company of his old...God, he didn't even know what to call Parker at this point.

"Are you comfortable with that, her being alone there?" Parker's question jolted Zane back from his thoughts.

"I have to be. Coming home to see my mother and

you needed to happen while the weather was good both here and there. This is an easier time of year for her as far as leaving the horses out on pasture."

"I get that, but aren't you worried about her safety?"

"She has six dogs in the house with her, and most of them go in and out with her when she does the chores."

"Six?" Parker sounded surprised.

"I think she got a little spooked when she first moved there, and she may have been trying to fill the void left when her husband suddenly died. She was pretty traumatized."

"I could understand that."

"Well, I don't think he'd do anything to hurt her. They had what appeared to be a good marriage." Zane certainly hoped so.

"Still, it would shake her up to see someone who is supposed to be dead."

"She won't recognize him."

"What do you mean?" Parker asked.

"They did reconstructive surgery. They do that to people now. They simply gave the poor sap a new face."

Parker whistled. "There is something wrong with that picture."

"I know, but that's what happens when you make a deal with the United States Government. They made him believe he was a national hero for protecting the people. Then they forced him to recreate himself and that included giving up his life and his appearance. I don't think she will know it is him until he tells her."

"That's really not right."

"I know. The worst part is that if he connects with her, she will figure out that I was keeping it from her and that might do me in."

Parker took a deep breath and let out a slow low whistle.

"No wonder you wanted to retire from that mess." Parker shook his head.

"This stuff with Catherine happened after I retired, but yes, that, and I felt responsible for Buck's near fatality, what with him being shot, then all the technology and crap that was going on. It was just time to get out."

"It doesn't sound to me like you are out of it yet."

Zane drifted off for a few minutes in thought and then he told Parker, "Who knew that a simple decision to say goodbye to Buck before I headed out here would evolve into something as screwed up as all this."

Parker answered, "You know that I believe everything happens for a reason. Speaking of which, that day you were in the cave, refresh my memory on exactly what happened in there?"

They were in an area of flat plains with grasses clear up to the bellies of their horses, who were grabbing bites as they walked along. Zane had forgotten the sweet smell that floated on the wind. There were wild roses and flowers of every color in all directions as far as he could see. The mountains made the perfect blue and green backdrop. There were still small caps of snow on the mountains up in the higher elevations. It was almost too beautiful to be real.

Zane took a deep breath of the sweet air and said, "I never told you all the details, did I? I left so abruptly because of my father....Shit, I can't even call him that anymore."

Lost in their thoughts Zane and Parker rode in silence for a while. Zane slapped a large horse fly off the shoulder of his horse with the end of his rein and finally spoke.

"When it became completely dark down in the belly of the cave and you started humming and playing your drum, something came over me. I had never seen darkness that black ever in my life before and then all of a sudden out of that black, a mountain lion came running straight at me. At first, it terrified me. The cat came three times. Every time his mouth was wide open and I could see his teeth, his tongue, down into his throat, and those big yellow piercing eyes. The third time as he charged me, he turned into a warrior. The top half of his face was painted red; the bottom half was painted black, and white circled his mouth. He had bear fur and feathers all around his face and two buffalo horns that were turned down, one on each side of his head. Like I said, I was terrified, and yet I couldn't stop looking at him. I stopped breathing. And then he abruptly thrust out his hand right in front of me up into my face. He said, 'The people are like the beads. They flow off your fingers into a beautiful pattern. So it is with the people. Now go and tell the people,' and just like that he was gone."

"That had to be intense for you."

"I didn't allow myself to think about it too much because it did startle me."

"And did you ever come to terms with it?" Parker asked.

"Later on, I thought that maybe it tied in with me working with people and trying to make things better.

The beads represented the people and it was my task to try and make them flow into a better pattern on the planet."

"That was profound thinking for a young man."

"I don't think I realized the true significance until later in life. Catherine has these medicine cards that she uses that tell about the power of the ways of the animals and I looked up the mountain lion in her book one afternoon. I was surprised that it also tied in with being a leader among men. It said something about placing you in a position to be a target for the problems of other people. That seemed to fit, given the work that Buck and I had chosen."

"I understand what you mean."

"It also talked about the abuse of power and not getting caught up in it. It said to follow where you heart leads you. It made me believe that I had made the correct choice in leaving when I did and even now with not totally abandoning Catherine. At any point, I could have easily loaded my horse in the trailer and driven my truck the heck out of there."

Parker asked him, "What made you stay?"

"It was the right thing to do for another human being who was in a tough spot. The book said that you must stand on your own convictions and take the time to review your own personal belief system. Being on her farm by myself while she was caring for her uncle gave me plenty of time to sit and ponder."

"I get it. That's what I do when I ride out here. I did miss you a lot when you left and I often wondered if we had made the right decisions about you."

"Did my father, I mean, do you think he ever figured

it out?"

"We can call him Foster, if you like. I think he had an idea about it, but he didn't ever say a word to me about it."

"I'm not sure I understand that. The final part about the mountain lion said that you can't make everyone happy unless you lie to yourself and to others. The first responsibility is to tell the truth. At the same time, isn't responsibility the ability to respond to any situation? I guess that's what the two of you did here and I did with my life. At least, that's my take on it at this point in time, Iron Crow."

"One thing for certain, Zane, there isn't a one of us that can go back and change it, but we sure as heck can make better decisions now."

"I hope we keep that in the forefront. I want Catherine to come out here and take a break from everything. I believe the wide open spaces would be good for her."

"What's his name wouldn't be able to get to her here, dogs or no dogs. Are you going to ask her to come out?"

"Catherine knew I needed to spend time with my mother, asking her to forgive me and making amends. And, I intended to go up on the hill and have a chat with the man I thought was my father. And last, I need to figure out whether to be mad at you or grateful."

"I'm hopeful."

"I don't think you will be disappointed."

Parker pulled up his horse. They dismounted and he and Zane pulled hobbles and their lunches out of their saddle bags. They sat on the rocks and watched the horses graze, eating what his mother had fixed for them and enjoying the sun and the winds of Montana.

They had ridden back into the yard dirty and tired, but content with just enough time to clean up for dinner.

~~~~~

That evening, Zane and Parker were sitting in the great room chatting over coffee.

"I'm telling you things haven't changed enough for the Blackfeet Nation. They say a nation is nothing more than a collection of individuals. What's happening is that many of the individuals are not on the same page. Plus, there aren't as many traditionals left."

Parker and Zane were deep in a discussion when Maggie joined them.

Zane said, "I understand that they didn't create these problems. I also understand that in today's world, survival depends on your ability to adapt to the competition. Their traditional lifestyle seems to be dying like the buffalo." He set his coffee cup on the old worn coffee table.

"One of the biggest problems is the ability of non-Blackfeet to buy tribal land. These pockets of non-Native owners can create problems."

"I thought all the land belonged to the tribe and had to stay within the tribe."

"Some of the people mortgaged their land. When they can't pay the mortgage, the bank forecloses, and then the land is out of the hands of the tribe. There is nothing we can do unless the tribe can negotiate with the bank."
~~~~~

"That's not right. I remember a time when the elders prided themselves on their physical prowess and ability to outwit the white people. Now it seems like the banks are taking advantage of an unfortunate situation." Zane was perplexed.

"I agree. Outsiders are also defying our holy places. For a time, they were allowing all people to go up McCann Butte at the Bear Paw Mountains. I know there is a big fight about it over there. Can you imagine? That is the sacred point of the four directions. The wind blows so strong up there you can't help but clear your mind of all thoughts and feel the unidentifiable presence of spirit."

Zane said, "Tell me that they didn't win that one."

"So far they have not. There was a strong outpouring of opposition. They eventually quit that nonsense."

"Thank God." Zane watched his mother quietly sewing beads onto a piece of deerskin. It sent him back to many nights when they had quietly sat together after Foster had gone upstairs to bed.

"The power is still up there, but it seems like it is more divisive and you have to look for it," Parker told him.

"Well, at least you can still go looking for it."

Maggie spoke softly, "I have enough going on here without having to go look for my power. Besides, I see God's power in this land and in the two of you." She had that expression on her face of secretly knowing something as she grinned at both of them.

CHAPTER 32

The dinner table was set and Catherine was busy in the kitchen putting the final touches on a garden salad. She placed a small bowl in a larger metal bowl lined with ice. They could come into the kitchen and serve themselves whatever food they wanted and then sit comfortably at the kitchen table. It would be cozy and conversation should flow easily from the round table.

Dr. Grant had managed to clear her schedule, and she and Lauren were arriving together. Effie Matthews called and said she was on her way. The dogs let her know that Dr. Grant's vehicle was coming down the driveway, and right behind her was Buck's white truck driven by his mother. It seemed strange to see a tiny white-haired lady climb out of a pick-up truck. Catherine greeted her company at the front door—something she seldom got to do.

"Come in. Come in. I'm so glad you could come. I'm excited to have you here."

Effie handed Catherine a small bouquet of flowers and Dr. Grant handed her a bottle of wine.

"Thank you. I'll put the flowers in a vase, and we will have this wine opened in no time. Come in and we'll sit here in the living room for now."

The dogs were making a nuisance of themselves, wagging tails and mingling between everyone. Catherine told them, "Come on, guys; give the ladies a break. Champ, come."

Lauren grabbed Champ by the collar and headed him toward the kitchen. The old dog liked her and was happy to be on the cooler floor as he quickly lay down near the doorway leading out onto the back porch. Lauren joined the other ladies in the living room once she'd sufficiently petted Champ. The other dogs had found their spots as well. Friskie followed close on Catherine's heels.

"Everyone want wine?" Catherine asked as she walked into the living room with a tray containing four gold-rimmed wine glasses and set it on the coffee table. She whisked the bottle of wine from under her arm and quickly produced a corkscrew from her pocket and removed the cork. They chatted about the recent storms, someone mentioned the sinkhole that had opened up in Micanopy, and then Catherine asked whether they were ready to eat.

After dinner while they were eating dessert, Effie brought it up.

"I am so happy Zane has finally gone to Montana to see his mother and Parker Iron Crow."

"Yes. I've only heard from him once since he left. I hope things are going well for him. He must be busy."

"We are hoping the same. Buck never understood how he could stay away so long."

"Well, I don't know too much about it, but I understand that he and his father didn't get along very well. He said the man was somewhat difficult with the way he treated people."

"He was a tough man, but he managed to run a very successful ranch. I have to say, though, he wasn't much fun to be around."

Mrs. Matthews hadn't elaborated, but Zane had told Catherine enough to give her an inkling of what that meant. Dr. Grant interrupted them, saying she and Lauren needed to call it an early night. They said their goodbyes and Effie and Catherine were left standing at the front door.

"Catherine, I have something I want to ask you."

Effie refused a cup of coffee, saying it would keep her awake and they sat in the living room in the barrel chairs on either side of the front window.

"Catherine, dear, are you doing okay with Zane gone?"

"Yes, I think so. It is lonely at night, but Lauren is here during the day and I have the chores to keep me busy. Plus the dogs are good company."

"My husband, Roan, arrives next week. He knows his way around a ranch, so if you need anything at all while Zane is gone, honey, you let me know and I'll get him right over here."

"That is so sweet of you, Mrs. Matthews."

"I would love it if you would call me Effie. Please, don't take this the wrong way, but how well do you know this Deb Albom?"

"I first met her when I was looking for property. She was my realtor. She wasn't too happy with me for a bit because she thought I was interested in Buck."

"You don't say. Well, I shouldn't mention anything, but there's something bothering me about that situation. Don't get me wrong—she's great with the two babies—but I can't quite put my finger on it. I have this feeling there is more to this woman. I don't want to say anything to Buck, but I certainly don't want him to be hurt."

"I haven't spent that much time with her. She was quite flamboyant when I first met her. She wore colorful flowing clothes, and she was loud and flirty. Once she and Buck settled in, she became quieter and dressed differently. That's all. And for someone who was pregnant, she really slimmed down. Her entire appearance and demeanor changed."

"Well, I suppose time will tell, my dear. Thank you. I better get back over there."

Catherine gave Effie a hug and watched until the truck taillights disappeared when she turned onto the main road and drove out of sight. Catherine had to admit that she had similar feelings at times about Deb.

~~~~~

It was after nine o'clock when she finished with the dishes and wiped the kitchen counter. She was about to go out to the barn to do night hay when the telephone rang. Once again, the caller ID said "Unknown Name."

"Hello." There was silence. "Hello. Will you please answer me?" There was dead silence. "Excuse me. Is anyone there?" The phone clicked. It infuriated her that someone would do that. What kind of person would do that? She couldn't help but wonder who it could possibly be and the person's intention? Then the phone rang again. She grabbed it.

"Would you mind telling me who you are?" she shouted into the phone.

"Sure, I mind, because by now you should recognize my voice."

"Zane, it's you. Oh my God! Did you try to call me a
~~~~~

minute ago?"

"No. Not me. Why?"

"Oh, that stupid thing about the phone ringing and no one is there."

"So that's happening again?"

"Yes, right now, a few minutes ago. This is the third time."

"I'm sorry. Are you okay? Do you need me to come home?"

She could tell by his voice that he was genuinely concerned. "No and what are you sorry about? Some idiot is trying to annoy me." As she spoke, she realized that he had said the words "come home."

"I just hate that you are being bothered by someone like this."

"I want to nail them, but their number is blocked, so I can't identify who it is."

"I'm serious. I will leave here tomorrow if you need me. How is everything else?"

"No. You just got there. I want you to have time with your mother. I think I'll be fine. I finished cleaning up the kitchen a few minutes ago. I had Mrs. Matthews, Dr. Grant, and Lauren over for dinner. I was just about to go out to the barn."

"Oh good, that must have been nice for you."

"Yes, it was very nice. Mrs. Matthews said her husband is coming and she offered to have him help me."

"You won't meet a finer man than Buck's father. Roan definitely knows ranching."

"She assured me that she'd get him right over here if I need him."

"How's the grass?" Zane asked.

"The grass, oh, you mean mowing? I'm keeping up with it. Lauren mowed the pasture with the trees. She's very good to have around."

"It makes me feel better that you have all these people backing you up until I get back."

"Was your mother surprised?" Catherine wanted to hear all about it.

"She was very surprised when this strange man ran up on the porch and grabbed her."

Catherine laughed as a tear slid silently down her cheek. She really missed him. Her emotions were raw, but she didn't want to let him know she was also scared.

"I bet that did shock her. Is everything else okay?"

"It's a long story. I have a lot to tell you, but yes, everything else is okay. It's very dry out here, so if you're having rain, send it this way."

"No rain so far. Are you really going to make me wait to find out what else happened?"

"Yes, I'm afraid so."

"Zane, you love doing that to me."

"No, it's more a matter of processing something this time. I need to process it myself. I promise you, I will tell you all of it when we can sit down together."

"I guess I don't have any choice then, do I?"

"None at all. So, do the dogs miss me?"

"The dogs? I think Trouble misses you more. Every time I open the back door, his head pops up."

"Yeah, I kind of miss him too."

"You aren't about to say it are you?"

"Say what?" He was teasing her.

"That you miss me?"

"You want me to say it to you on the phone?"

"Zane, seriously?" she interrupted him.

"I do love messing with you, Catherine, and, of course, I miss you." He chuckled.

She loved hearing his voice and imagined the twinkle in his eyes, the curve of his lips and his dimples. She also knew that going to see his mother was exactly what he had needed.

He told her "Okay, then. I guess I'll check on you again tomorrow. Call Buck right away if you need anything. Ask him if he knows of any way to trace that caller."

"All right, I'll ask him the next time I'm in the feed store."

"Don't wait. Call him in the morning. Okay?"

"I'll be okay."

"I promise you, I will come home in a heart beat if you need me."

She didn't want to hang up the phone. Catherine wanted to tell him to catch the very next plane. She wanted to tell him that she really felt scared. Instead, she held her breath. She had this sinking feeling in the pit of her stomach that everything was about to change again. Champ pushed her hand with his cold wet nose. She opened the back door, let all the dogs out into the still evening night, and hurried to the barn.

CHAPTER 33

James had finally figured out a way to contact Catherine. He dialed her number prepared to speak this time. When she answered, he disguised his voice. "Hello, Mrs. DeLong. My name is James Robert Campbell. I'm a freelance writer and I was wondering if I could interview you for an article I'm writing for the local paper."

"I'm afraid I'm not sure why you would want to interview me."

"I understand that you recently moved to Highberry and I'm writing about career changes and what is bringing people to this area."

"I really don't believe anyone would find me all that interesting."

"I beg to differ. I have heard that you were involved in publishing, started your own non-profit organization, and now you are operating a small ranch. That's quite a career change."

"I can't argue with that, but I promise you, my life is pretty boring."

"There isn't any way I can convince you to let me interview you? I'll come to you."

He could hear the hesitation in Catherine's voice. He had to convince her to let him talk to her. "I promise that you will find it worthwhile to sit down with me." He certainly wasn't lying about that. He'd make it worthwhile because he would finally have the opportunity to explain to her what actually happened with their lives.

"I'm not sure I want to expose myself. Where is this article going to be printed?"

"In the little town newspaper, nothing huge, we are simply trying to lure other people into the area by showing our diverse population."

"I didn't know the town has a newspaper."

"See, all the more reason to let me come speak to you. Can I set a time, maybe later today?" James was desperate.

"Oh, I'm not sure."

"I can come this afternoon. I only need thirty minutes." He was sweating.

"Oh, I hate this, but I guess I'll do it."

"I promise it will turn out okay."

"How is two o'clock?"

"I'll make it work."

James didn't want to seem anxious, but he was. He had been hoping for this opportunity for a very long time.

"Do you need directions to the farm?" Catherine asked.

"No, no. I'll use my GPS." James was relieved when Catherine relented. He would finally get the moment with her he'd been fantasizing about. He had nothing to lose at this point in his life. He could feel and hear his heart pounding in his chest.

<div style="text-align:center">~~~~~</div>

Catherine wrote his name on the pad by the telephone. She had purposely agreed to meet James Robert Campbell at two o'clock when she was certain

Lauren would be there. She didn't need some strange man coming around when she was alone. She wished she had asked the name of the paper so she could have called to make sure, but it was too late now. His name made her feel uneasy. James. James. James. What the hell happened to their life? Every time things began to level out, something as simple as someone's name would set her off. The unexplained silent phone calls and Zane being out of town made her feel edgy. As soon as Lauren pulled her car up to the barn, Catherine called her over to the house.

"Lauren, there's some reporter coming here at two o'clock from the town newspaper to interview me. I would appreciate it if you could keep an eye on the situation. I'm very gun shy since because I've had some mysterious phone calls."

"I understand, Miss Catherine. What town newspaper?"

"He said he was writing a story for the town newspaper."

"I'll have to ask my dad, but I don't know of any town newspaper, Miss Catherine, unless you are talking about the *Gainesville News*. That's the paper we read."

"He didn't mention the name and please, don't tell me that. I'm already nervous about this anyway. Just please keep an eye out for me. I'm going to keep him outside. We will sit in the lawn chairs up by the house."

"Do you want me to call Dad? I have my cell phone."

"No. I'm sure it will be okay. People don't go around making things like that up, do they?"

"I'm not sure about anything these days, ma'am."

~~~~~

Catherine let the dogs out the back porch door and walked around the house into the front yard. As promised, James Robert Campbell pulled up to the front of her house promptly at two o'clock. As soon as he exited his vehicle, the dogs ran up to the man. He was turning in a circle, trying to keep his eyes on them. Several of them were barking loudly.

He was about 5'10" or 11", brown hair, slender build, wearing what appeared to be brand new jeans, a crisp long-sleeved red plaid western-style shirt and brown boots. He had on a belt with a large silver buckle.

As she approached him, she caught the scent of a very familiar aftershave. She thrust out her hand, which he took in his, but he didn't shake it. Instead, he gently held on to her.

"Good afternoon," she said. "Would you like to join me here in the yard? I have some nice lawn chairs." Catherine slid her hand out of his grasp and turned away from him.

"Sure. No problem," he said. As he followed her, some of the dogs began to growl while others were sniffing his pants. Catherine told them to settle down.

"Here, sit right here. This will be fine." Catherine sat on one of the cushioned chairs and motioned for him to sit across from her on the loveseat. There was an ornamental metal coffee table with a glass top between them. James sat down obediently and she stared at him for a few seconds, studying his face. Something made him seem oddly familiar. His features were chiseled. He had a high forehead and slender, pointed nose. She
~~~~~

glanced away when he looked directly into her eyes. There was something about him that made her feel uneasy. She shook her hair back out of her face, pushed it behind her ears, and said, "Well, where do you want to start? Fire your questions at me."

It was at that moment that Catherine wondered why someone who was about to interview her didn't have a notebook. He had absolutely nothing to write on or with, and he didn't even appear to have a tape recorder. It made her uneasy again, almost heading into a bit of panic.

"Catherine, I need to explain something to you."

The way he said her name was eerily familiar. A chill traveled quickly up her spine, and she felt something stir in the middle of her gut that made her sit up straighter.

"Is this some sort of trick? Are you really with the newspaper? Is there even a local newspaper? Why are you really here?" She grasped the arms of the chair and started to get up.

"Wait just a minute. Stop and sit here for a moment and I'll explain it all to you. Just give me a second. I'm not trying to upset you."

She didn't like the tone in his voice.

"Upset me? Upset me about what?"

"I'm not sure we should be doing this out here in the open. Could we go inside?"

"No. I don't know you. I'm not comfortable with this. I think that you should..."

He quickly interrupted her. "Catherine, there's no easy way to say this to you. Don't you recognize my voice; the scent of your favorite aftershave?"

She sank deep into her chair, slid her hand to her throat. Then she covered her face with both of her hands. She didn't want to hear what he was about to say.

"If you will listen to me, I can explain everything."

Catherine sat with her hands still covering her eyes, but worse, she had the urge to cover her ears so that she couldn't hear a thing he was about to say. She didn't want to look at him.

"Look at me, Catherine. You do know it's me, don't you? I know this isn't making any sense to you. I know you didn't recognize me, but I can explain. I need to explain this to you. I need you to look at me."

She hadn't said anything. She didn't want to. She didn't want this to be happening at all. She slowly lowered her hands from her face, looked at him, and said, "Your face. What happened to your face, James? The accident? My God, I thought you were dead. You were dead."

"No. The surgery on my face didn't have anything to do with the accident. I wasn't in the car. I wasn't in any accident."

She could feel the blood draining from her face. "But there was a body in the car. You are supposed to be dead. They told me...." Her voice trailed off.

"Yes, but that wasn't me. That man was already dead when they put him in the car."

"You, you weren't even in the car? You...but they told me you died in the accident. I saw your body at the...." She stopped talking.

"Just let me tell you the story."

"The story? This isn't a story, James. This was

about our lives."

"I know. Believe me. I know. I didn't have any idea about the control the government was going to have on us, on me."

"You didn't know? You kept all this from me and then it became one more lie after another as you manipulated me with.... Oh, my God, James. It is you. I can't believe this is happening. The phone calls. Are you the one who's been calling me? And..., and the picture? Did you put the picture on my computer? Have you been stalking me?"

"Stalking you? No. No! I was trying to figure out a way to talk to you without scaring you. I wanted to hear your voice."

"Scaring me? Didn't you think that finding out that you had careened off a cliff and died was going to scare me? Do you have any idea how scared I was? I never had to live alone before. I never made decisions like this alone before. Don't you think the phone calls were scaring me now?"

"I know."

"You know. That's all you can say. That you know. You have no idea. I gave up our apartment, everything we owned in the apartment, my life, my job. And all you can say is that you know and all the time you were actually alive. Oh, and now you want to waltz in here and tell me a story. Well, tell me the story about where you have been all these months. Better yet, tell me who you have been with."

"Catherine, it's not like that. It's not like you have been by yourself either. I know all about him."

"Oh, my God, you think you know what about him?"

"Yes, I know about Zane what's his name and I know about Roger and Buck too."

"How dare you? I attended your funeral and now you think you are going to stand there and chastise me as if I've done something wrong. I had no knowledge that you were alive. I buried you and now you want to treat me like I did something wrong by moving on with my life. Oh, no! You don't get to do that to me! What the hell were you doing? Please tell me that you honored our marriage vows because you were alive and you knew that some day you'd be able to explain this to me. Tell me that you...."

He thrust his hands up in the air and blurted out, "You can't expect me to have..."

She cut him off. "Oh, my God, James, our entire life became a lie. You threw away everything. You were the one who made the decision not to include me. From the minute you discovered that chemical combination to create that drug, you decided to exclude me from all of it. You didn't trust me, and yet here you are now, expecting me to trust you. Look what a mess you made of our lives. Oh, no you don't! You don't get to do this. And I suppose you want me to forgive you. Is that why you concocted yet another lie in order to come to my house?"

"Catherine, I love you. I have always loved you. I never expected it to turn out this way, but I certainly never stopped loving you."

Lauren suddenly appeared and interrupted them. "Is everything all right, Miss Catherine? Do you need me for anything?"

Catherine watched James' head pop around toward

the young woman standing at the rear of his car. She quickly answered her. "Thank you, Lauren. I'm okay at the moment, but I do appreciate your checking. Thank you."

"Well, I'll be right nearby if you need me."

"Yes. That will be good. Thank you."

As soon as Lauren walked away, James snapped at her, "Who the hell is that?"

"That is none of your business. James, honestly, what did you think was going to happen? You suddenly come back to life and I'm supposed to run into your arms? No. I don't think so. I've had a lot of time to think about this. I've been sick about it for more than a year and a half. No! You are the same man who stood holding my hands on our wedding day looking into my eyes and making those promises to me. You broke every one of them. I was heartbroken, suffering, and you must have already been with Arianne. When I couldn't get an answer on her phone and she wasn't at her apartment, I began to wonder where she had gone. Now it's all beginning to make sense to me. She was with you."

"Catherine."

"Don't say anything else, James. Please."

She was shaking uncontrollably. She couldn't get over how different he looked. It was very difficult to see any similarity to the strikingly handsome face that she had loved so much. He simply didn't look or behave like her beloved James.

"The fucking government had me under protective custody. They have been controlling me. They just released us from protective custody."

"Oh, so you are admitting she was with you. You

just said 'us.' How convenient for you to be able to blame them, the United States Government, for forcing you to sleep with Arianne. I thought I knew you, James, but honestly, I literally do not recognize any part of you anymore."

He appeared stunned as he slumped back onto the loveseat. She knew he deserved every squirming minute of it.

"James, you can pretend that you can fix this. You can think that I will forgive you, but how could I ever forgive you? You completely lied to me and for a long time."

His tone of voice had changed. "Catherine, I lied to myself. I thought it was the most remarkable opportunity to prove myself to my country."

"That is possibly the only thing you've said that's believable. But you certainly must have known you could have trusted me."

"I thought it was the only way to protect you. If you didn't know, they wouldn't come after you. It was my way of keeping you safe."

"How would they have known that I knew about the drug? It makes no sense. I was in danger anyway. Do you know if we are still in danger?"

"Nothing makes any sense anymore, Catherine."

"I beg to differ. My life is making more sense right now than it ever has. I'm happy. I'm happy and I'm not going to let your decision to come here stop me from doing exactly what I am doing. I like my life now."

"I can't imagine why you want to be in this ridiculous community."

"I don't care what you can or can't imagine. You

don't get a say in my life anymore. I loved you. I trusted you, but I could never trust you again."

"I understand that I ruined everything for both of us."

"Not just for us, James. You ruined things for yourself and a lot of other people, but I refuse to allow you to ruin it for me."

"Where do we go from here, Catherine?"

"We? We don't go anywhere from here, James. We don't exist anymore. That died that night the car careened off the ravine, and unfortunately for you, this is my story."

"Catherine, we could make this work. Don't you want to make this work? We were so good together."

"No, James. It's far too late for us. I don't want to be connected to any of that or you ever again."

"Catherine, please...."

"No, James. I can't go back. We can't go back. It is truly over. It just is. It is simply what happened."

"I didn't think it would end like this."

"Maybe it would have turned out differently if you had trusted me and we had walked the entire walk together, making decisions along the way, but you decided to leave me out of it. This is where I am, James. I'm out of your life. Please, you have to let it go. You have to let me go."

"Catherine...."

"No, James. Please, just go."

"I want to hug you. I need to hold you. Please, just let me kiss you goodbye."

"No. Not any more, James. Please go. Go now."

She caught the motion of a car as it began to drive

slowly down the driveway toward them. The small black car pulled right up to where they were standing. The door quickly opened and Arianne stepped out. Catherine couldn't believe that Arianne had come to her house. "Oh, my God, are you going to put yourself in the middle of this now. Get out of here, both of you. Just get out of here."

The dogs came running from all directions and Lauren came hurriedly across the yard from the barn as Catherine raised her voice. "Please get out of here now!" she shouted. "Both of you get out of here!"

CHAPTER 34

The feed store was particularly slow, and Buck was thumbing through a magazine with his feet propped on the counter when the phone rang. It was Deb.

"Hi, Buck. How's it going?"

"Slow; it's very slow. I think it's because it's so hot. Everyone is waiting for late afternoon so it's cooler."

"I bet you are right. The babies just went down for their nap and I noticed a little heat rash around Diddie's neck. Can you bring home some baby powder that has corn starch in it?"

"You betcha."

"Okay, honey. Thanks. See you this evening."

"No problem. Love you."

He had barely placed the phone on the cradle when it rang again.

"What did you forget?" he asked without saying the store name or even hello.

"I didn't forget anything, Buck. It's Bill."

"Sorry, I thought you were someone else calling me back."

"Say, what's the status on your buddy and his broad?" Bill asked.

"Who are you talking about—Zane?"

"Yeah, what's going on with them?"

"Zane is in Montana and Catherine is here. Why?"

"Oh, I heard a rumor that James was on the move. Someone saw him on a flight out of New York; seems he was headed to Jacksonville."

Buck was trying to pull the pieces of the puzzle together. "I thought you said they weren't tailing him."

"Pure happenstance as one of our guys who had been in Montana with them saw him at the airport, recognized him, snapped a photo, and checked it out."

"Shit."

"I know. Where do you think he's headed?"

"You know exactly where's he's headed. Let me call you back."

Buck hung up the phone, found Catherine's number on the computer, and dialed. He barely recognized her voice when she answered.

"Hello, Catherine; is that you?"

"Yes, I have a cold."

"They say those summer colds are the worst. You sound terrible." He wasn't buying her story.

"Yeah, it's not much fun. Can I help you?"

"I was calling to see if everything is okay."

"Yes. Sort of," she lied.

"What does that mean?"

"Oh, it's okay. I think it will be okay."

"Did something happen? Is Lauren there?"

"Lauren just left. No, she's not here. Everything is okay, though."

"Well, all right then. You would tell me if I could help with anything, wouldn't you?"

"Yes. Yes, I would. Thank you, Buck." She was relieved to get rid of him so easily. She had a headache from trying not to cry.

~~~~~
~~~~~

Buck pulled out his wallet and located a hand written tattered card with phone numbers. He quickly dialed his old store phone.

As soon as she answered, he said, "Hi, Mrs. Wheeler, this is Buck. Is Zane around?"

"Well, hello, Buck. How are you?"

"Oh, I'm good, Mrs. Wheeler. Everything is fine. I just have a question for him."

"I'll get him. Hold on a minute. It's good to hear your voice."

Buck heard Zane walk across the wooden floor.

"Hello."

"Hey, Zane, it's Buck."

"Hey, man. What's up?"

"I'm just giving you a heads up because you need to give Catherine a call. It seems that James is on the move. They got an eyeball on him and he was headed to the Jacksonville airport."

"Oh crap!"

"My sentiments, exactly. I called Catherine and she said she was coming down with a cold. She doesn't sound right. Something's not right there."

"Okay, buddy. I'll give her a call right now."

"Let me know what you find out."

"Thanks, Buck."

"No problem, man."

Buck scrolled down on his cell phone, found Bill's received call and pushed the button. "Hey, Bill. I haven't found out anything, but I'll get back to you if I need you."

"Good deal. Keep me posted."

~~~~~

Zane quickly dialed Catherine's number.

"Hello."

He was relieved to hear her voice. "Catherine, it's Zane." He heard her take a deep breath.

"Zane, oh my God, I was hoping to hear from you."

"Are you okay? What's going on? Are you sick? You don't sound right."

"No, I'm okay. I just had a bit of an upset."

"What happened?"

"I don't know if I should tell you."

"Of course, you should tell me. What's going on?"

"This man called earlier and said he wanted to interview me for the local newspaper and I can't believe I fell for it. I made sure he arrived when Lauren was here, but it turned out he wasn't with the newspaper at all."

She was talking rapidly and he could hear the fear in her voice. "Okay, so slow down and tell me what happened."

"Oh, my God, Zane; it was James. James was here. He's alive and I didn't even know it was him until he started explaining."

She began to cry, making him feel helpless and angry.

"Catherine, did he hurt you. What the hell did he do to you?"

"Hurt me? No, he didn't physically hurt me. He didn't do anything to me unless you call pretending to be dead....I just can't believe how naïve I was about this whole thing. I must be the stupidest person on the planet."
~~~~~

"No, honey, you are not. He blindsided you."

"Did you know about this? Did you know he was alive?"

"Do you really need for me to answer that now?" He wasn't about to tell her the truth over the phone.

"Yes, you might as well join the list of people who have lied to me. Why wouldn't you?"

"Catherine, I didn't lie to you. There was a confidentiality issue. It was classified information."

"Don't tell me that. You could have told me."

"It was too soon. You needed some distance from it—all of it. You were still fragile."

"Fragile. That's an interesting thing for you to call me."

"I know you are upset. I wish I had been there to protect you. What happened?"

"Oh, he tried to tell me this story about how he had been victimized by the government. I can comprehend some of it, but there is no excuse for him not to have trusted me from the beginning. And, I know he was with Arianne. I'm supposed to act like that never happened either and forgive him."

"Catherine, I think it's good for you to be this angry."

"You bet I'm angry. And I'm not too happy with you keeping this from me either."

"It wasn't my place to tell you, Catherine. Think about it. I mean, that's a lot to dump on someone. I saw how vulnerable you were."

"You let me think that he was dead all this time and there I was face-to-face with someone I didn't even recognize. I thought I was going to pass out. It was shocking."

"I'm sure it was. There wasn't any easy way for him to tell you. I think it would have been worse if I had told you."

"I don't know why you wouldn't have warned me. I don't know what I should think or feel about that. I told him to leave and he actually asked if he could hug me—he wanted to kiss me goodbye."

"And...?" he asked, although he didn't really want to know.

"Of course I wouldn't let him. I couldn't even think of touching him, kissing him. He didn't even look like James. It wasn't him. Not my James. I didn't feel anything for him except a strong sense of mistrust and pain."

"I'm so sorry, Catherine. I don't know how I could have protected you from this."

"It gets worse. I was telling him to leave when a car came up the driveway. I couldn't believe my eyes when the car stopped right in front of us and Arianne jumped out."

"Then what happened?"

"Well, I started yelling at both of them. Arianne just put her hands up and asked me to stop. When I finally got myself under control, I couldn't believe what she told me. She asked me to calm down. She said she was there for me, not for him. She said James isn't who I think he is; that he has changed. That she was hoping that I didn't allow him back into my life. She said that she had been with him up in Montana, of all places. That he had been nice in the beginning, but had become very abusive to her and that she didn't want what he'd done to her to happen to me."

"Seriously, she said that."

"Yes. James was just standing there, and all of a sudden, he lunged at Arianne and grabbed her by the arm and told her to shut up. I think she completely knocked him off guard. He wanted me to believe he was remorseful, but how could I ever trust him? He grabbed her."

"What did she do?"

"Arianne twisted out of his grip and pushed him. He stood there, looking at the two of us. In that moment, he suddenly seemed defeated. I think he realized what he had done. I'm sure he could tell by my face that he frightened me. He didn't speak to either one of us, and he just turned and got into his car. He closed the door and started to back out, but then he stopped, pulled up to me, and put down his window. He told me he was sorry and he'd figure out a way to make this right, and then he drove away."

"Thank God."

"I know. I can't get over how he looked, and now I'm worried about being here alone. I know the dogs won't let anyone into the house without making a lot of noise, but it is scaring me that he might be lurking around. Arianne apologized and said she couldn't undo what had been done, but she was truly sorry. She said she had gotten caught up in trying to ease his pain over losing me. I didn't say another word to her after James drove away. She stood there, tears in her eyes, and got in her car and left. She came all that way just to talk to me for five minutes. I don't even know how she found me."

"If James is smart, he won't stay around either."

"Do you really think he will go?"

"Well, Buck just called me and said someone had seen James in the New York airport and that's how they tailed him to Jacksonville. They alerted Buck to the possibility of your having a visitor. Maybe now, they will put him back under surveillance."

"So when did you find all this out?"

"Just a few minutes ago when Buck called."

"So that's why Buck called me. He was checking on me, but it was too little, too late because James had already been here."

"They stopped tracking James once he and Arianne were released from protective custody. It was a fluke that someone saw him and recognized him at the New York airport."

"Well if that's supposed to be comforting, it's not."

"What do you want me to do? Do you want me to come home now?"

"No, Zane. You just got to Montana, to your mother. You waited a long time to get there. I can't be that selfish. I'm sorry that I'm so upset."

"Your situation is much more pressing than anything happening here."

"I think I'll be okay. It's just kind of spooked me."

"I'm coming home. I'll catch the first plane out. Hang in there for me."

"No. I won't hear of it. No. Please stay with your mother."

"Catherine, then come out here. Get in touch with Lauren, Dr. Grant, and Buck. Tell them you have to leave and you are coming to Montana. Get on the next plane and come here. James won't expect you to do that. They can handle anything that comes up on the ranch. Buck will help. I have complete confidence that he can handle it. Besides, when Buck's father gets there, he will pitch in too."

"I can't leave my animals. I'm staying here and you are staying there. I mean it."

"Champ stays with you in your bedroom anyway. Just shut and lock the door at night. There's a pistol in the drawer in the guest bedroom under my jeans."

"I don't know, Zane, a gun?"

"Put it in your nightstand at night."

"Okay, but I haven't shot anything since I was a young girl and my uncle and cousins used to let me shoot their guns."

"You'll be fine. Just point it and squeeze the trigger."

She was very quiet and then he heard her take a deep breath. "I don't know that I could shoot him. Tell me you don't think he will come back here."

"I don't think coming back would accomplish anything for him. What did you tell him?"

"I told him to leave, to just go, that it was over."

"I think that's fairly clear."

"He said he would figure out a way to make it right and slowly drove away. I don't want to feel anything for him. Lauren was here and she came running when she heard the commotion and so did the dogs."

"Commotion?"

"I couldn't help it. I know I raised my voice at him and then at Arianne. I was completely shocked by the whole situation. I have the memory of standing in front of his casket, staring at his burned and distorted head. It was so unbelievable that I fainted. Now, I find out that all the time I was grieving for some poor dead man that I didn't even know."

"I understand how you must feel."

"No you don't. No one can understand how betrayed I feel by everyone."

"I hope not by me. Do you feel betrayed by me?"

"Yes, yes, I guess I do."

"Please don't. Everything I did was to protect you. I never did anything that I thought would hurt you."

"Yes, Zane, but aren't you guilty of lies of omission?"

"It was all about keeping you safe and not exposing you to anything that would harm you."

"I'm trying to understand that, but this is all such a shock. And, what you are saying is exactly what James said to me. He said that too, that it was about keeping me safe. I don't know how to feel."

Zane was scrambling for anything to make her feel like she could depend on him.

"I think it's for the best. You'll be able to get on with your life now that the truth is out in the open."

"I don't know how he could do this to me, and now I feel like you withheld the truth from me too."

"I don't think James had a choice, Catherine. I'm certainly not sticking up for him, but they really had him between a rock and a hard place."

"I'm not going to easily forgive him."

"No one said you had to forgive him. If you do, it has to be for you, not for him."

"I have to hang up. I'm exhausted; I have a headache from crying and I feel nauseated, and I still have some chores to do. I need to go."

"I can come home tomorrow."

"No. Don't do that. I'll call you. Give me some time."

"Catherine, please. Come to Montana. And if not, call me and I'll get right on a plane."

"Good night, Zane."

He didn't have a chance to tell her anything else as he heard her quietly hang up the phone. He sat down at the old familiar kitchen table. He was worried that this was going to change everything for both of them.

~~~~~

Buck answered the phone with half of a "Hello" when Zane blurted loudly, "He was there at her house. That son of a bitch weaseled his way in there and tried to get her to forgive him."

"Shit."

"I know."

"How'd she handle that?" Buck sounded concerned.

"She kicked his ass out of there. She said she told him to leave. He really shocked her and then Arianne showed up."

"You've got to be kidding me."

"No, but it turns out Arianne was there to tell Catherine not to trust him. Apparently, things didn't go so well between those two. They had been holed up somewhere in Montana of all places, but it apparently didn't end well for either of them. So, now what do we do about him?"

"Nothing, Zane."

"She doesn't feel safe at her own house. I told her to lock herself in the bedroom at night with Champ. Friskie will make a hell of a lot of noise. All the dogs will."

"She'll be fine."
~~~~~

"I hope so."

"Zane, I don't think he will do anything to her. I think she will be okay. If he wanted some sort of revenge, he'd go after the people around her, not her. Or, he'd go after the people who destroyed his life."

"I'm not worried about him. I don't think he'll come after me."

"I doubt it, but you never know."

"Well, there's not much I can do from Montana. I asked her if she wants me to come back there and she said, 'No.' I asked her if she wanted to come out here and she told me 'No.'"

"We will keep a check on her, but there's not much we can do either. What did she tell him?"

"She told him to leave—that she didn't want anything to do with him anymore. Can Bill check on James' whereabouts?"

"I hope that gave James the message, but sure, I can ask Bill. I'm not sure what they will do now that he has made contact with Catherine."

"Okay, and thanks for giving me the heads up."

"No problem. I'll keep you posted. Say, tell your mother and Parker I said hello."

"I'll do it. Try and get Catherine to open up to you. I'd like to know what's going on in her mind. She's still pretty shaken up."

Buck promised to check on Catherine and said he would fill Bill Brannan in on what had happened and ask him to try to locate the son-of-a bitch. He could only hope to hell that James would leave Catherine alone.

CHAPTER 35

Zane sat on the back porch after dinner with his mother and Parker. The ranch hands had gone off in different directions, weary from the long hot day. The three of them were enjoying the late afternoon sunset. The pink clouds were hanging just above the mountain ridge in the last moments of daylight.

"I don't even know how to begin to tell you about Catherine. What I know for sure is that she is a woman of conviction. She is sensitive, passionate, and romantic. She knows exactly what she wants and believes in, which makes her very strong, and yet, at times, she is very vulnerable. This very special woman came into my life and definitely changed it. What amazes me is that she immediately trusted what she saw in me. Maybe I should start with what's happening now and work backwards. Catherine had a visitor today. It's someone I've known about, and I had hoped this day would never occur. It seems that her deceased husband, James, showed up at her house today to ask her to forgive him."

"The federal government faked his death in order to keep the two of them safe because of something her husband was involved with. As far as she knew, he was dead. She identified what was said to be his body and held his funeral."

"So how did she handle that?" Parker asked. "She must have felt like she saw a ghost."

"She was completely shocked. He tried to tell her he

had been in protective custody, had been forced to make certain decisions, and asked her for forgiveness. She wanted nothing to do with any of it or him. Then this woman who has been staying with him showed up to warn Catherine not to trust him. Catherine asked them both to leave. She was completely overwhelmed. She has this memory picture of the horrific sight of his burned body in the casket, and then today this stranger shows up in front of her, saying he's James. As I told you, Parker, part of the government deal was to give him a new identity, which included reconstructive surgery on his face. He doesn't even look like her husband. It completely freaked her out. She said after they drove away, she was horrified."

Zane's mother listened intently, rocking softly back and forth. "I can't even imagine all the things going through her head as she was realizing that he was alive. She had to have been in shock."

"Oh, she was. She said she thought she was going to pass out. She's spooked now to be in the house alone at night. I told her to lock the dogs in the bedroom with her. She has a big yellow retriever and then her little fuzzy mutt, Friskie. They will bark and make a huge commotion. She has six dogs altogether. The rest stay downstairs at night. I don't think anyone will get in the house. Plus, I told her where to find my pistol."

"Son, do you think you need to go to her?" Parker stood to get a better look at the sunset.

"No. I'm thinking she would be safer here. I think she needs to come here."

"Then you must tell her to come," his mother insisted.

Parker nodded his approval. "Yes, you should tell her to come. She will feel safe here."

"I'm sure she will want to iron out the problems with her farm. She has her animals that need to be attended to. I don't think she will leave them unless she has the perfect farm sitter. She will worry too much. Either that or I have to go get her. I have a trailer and so does she. We could haul everything out here."

"Isn't Roan Matthews joining his wife at Buck's place? I can't imagine why they couldn't help her, plus all of them living in Buck's house together?" his mother asked.

"Mom, I'm not sure what they are going to do or for how long?"

"Effie told me herself that she and Roan wanted a change in their lives before it was too late. You should ask Effie. They'd be perfect farm sitters. They won't let anyone onto that property, and she'll be safe right here with us. Plus, her animals will love them. She won't have to worry."

"That's a lot to throw at someone. Catherine has three horses, I have Trouble, and we have a barn cat and six dogs in the house."

"Seems like a piece of cake for those two," Parker added, smiling at Zane.

"I'm not sure what she will think of all this."

"Roan and Effie would think it's a picnic compared to their spread," his mother added.

Zane knew they were right. The Matthews could easily take care of everything at Catherine's.

"I'll see, but I'm inclined to think I need to go home no matter what she decides."

~~~~~

Catherine hurried through the night chores and rushed into the house quickly locking the porch door behind her. She dialed the phone number Zane had written on the pad in the kitchen.

"Yes. He's right here, just one moment. Zane, it's Catherine," his mother said as she handed him the phone.

"Hello, Catherine. Is everything okay?"

"Yes, I just got back in the house from night chores. I'm fine. I got a call from Effie Matthews just a little bit ago. She said you had talked to her and she had talked to her husband and they would be more than willing to stay at the ranch if I needed to take a break. Did you ask her to do that?" She was a little perturbed with him about it.

"Yes, I did. I know I should have talked to you first, but there was no point to it if they weren't receptive."

"I don't understand how I can just walk away from my animals."

"You don't have to do anything you don't want to do. Invite the Matthews over and see how it goes. You don't have to make a decision this minute. If you decide not to do it, I can come home."

There, he had said it again. It made her feel a little better to hear him say it.

"I know. It's just that I don't feel like I can relax here. I'm feeling like I have to be constantly watching over my shoulder. It's not the same for me right now."

"I understand, Catherine. You might want to talk to Buck, but the Matthews care for all the same animals
~~~~~

that you have, only on a much larger scale. They manage them all very well. They won't let anything happen to your critters. Besides, if you really feel that uneasy, I will fly home and we can haul everything out here. We have the two trailers."

"I appreciate that you would do that. I don't think we need to get carried away just yet. I'm worried about Champ and Friskie the most. They are so attached to me."

"I get that, but Mr. Matthews is very good with dogs. I've been around him and his dogs. Why don't you think about bringing Friskie here with you? Then you'd only have to worry about Champ. I'm sure they would let him do exactly the same routine. It's not like it's going to be forever."

"I know that, Zane, but I'll be all the way in Montana."

"Catherine, you will love it and you can relax here."

"I don't know."

"Take your time. Have the Matthews come over. Remember when you walked out of there and let me stay in your house?"

"I thought about that, but then I didn't think I'd be gone more than a few days."

"Yes, and you were gone for months and I took care of everything just fine, now didn't I?"

"I know."

"Well?"

"Okay, I'll think about it."

"I'll be waiting to hear you say that you are coming."

"I'll talk to you soon."

Neither one of them could say the words they longed

to say to each other.

~~~~~

Catherine was both surprised and relieved that the dogs got along with Mr. Matthews so well. It was an affirmation that it might be okay to leave them and join Zane in Montana for a little while. She didn't have to stay long. Effie had walked right into the tack room and scooped up Sweetie, who started purring and rubbing up under Effie's chin.

"What a sweet cat," Effie said as she sat her on one of the saddle pads.

"Actually, you have that right because Zane named her Sweetie. He found her in a wood pile while I was away taking care of my uncle. I can't believe he kept her safe from the dogs."

"Oh, I can believe it. Zane always loved critters and that Foster Wheeler was so mean toward him about it. His father would never let him have a dog of his own. It was ridiculous."

"Yes, I've heard a bit about that."

Roan Matthews was rubbing the neck of Zane's stallion, Trouble, over the stall door. "Got no idea what that boy was thinking when he picked up this ugly son of a gun. And a stallion at that! Total trouble."

Catherine must have had a startled look on her face because Effie started laughing and said, "Roan, stop teasing her. Catherine, Zane told him the horse's name, and we actually have several Arabians. We have used them for working cows for years. He's messing with you."

"Oh. I was worried you would be unhappy with
~~~~~

having to take care of my Arabians. Zane actually named him Trouble when he rescued him."

Roan patted the stallion's neck, "I like this feisty guy. He and I will get along just fine."

They seemed to absorb every single detail Catherine threw at them. They weren't upset about the house being a two-story. They didn't mind the dogs being allowed inside, and they understood who was allowed upstairs. Roan said he would keep the fence lines cleaned and the fences repaired, would run the tractor and mow if needed. Whatever she wanted, just make a list. It all seemed so easy.

"I'm just worried about my little dog, Friskie. He's so attached to me."

Effie told her, "Take him with you. There was a little dog in a crate on your flight here, isn't that right, Roan? I saw it when we picked you up at the airport. "

"Can't say as I noticed," Roan said.

"I don't know. Do you think he'll do okay in Montana?"

"Oh, honey, he'll be just fine. Maggie won't mind having that little dog in her house. She is the sweetest woman you could ever meet, and that little dog isn't going to bother her one bit. She has all those ranch hands tromping in for lunch and dinner every day. Your dog will be just fine. Whatever you decide will be just fine."

Every question she had was answered.

"I suppose I could go to Montana for a little while. Just to get away. Take a break."

Roan spoke up. "Catherine, let me tell you something; Zane Wheeler is a good man. If you think you are the least bit interested in him, I wouldn't be wasting any time worrying about a little dog. You won't be sorry when you get out to the ranch, either. It is one of the most beautiful areas in the world."

Catherine took a deep breath and said, "Well, I'll sleep on it and let you know tomorrow."

They slowly walked back through the barn and out to the front driveway. Catherine stood and watched them drive away. Then she turned and looked at her house, the pastures, and wondered what she was going to do.

~~~~~

That night, after she'd finished dinner and just before eleven, she slowly opened the back door and let the dogs out. She didn't feel very comfortable walking down to the barn alone, even though the lights gave her a clear path. It was what might be lurking in the dark that frightened her. She threw hay, checked the water buckets, and turned off the barn lights. She called the dogs and hurried up the path to the house. She clipped a leash onto Friskie and quickly took him right outside the back door while Champ stood on the top porch step and watched them.

With Champ on the rug next to the bed and Friskie on Zane's pillow, Catherine closed and locked her bedroom door, opened the nightstand drawer, and felt for the pistol; then she stood the flashlight upright on the nightstand. This was not how she imagined her life would be. Morning couldn't come soon enough. She knew she'd be making phone calls and heading to the airport as soon as she could. She patted Friskie on the
~~~~~

head as tears slid down her cheeks and plopped onto her pillow.

She lay there for a long time in the darkness, thinking about what had happened, not only to her, but to James. It couldn't have been easy for him to be whisked away suddenly to a strange place and kept under surveillance. She couldn't help but wonder how they had convinced him to have the surgery on his face. She had to admit that he had always been somewhat vain when it came to his looks. He had often spent more time in front of the mirror than she did. It had to have been disconcerting for James to discover the drug concoction, decide to provide the formula to the government, and then have to maneuver around her. She had a hard time grasping how much he had changed not only physically, but also psychologically. His new appearance made all of it even more difficult to accept. She eventually fell asleep from sheer exhaustion.

CHAPTER 36

James felt completely devastated, but there wasn't anything he could do about Catherine's decision. Clearly, she had been severely traumatized by losing him, their apartment, her uncle, and then by all the changes in her life. It was killing him to admit it, but Roger had hit the nail on the head. Did he love her enough to stay away and let her go? He couldn't stand how she had looked when she was shouting at him and Arianne. She was not the Catherine he had once loved. She had blatantly told them to get out of there. She was right, of course. He had violated every promise he made when he said his vows to her. In the beginning, he had been blinded by his desire to do the right thing. There was nothing wrong with patriotism. Hell, when he was in high school, he'd written a paper about it. He could still rattle off the first sentences from memory.

Patriotism is the love of country. The patriot is a person who loves and is devoted to his native country and its welfare.

He had been committed to those two statements. That was why it had been so easy to turn over the formula for the fatal drug. Now, because of it, he was facing his worst nightmare. Life as he had known it was completely over. Any chance he had imagined with Catherine was gone forever, and even Arianne had unexpectedly turned against him. The two of them had become very strong women and formidable foes.

He had to admit that the entire ordeal had changed him. He felt bitter, frustrated, completely out of his element. It had been a long time since he was completely alone, but that's exactly where he found himself again. He couldn't even count on Roger. All he felt for him was contempt. Roger had orchestrated this entire situation. All fault should fall on Roger's shoulders. He had been resistant in the beginning, but his buddy, Rog, had persisted and eventually talked him into it. Now, he had one thing left to do and it meant returning to New York.

He stood in front of the distorted mirror in the shabby room at the old motel north of Highberry and picked lint from his suit hanging on the back of the door. He buttoned the top button of his white shirt, pulled the tie around his neck, and tied a perfect knot at his throat. He ran his fingers through his hair and leaned closer to the mirror. He didn't remember when he started turning gray. It was still difficult to look at his image and accept the reflection looking back at him. His hairline was different. His nose was thinner and more pointed. It even felt strange when he touched his face. It surprised him every time he looked at himself.

He placed his brand new pairs of jeans and his shirts across the bedspread and set the boots at the foot of the bed, rolled the belt, and slid it down into one of them. Maybe someone would get some use out of them. He wasn't going to need them anymore.

He quickly slid his arms into his suit coat, took a look around the room to be sure he hadn't forgotten anything, and pulled his suitcase out the door. All he wanted to do was get to the airport in Jacksonville and catch the first plane to New York.

~~~~~

As soon as Roger answered the phone, James cut right to the chase. "Hey, Roger, it's James. I'm back in New York and I need to talk to you. What's your new office address and how soon can I come by to see you?"

"Wow, James, I really didn't think you'd want my opinion on anything after our last conversation."

"Au Contraire, Pierre! I'm taking your advice and reinventing myself and I need your thoughts on a few things."

"Well, I can do this pro bono if you meet me away from the office. If you come through here, I'll have to bill you or my new partners won't be too happy with me."

"Fair enough. Where do you want to meet? Where's your apartment?"

"I'm actually staying at the Fairmont Hotel until my new apartment is painted."

"What's the room number?"

"Suite 313."

"That's interesting now, isn't it?"

"You have a memory like an elephant, James. Go ahead and tell me how brilliant I was when I got us a better room at college."

"Yes, you were genius by using your phobia of the number 13. Once they moved us, we could look right into the girl's dorm windows."

"We were an unstoppable duo."

"And the plot only continues."

"Okay, so what time?" James asked.

"How's seven o'clock tonight? Want me to get take-
~~~~~

out?”

“No, I can't stay for dinner. I have something I want to run by you. It won't take long.”

“Okay, James, seven o'clock it is. See you later, buddy.”

~~~~~

Roger answered the door and stood there stunned for a few seconds.

“Wow, glad to see you too!” James said and pushed his way past Roger into the suite.

“Why don’t you come in, James,” Roger said as he closed the door and spun around to follow James. “Forgive me, but I was startled for a moment. You know, I never saw you looking like this before.”

“Don't make me any more uncomfortable than I am. I'm not even okay in my own skin yet.”

“I understand. Although, you have to admit they did a heck of a job. I mean, if I hadn’t recognized your voice, I would never have known it was you.”

“I get it. Don't you think I'm startled every time I look in the mirror?”

“Yes, I’m sure you are. But look at it this way—you can actually date some of your former babes and they won't even know it's you.”

“Always the optimist, Roger; you never stop seeing that silver lining.”

“Speaking of that, what's this about? What did you want to talk to me about? Do you have a contract or prospectus?”

“Honestly, I was hoping we could brainstorm. I'm sort of at a loss as to what to do with myself now.”
~~~~~

"Hey, you want a drink? We can sit out on the balcony and watch the sun set while we talk."

"Sounds like a plan."

Roger led the way to a small kitchenette and pulled out a few liquor bottles and glasses. "What's your pleasure?"

"I'll have a shot of that bourbon over ice. You do have ice, don't you?" James was unimpressed with the place.

Roger poured them each a glass and they walked out onto the balcony. The buildings were vividly outlined against the darkening sky. It had rained earlier in the day so the air was unusually clear over the New York skyline.

"Okay, James. What do you need from me?" Roger was attentive.

"I've never done anything other than computer technology and pharmaceutical research. I have no idea what to do."

"Why do you have to do anything? Your pay-out was an incredible amount."

"Yes, but I can't sit around every day twiddling my thumbs. I'm used to working. I mean really working."

"Well, when you were a kid what did you dream about?"

"That's not even funny, Roger. You know damn well that when I was a kid all I wanted to do was get out of the hell holes I lived in with the endless march of foster parents."

"Yes, but let's fast forward to the family who actually adopted you, because that wasn't a bad situation."

"No, not really, but look where it got me—

unemployed and with nothing but time on my hands." James sounded disgusted.

"You don't need to be employed. You can do anything you want to do."

"That's the problem. I have no idea what to be when I grow up this time."

"James, the whole world is right in front of you. Just look. Right here is all of New York City. Think positively for once."

"Yeah, and when you look at it from up here all those people down there look the same."

"They're not. Every one of them has a dream and so can you again. Lots of people have started over."

"I don't want to start over, I don't want to look like this and I sure as hell didn't expect to give up Catherine."

"I'm sorry. I didn't know this would happen either. What about getting back into research? You loved it. We'll doctor your résumé to cover the dates you were in protective custody."

"That's what I love about you, Roger. You have a solution for everything, even if it's a lie."

"It's not a lie. You weren't unemployed. You were working for the United States Government. We can say you were working on a highly confidential project that can not be disclosed and that you were on loan to the feds. I'm sure they will back you up."

"Roger, you're not thinking clearly. I don't exist. Did you forget that I'm dead?"

"This James isn't dead. The new you is sitting right here right now. Why don't you start your own company and do research yourself. Then you won't need a resume. You can hire your own staff."

"Do you want another drink, Roger? I'll go fix us each another drink." James took Roger's glass from his hand and walked into the small kitchen and poured them each another shot over the rocks. He walked back out onto the balcony and handed Roger the glass.

"Listen, James; I have all these new contacts. Let me work on this for you. I can get you some interviews. I can make this happen for you."

"Brownie points? Is that what you are looking for? Trying to make it all better?"

"No, James. I really think I can help you. You have such a chip on your shoulder."

"Well, for Christ sakes Roger Dodger, wouldn't you? Everything in my life has completely changed. Every single *thing*!"

"I haven't changed. I have always had your back."

"Really? You would have had Catherine on her back if she would have let you." He was sounding hostile.

"That's not fair, James. Wouldn't you rather have me be with her than that cowboy?"

"It shouldn't have ever been an issue. None of this should have happened at all. I should still be with Catherine."

"We can't do a damn thing about any of this now. All any of us can do is go forward from this moment. We made these decisions and now we have to live with them."

"Point of entry," James said.

"What? I don't understand what you are talking about."

"It's our point of entry. We all start from right here

right now. That's so damn optimistic, isn't it, Roger?"

"Look; just give me some time to work on this. Give me a week or two? Will you do that?"

"Oh, yeah, let's just see what happens. I have to go."

"You don't have to rush off."

"Yes, actually I do. It's been real, Roger."

James set his glass down on a small table between their chairs, walked from the balcony straight through the suite, and out the door without looking back.

Roger walked into the kitchenette with the two glasses in his hands and poured the ice into the sink. As the remaining fluid dripped out of the glasses, he noticed a drop of thin white liquid fall onto the stainless steel sink from his glass. He held the glass up to the light, stuck his finger inside, and scooped out a milky-white fluid. He rubbed it between his index finger and his thumb and then he lifted it to his nose and smelled it.

"That stupid son of a bitch," he said.

Roger quickly walked across the room, grabbed his cell phone from the table by the door, and pushed 911. As he heard the voice answer at dispatch, the room began to spin, making him feel very dizzy.

"Hello, hello. I need an ambulance. I'm at the Fairmont Hotel..."

He barely got the words "Fairmont Hotel" out of his mouth, tried to say his room number, when the cell phone suddenly dropped from his grip. He wanted to tell them about James, that he thought he'd been poisoned. The left side of his mouth began to droop and saliva oozed out onto his chin. He grabbed for the table as he began to careen to the floor. There wasn't a thing he could do to stop the fall as he hit the floor in a crumpled heap. He shouldn't have met with James, shouldn't have let him into the suite. He shouldn't have let him fix them another drink; he shouldn't have trusted.... The room was spinning—spinning ever so fast as down and down he went. There was this deafening roar in his head, and then suddenly everything turned totally black.

~~~~~

Catherine felt sick to her stomach. She didn't know exactly when she finally drifted off, but she had barely slept at all the entire night. This was her second night in the house alone since James had suddenly appeared. Her bed had seemed like an enormous roller-coaster as she went from one dream to the next. First, she was falling off one of the horses, but she didn't recognize where she was or the horse. Then someone was pushing her off the railing of a boat into a foaming, roaring sea. She was hanging onto the rail in a panic. When she opened her eyes, Champ was standing in the middle of her bed, staring into her face.

"I know, Champ; I do. I simply don't know how I am going to leave all of you, but I don't know how I can stay either." She grabbed him by the sides of his neck and pulled him down next to her on the bed and began to sob uncontrollably into his thick golden retriever fur. He rolled over on his back and stuck his feet in the air asking her to rub his chest. "Oh, Champ, you are the best boy in the whole world. I don't know how I am going to get into the car and drive away. How can I do that to you and all of them?"

The big loving dog gently began to lick the tears
~~~~~

from her face, which only made her feel worse.

"I know how much you love me, but honestly, I won't be gone forever. And besides, Buck's parents are lovely people. Really they are. They will take good care of you. I know they will. You have to promise me that you will be here when I come home."

She wrapped her arms around him as Friskie wormed his way down over her shoulder and up under her chin.

"I wondered where you were, you little cutie, but thank you for giving Champ and me our moment."

She had to laugh, even though she didn't feel like it.

"You are both something else. I just wonder what Buck's father and Effie will think about you two trying to sleep in the bed."

She wasn't prepared emotionally for leaving. Yes, she had her bags packed and her plane ticket was printed downstairs, waiting in her purse, but she didn't know how she was going to do this.

"I know. I have to be strong, but it is ridiculous to feel so sick to your stomach about doing something. Still, I don't know how I can stay. I'm so confused. I don't know when I've ever felt so out of control."

The dogs were looking at her intently, waiting for her to sit up and signal going downstairs. She threw off the covers and slid out of bed.

"I really don't want to face today. This is awful."

She forced herself to make her way into the dressing room and quickly threw on last night's clothes.

"No sense making more dirty clothes. I'll just wear these today."

The dogs followed her down the stairs and greeted

the other dogs in the kitchen. She was wrestling with every aspect of what was happening to her, trying to make sense of it. First, was the unbelievable and startling appearance of James. What in the world had possessed him? She couldn't imagine his being alive and not telling her. Plus, why had he agreed to keep her completely in the dark? He had been alive the entire time–the entire time that she was grieving—the whole time that she had been sick, and even while she was falling in love with Zane. She was, had been, still married to him, and there he was now, in her face. Her mind still couldn't grasp how he looked, how he spoke to her, how he could do this to her. How could he do this to her? She was furious at herself for being such a fool.

He had looked so different. He actually looked awful. He had been handsome. Now, his hairline made his forehead look larger and they had done something to his nose and it was smaller and pointed. And his eyes weren't brown anymore. They were a weird green color. She couldn't begin to figure out how he had allowed them to do all that to him.

Then there was Zane. Oh, my God! He must have known about James being alive all along, and yet he had been willing to live in her house and make love to her while she was still married to James. Technically, if you had an analytical mind like he did, she could understand how Zane could convince himself that she wasn't really married to James because that James didn't exist anymore. He was someone else. Still.... And how much exactly did Buck Matthews know? And what about Roger? That stupid piece of crap was right there trying to make his ridiculous moves on her when all the while he knew James was alive.

Her mind was racing in a hundred directions. Was the entire world going crazy? How in the hell did life turn out so convoluted? She ran her hands through her hair and stared out the kitchen window.

She wasn't ready to do this. She finished her cup of coffee, set the cup in the sink, and walked to the front door and peered out the small glass pane. She watched the truck turn down the driveway. She couldn't believe she was about to allow someone else to stay in her house once again while she tried to figure out what to do. All she knew was that she had to leave Highberry for a while. She also knew that, in spite of everything she had recently discovered, she couldn't wait to feel Zane's arms safely surround her.